USHER HOUSE

RISING

A MADELINE USHER NOVEL
BOOK ONE

DON ROFF

ISBN: 979-8-88757-013-6

Cover: Lynne Hansen

Editors: Kassie Metivier and Hayley Frerichs

Brambleberry Books

www.brambleberrybooks.com

This is a work of fiction. Names, characters, places, brands, media, and incidents are either the product of the author's imagination or are used fictitiously. Any resemblance to similarly named places or to persons living, dead, or living dead is absolutely, positively unintentional.

"During the whole of a dull, dark, and soundless day in the autumn of the year, when the clouds hung oppressively low in the heavens, had been passing alone, on horseback, through a singularly dreary tract of country; and at length found myself, as the shades of the evening drew on, within view of the melancholy House of Usher."
—Edgar Allan Poe

For Wilder Taylor Roff—who loves creaky old houses and all of the shadows that lurk within them, too.

ONE

1

The journey to Usher House began with a simple, plain envelope that sat in the mail basket for nearly a week. Looking back, that's where it all started. It all seemed like a dream within a dream. My entire life had done a 180-degree turn. It's strange how that happens. One minute you're going along, working your little job, living your life, and the next someone close to you dies and you get a strange summons to a place that you've never known of previously. If anyone tells me that they have life figured out, I'll be the first to tell them they're a liar or they're trying to sell me something—like an app advertised on Instagram for $19.95.

2

When the catalytic envelope had been slipped through the mailbox slot, I wasn't in the right frame of mind. You see, the only person in my life, my adopted mother Peggy Bland, had died. Peggy and I weren't super close, even though she adopted and raised me for the last four of my eighteen years. I'd been given up for adoption not long after I was born. And when adoption didn't happen, I had gone through a plethora of foster families. They sucked—lots of abuse physically, verbally, emotionally, and psychologically. I guess, looking back at that, it did kind of give me some coping skills. But it also messed with my head, bad. My self-esteem took a swirling dive down the toilet, and I ended up seeing a lot of school counselors and a few psychiatrists. The ineffectual shrinks the state would pay for anyway. My foster families weren't wealthy enough to afford a private psychiatrist. And I found out later that many of the foster families weren't really even interested in raising kids. They only did it to get money from the state. Lucky me.

The Bland family was different, though.

Peggy and her husband Jeff had their own financial advisor business. Now, usually, people in those kinds of ventures do relatively well, but Jeff and Peggy struggled to make ends meet. I found the whole thing ironic that they advised people and companies how to save money on their taxes, but they couldn't even help themselves to some of that advice. Still, though, they had adopted me a year after staying with them, when I was fifteen.

The Bland house was about the size of an animal cracker box— under 900 square feet with three cramped bedrooms. Peggy's favorite colors were pink and yellow, so the house was painted a bright, canary yellow and adorned with two big, pink rhododendron shrubs on either side of the walk-up porch. Though it was a tiny house, Peggy had made it as cozy as she could for Jeff and me. The aroma of fresh-baked bread and cooking spices always hung in the air.

Later, I discovered Jeff had a gambling problem, as well as being a binge drinker. He hid it well, especially from me. I was already aware of the signs of a neglectful parent—the frequent lying, the unexpected absences, and the withholding of details about where he was and what he was doing. Jeff Bland was already a secretive guy. In fact, when Peggy had come home one day—all of his stuff was out of the house. He'd vanished without a word.

Peggy and I were left alone.

That happened a couple of years ago when I was sixteen. I was still in high school, good ol' Carver High School in Pickman Flats, Washington State. I took a job working at the local grocery store, Williamson's Market. I filled the bulk bins, which was a tedious, thankless job, but it helped to pay the bills and it gave me a sense of independence. Maybe even a little self-worth. How sad is that? You know that story you'd probably read about in Greek mythology about Sisyphus having to push the boulder up the hill in Hell over and over again? That's pretty much what working in the bulk section of Williamson's was like. I'd have to scramble to fill up the raw almonds, the gluten-free rolled oats, the organic white Basmati rice, or the organic honey dates. I'd fill one bin—and then another was empty. I felt like that Dutch boy who plugged the dike with a finger to prevent his country from flooding. Yes, I'm aware I'm mixing my metaphors with Sisyphus and Hans Brinker, but give me a break—my adopted mom, who was my whole world, died.

It was September, and Peggy was complaining of chest pains. I had asked her if she wanted to go to the hospital. She'd once mentioned having chest pains before but told me they were "nothing". Maybe in passing when we'd have breakfast and she'd say, "I'm having chest pains, oh, and pass the sugar."

Death has a way of making you look back on a person's life. It's almost like a series of scenes in a movie; trying to remember if there was any little clue that might have led to their surprising and inevitable passing. With Peg, I can't think of that many. She was pretty tight-lipped most of the time, which is what I liked about her. She minded her own business, but was there when I needed her. Let me tell you, math wasn't one of my stronger subjects, and I probably wouldn't have even graduated if Peggy hadn't helped me out with my algebra homework every night. She said she was having chest pains, so I told her I'd drive her to the hospital. She said if she felt the same way in the morning, then we would go. I tried to get her to go to bed, but she insisted on sitting on the couch binge-watching some Netflix show.

When I woke up the next morning, I found her in the same place, the yellow and pink fleece blanket I had draped on her still there. On the screen, Netflix was impatiently asking if she was still there. She was not. Peggy had passed some time in the night. Her eyes were closed, and her mouth was agape as if she were in a deep sleep. Her skin had a greenish hue, though, where the blood had washed out of her face. That's how I knew she was dead instead of sleeping—the ghastly pallor of her skin. No healthy, sleeping person looked like that.

I still see that dead face in my thoughts from time to time.

Poor Peggy.

I hope, at least, that before she died, she got to see how the season of *The Crown* ended. She loved that show, and she would be disappointed in the afterlife, I'm pretty sure, if she was left hanging.

Her funeral was a small affair. Mostly clients Peggy had done their taxes for. I had seen them at the house from time to time, where Peggy mostly worked. They didn't really know me, so they gave me the awkward, "I'm sorry for your loss," and all that. There was this ramshackle buffet at the community building downtown where people ate in her memory. Death's kind of weird that way. People throw you the best shindig of your life in your honor, and you're not there to even savor it. Yeah, people say that "you're there in spirit," and all that. But I don't believe that. Dead was dead. And Peggy Bland, rest her soul, was not with us anymore.

3

I was working my least favorite shift at Williamson's—noon to nine o'clock. We usually got out of the store by about 9:20. It made for a long day of filling up bins and answering a lot of stupid questions from customers who could probably answer them themselves if they only bothered looking. I was on my lunch hour, which was three o'clock to four. I would always slip out and go to the Taco del Diablo down the street. I loved this local restaurant, which was small, painted in golds and reds, with red chili lights strung inside. The lighting was kept low, which was a nice break from the bright fluorescents of the grocery store. I would scrunch down in my favorite booth in the corner and hide from the world in the dimness for most of an hour.

Carly Mackenzie, my best friend, strolled in, ordered a grilled chicken burrito and a Cherry Coke, and sat down across from me. She worked at the clothing shop, Harrington's, in the strip mall. Her manager was pretty chill and would let her take her lunch at the same time. Carly had curly, flaming red hair and always dressed tastefully. Today, she was wearing an eggshell white scarf with a matching blouse, dark leggings, and two-inch black pumps. As usual, I was in frumpy khaki work pants and a shabby green polo shirt.

"Why the long face, Horsey?" she asked. She was also quick with the tongue sword, which often made me laugh.

I threw a French fry at her. "Bite this."

"So, are we on tonight?"

"I don't know," I said, suddenly feeling more tired. "Kinda feel like staying at home."

"It's Friday fucking night. Are you serious? We're going to Marty's to get some cute college guys to buy us a few rounds and get totally shit-faced."

"You're the one who likes to get shit-faced, not me."

The one time I did get "shit-faced," I puked SpaghettiOs down the side of Carly's red Prius. And that's not figuratively—it was literally a big can of SpaghettiOs. She thought it was funny until we had to scrub it off the next morning. That shit is hard to get out when they dry up overnight.

"Think he'll be there?" I asked, trying to quell my anxiousness.

"It's National Give Zero Fucks Day, darlin'," Carly said, playing with the kinky locks of her auburn hair. "You should really celebrate."

"I was being serious, asshole."

"Obviously," she said with a shrug. "I don't know how you can obsess so much over a mediocre Chad with two first names for a name anyway."

Over the summer, my ex-boyfriend, Parker Scott, broke up with me. He said it was because he was going to go to Washington State University in the fall and he didn't want to commit to a long-distance relationship (I certainly didn't have the cash or the GPA to attend WSU myself), but I'm pretty sure it had to do more with Mary Calloway's tits. He'd had his eyes on them all through our senior year. She was a cheerleader on Parker's football team who always wore tight shirts and sweaters to accentuate them. Parker was a star running back and was awarded a scholarship. I didn't even have to ask if Mary was going to WSU. She was. *Go Cougs!* A couple of weeks later, my adopted mom drops dead in front of Netflix.

If I had a dick, life had given me the biggest dick-punch ever.

I don't pay much attention to my weight, but I had seriously dropped like 17 pounds from being upset. My stomach was still agitated from my post-breakup anxiety. Some salty French fries and iced tea was about the only thing I could handle for lunch. Pickman Flats is a small town, and even seeing Parker's silver Ford pick-up, or one that looks like it, throws a shitload of anxiety into my day. I don't know if it's post-traumatic stress or what. Sure, I'd had a few boyfriends in my life. Many of them were just "boyfriends" in an unofficial sense. I dated them primarily to get away from my fucked-up foster families. The eager embrace of boys was someplace I could go to escape from my faux parental units. That's all.

But Parker was different.

I met him a couple of years after I started living with the Blands. So that means we were going out for a little over two years. It was bliss. The first three months Parker and I were dating, I lost my virginity. Since then, we were pretty regular with the "cuddling plus," as I called it. But Parker wasn't your typical dumb jock either. He had perfect grades, came from a family of means, and had good personal hygiene habits. I was kind of hoping for more from Parker, like maybe an engagement ring. But during the last few months of our relationship, he always seemed distracted whenever we were together. Sex was pretty much automated. And many times, he'd hide his phone, and he'd changed his passcode. I was kind of a trusting fool, and I didn't think much of it. I had figured he was worried about attending college in Pullman in the fall—and I'd let my guard down with him because I was in love. But no, it was all about Mary Calloway. I'd seen them together a couple of times before he finally came into work. Yes, that's right, he actually came into work—and broke up with me. I know he did it because I couldn't talk much and make a scene, and risk being fired. He was standing there with a quart of non-fat milk and a sack of sesame seed bagels and told me he was breaking up with me because of Pullman's distance, which, by the way, is only a couple of hours away. It's not like he was going to Harvard or UCLA. It's an afternoon drive. We could've spent weekends together. But yeah, I put all the pieces together and figured it out. I guess it would have hurt less if he had told me to my face rather than the sneaking around and lying. He didn't even respect me enough for that. The dirty, lying bastard.

"If Parker happens to be home for the weekend and shows up—we bolt and go someplace else," I said, contemplating my last fry, and then dropping it into the oily plastic basket. "And I'm only going out for, like, an hour."

"Dealio," Carly said.

"Did you really just say 'dealio?'"

4

That night, when I was getting ready for an hour on the town with Carly, I happened to check the mail. It'd been a week since Peggy had been buried out in Pickman Flats Cemetery. It was always kind of bizarre that she was lying in her "new apartment" six feet underground and I was in her house. It was in her will that I inherited the house (and the bills). But I was barely making enough money to cover the mortgage and was seriously looking to rent out two of the bedrooms. Carly, and possibly another friend, were still trying to put some funds together to share the house expenses. Otherwise, I'd have to sell it before the bank foreclosed on it and try to find an apartment. Probably a shitty studio in a low-rent part of town with my wages from Williamson's Market.

I was looking through all the mail in the basket. Mail slid through the letter slot and dropped into a wire basket in the front closet. With the door to the closet closed, it was easy to forget that you actually got mail. The basket overflowed with junk mail, gift catalogs, and overdue bills. The bills depressed me—sewer, water, garbage, power, et al. Thankfully, nothing was shut off—yet.

And then this envelope among them in the heap.

It was addressed to me. The postmark was from Barlow, Georgia. It didn't have a return address on it. I almost threw it away, thinking it might be some junk, but something told me to open it. It's not like I received a lot of mail anyway. It was a folded piece of stiff cardstock paper, antique white in color, and along with it, an airline ticket. The text on the card looked old-fashioned and handwritten. Was it? I couldn't tell. The letter had an old smell, a musty smell—like the paper stock had been kept in a leaky basement. I didn't know what to make of it. There was an address to RSVP back. But this didn't seem like a party. I read the letter, and didn't know what to make of it. It read:

YOU ARE CORDIALLY INVITED TO AN INTIMATE GATHERING AT USHER HOUSE. OCTOBER 13. THIS IS AN AFFAIR OF SOME URGENCY THAT IS A PERSONAL MATTER. PLEASE ARRIVE AT 6 PM ON THE DATE. NO GUESTS PLEASE.

TWO

1

"You mean, like, Usher the hip-hop singer?" Carly said as she was wolfing down some buffalo wings and sipping a Cosmopolitan. We were at Marty's Bar & Grill. The Friday night crowd mostly consisted of overenthusiastic college students and desperate loners looking to hook up. Cigarettes After Sex were crooning about giving someone all of their love. The Lakers were playing the Trailblazers on all of the flat screens. The music and chatter was so loud that we had to shout. "Maybe it's, like, from a long-lost relative who died and you're about to inherit a fortune," she continued, "and you're going to meet a handsome prince and live happily ever after."

"Give me a break."

"You work in a grocery store, Mads, you were meant for so much more than the cards of life have dealt you." She placed a hand on my shoulder and leaned in closer. "You're a sparkly little diamond in the rough, darlin'."

"Now you're being ridiculous."

"I'm totally serious."

"You're totally drunk."

"That's beside the point," she said as she hoisted her glass in the air. "And you said there is an airline ticket?"

"Yeah, it's for the day before I'm supposed to go there, October 12th. The plane flies out of the Pickman Flats airport, connects in Seattle, then it lands in Atlanta. I looked up Atlanta to Barlow, and it's about five hours, so I guess I'd have to rent a car. Maybe stay in an Airbnb or something in Barlow. I don't know."

"If they're willing to pay for your air travel, love, I'd say it's pretty damned serious. You should go. What do you have to lose?"

"I don't know," I said. "It's weird and it doesn't make a lot of sense. And I couldn't find out much about the place online."

"All the more reason to board that plane, say fuck it, and go."

"Easy for you to say, Ms. Spontaneity."

She shrugged. "We all have our superpowers."

Yeah, I couldn't stop thinking about it. My brain reeled with thoughts of what the hell this invitation was. Maybe it was a mistake? Maybe it was meant for a different Madeline Bland and it was sent to the wrong house. Pretty sure I could Google the name and find at least five Madeline Blands somewhere in North America. At any rate, I didn't want to be here at Marty's. Normally, I would have loved doing this with my best friend. After Parker breaking up with me and then Peggy dying, though, I've just wanted to curl up in bed with my laptop and watch cat videos on YouTube pretty much nonstop with a cup of hot chamomile tea. Damn, that sounded pretty good.

A few college guys were eyeing us. Move along, guys, move along.

"Do you want to get out of here?"

Carly sipped her Cosmo. "Are you *serious* right now?"

"Yeah," I said. "Maybe there's still time to, I don't know, go see the late movie or drive around or something. I kinda need to clear my head."

"You are so *lame*," she said. "I go out of my way to show you a good time and cheer you up and you want to act like a granny and go to a movie or on a drive? These fake IDs I had made weren't cheap, hun."

"Yeah, and I appreciate them. But some other time, OK?" I said.

"Or you can take me home and then come back. Pretty sure that I'm killing your devil-may-care vibe with all of these cute college guys."

"Oh, please."

Carly rose as a couple of bright-eyed guys watching us sidled over to our table.

"Hey," one of them said to me. "I'm Brad."

My head started to throb. I wasn't sure if I was going to pass out in his arms or throw up on his snazzy-looking polo shirt. With everything going on, I was not in the mood to be on the rebound with some random stranger wearing khaki slacks and sporting a trendy haircut.

"You seem like a nice guy, Brad. But we're leaving."

Brown-eyed Brad gazed at his blond-bearded friend with the piercing blue eyes. "But the party's just starting, right, dude?" His friend nodded.

"That's what I told her," Carly said. "But she has her granny panties tied in a knot."

"Aw," Brad said in mock concern. "What's the matter, Granny Smith? Need some help unknotting those bad girls?"

"Forget it," I said, pushing past Brad and Yellow Beard. I had to practically body slam my way through the warm bodies huddled around the bar to find the exit.

Outside the night air was cool and crisp. That promise of autumn on the wind. This was my favorite time of year. Wool scarves. Apple cider. Rubber boots. Colorful leaves. Fingerless gloves. Hot cocoa. Bright orange pumpkins in green fields. Rainy days. Longer nights. I had a love affair with the season. I sucked in autumn's promise and blew out the lingering summer from my lungs.

"That was some seriously, righteously rude shit," Carly said storming out of Marty's and clicking down the sidewalk in her heels.

"I'm pretty sure Brad and Yellow Beard will survive."

"You can be such a selfish bitch sometimes, Mads. I swear to Christ. Lighten up and enjoy yourself for once."

"Then take me home and come back if I'm such a pain in the ass."

Carly scowled at me like she wanted to punch me in the face. Frankly, I kind of wanted to punch her back. Then her frowning face cracked into a laugh. She pointed. "Holy shit. You should see your face right now. It's all puckered up like a cat's asshole."

I shot her the finger.

"Seriously, though, I *had* you going."

"I hate when you do that shit," I said, trying to conceal a laugh.

She slapped me on the back. "You fucking love it otherwise you wouldn't keep laughing."

"Who's laughing?" And then I did. She knew me too well.

"'Yellow Beard,'" she laughed. "Now that's some funny shit, hun."

2

After we left Marty's, we drove past the multiplex theater. All of the movies looked lame, so we got a couple of greasy burgers at Burger Bliss instead. They're the best greasy-spoon joint in town—and then we headed for my house. I asked Carly to stay the night so we could sit up and talk, but she had to go to work early. Her store manager had texted her. She said she wasn't going to be there in the morning, that she was "feeling sick." Carly said she knew that the manager's boyfriend was in town.

"Whatever that Usher House invitation thingy is," I told her as she was leaving, "I'm not going."

"Why not?"

"Well, for one thing, it's weird. For a second thing, I can't take any time off work, and for a third thing, I'm broke. I couldn't even afford to go if I wanted to."

"You have such a defeatist attitude, darlin'," Carly said. "It's a *free* airline ticket. The car rental can't be that much."

"Yeah, but it's a ticket for *one* way," I said. "Don't you find that a little creepy?"

"Maybe whatever's going on will take a couple of days or whatever," she said. "If they're willing to pay for your ticket out there, I'm pretty sure they'll pay for it back."

"I still don't like it."

Carly rolled her eyes. "See you at lunch tomorrow, hun?"

"Yeah," I said. "Good night."

The burger I had forced down from earlier didn't sit well. All the grease and bread made me feel like I had swallowed a rock. So much for bliss from Burger Bliss. I slipped into my nightgown, put the sleep timer on an audiobook for 30 minutes, and went to bed. I probably heard about the first ten minutes of *Anchors Aweigh: Releasing the Past for Future Smooth Sailing*, a lame self-help book by Philip Norville, who was a local author, before I conked out.

It was about 3:13 when I was awakened by a noise. It sounded like someone had come into the house through the front door. Did I forget to lock it? I usually never did. But I had had a couple of drinks at Marty's so I could've been too tipsy to remember.

I grabbed my phone and prepared to dial 911 just in case.

Sleeping alone in the house wasn't fun. The nights seemed so much longer and darker now. That safe feeling of knowing that someone else was near. I really missed Peggy.

Rising out of bed, I crept out of the bedroom and down the dark hall.

The front door stood open. It flapped back and forth like a bat's wing in the darkness. The wind outside had picked up. The wind chimes jingled. Tree branch shadows danced on the open door from the blue streetlight across the street. Whenever the wind did pick up, the birch tree rubbed up against the wires creating a squeaking sound that always scared me a little bit. I held my phone close. One shadow from outside the door and I was punching in 911. I shut the door and locked it. *Whew!*

As I started to turn, the shadows of several figures stood in the living room. There had to be about five or six of them. One of the shadows grabbed me. It was a large-headed bald man wearing a dark overcoat. "We have you now, witch."

He pulled on my arm. I tried to get away. But he was too strong.

I hit 911 on my phone but nothing happened. The phone wouldn't dial.

Then the other men grabbed me. They pulled me through the living room and out the back door to the backyard. A sprawling oak tree dripping with brown Spanish moss stood in the middle of the yard. A tree that wasn't there before. Its thick, crooked branches outstretched into the night sky. The tendrils of moss seemed to shake at me. A layer of fog clung to the ground like a pale shroud. The wrinkled-faced men all seemed enraged. They wore overcoats and trousers. Their clothes appeared old and out of date, like from a previous century.

The bald man pushed me against the rough bark of the tree. Another man had a coiled length of rope with a hangman's noose tied on one end. He threw it up into the tree. The rope swooped over a sturdy branch with a whipping sound. The noose fell close to my head, undulating back and forth like the pendulum of a grandfather clock. Another man grabbed my hands and tied them behind my back with what felt like a leather strap.

The bald one spit on me. *"Hang the witch!"*

And that's when I woke up—the morning light shining in my face.

Holy shit, it was a dream. Ugh, it had felt so real. The night wind on my face. The rough bark of the tree. The whisper of the wind on my cheeks. What a strange dream. I've never had anything like that before. Maybe it was the indigestion from the burger? I once read that eating heavy foods before bed can give you bad dreams. It was still early, the clock read 7:06, but I didn't want to go back to sleep. I was afraid of dreaming it again.

I got up and shuffled into the kitchen. I made some coffee and watched *Regular Show* on Hulu. The moronic escapades of a dubious bluebird and a rambunctious raccoon got my mind off my nightmare. The coffee helped to scrape away the cobwebs that had settled inside my skull. I wished I could call in sick to work like Carly's manager did so often, but I needed the money. I didn't work, I didn't get paid. Besides, it was Saturday, the busiest day at Williamson's Market. My manager probably wouldn't let me stay home. We had a skeleton crew since he'd cut employee hours to the bone to save money on payroll. There wasn't exactly any coverage in the bulk department if I stayed home. Someone else from another department would have to cover. Not cool. We were all overworked there enough. Besides, if I hung around here, I'd have too much time to be depressed about being alone.

3

Thankfully, the first few hours of work flew by quickly. It was busy—I answered a lot of questions and filled lots of bins with nuts, flours, rice, trail mixes, and candy. The customers seemed to be in a good mood today. Before I knew it, it was three o'clock—time for my lunch break. I went to Taco del Diablo, ordered my usual of French fries and an iced tea, though I wasn't super hungry, and waited for Carly. She always perked me up. Then I got a text that she'd be late. A sales clerk was a no-show and Harrington's was busy, so she couldn't get away.

So, as I came out of the bathroom, I ran into Parker as he was coming into Taco del Diablo. My food leapt up to my throat and knotted there. I wasn't exactly expecting to see him.

"Hey," he said.

"Hey," was about all I could think of to say back.

"You working?"

I wanted to say obviously since I was in my khaki work pants and green polo shirt with the Williamson's Market logo embroidered on it. But I didn't. I nodded.

"Sorry," he said. "I guess that was a little obvious of a question."

"Yeah." I looked around. "Where's Mary?"

"Oh, she's up in Pullman," he said. "I came home for the weekend."

My heart did a little flutter. Did that mean that they broke up? Oh, that would be so wonderful. I don't exactly want to get back with Parker. But, if he begged and pleaded, shedding copious amounts of tears, and then fell to his knees to confess his undying love for me, I just might, stupid me. Even though our last few months together weren't exactly heaven, they were still better than moping around and being depressed in post-relationship hell.

"She's gone?"

"Huh?" He shook his head. "No, she's spending a couple of days with a friend who's going through a hard time after her boyfriend dumped her." He grinned. "And I needed to pick up a few things I left at home."

"Oh."

He laughed. "You thought that we had…?"

I shrugged. "Can't say that I didn't hope."

"I didn't know you were here," he said. "But since you are, I'll tell you that breaking up with you had nothing to do with me thinking that you were a bad person."

"Uh, I appreciate that."

"I just, I don't know, wanted a change. You know, like, it's when you have Corn Flakes every day for breakfast and you want to try Fruity Pebbles."

"So now you're comparing me to a boring breakfast cereal that was invented so white people would stop masturbating?"

"Uh, no. What? Really? I didn't know that. Weird."

"Yeah, you know your weird ex-girlfriend. Collector of random facts."

"No, hey, sorry, bad analogy. I just, I don't know, wanted a change. But it wasn't you, Mads, it was me. I just felt, you know…"

"Freaky for Fruity Pebbles?"

"Restless."

I was so pissed at Carly right now for being late. "Well, Park, I need to get back to work."

"Yeah, OK."

"I, uh, hope you and Mary are happy and you know, have like a zillion babies. Enjoy Pullman."

Parker studied me like I had revealed to him that I had an incurable disease.

I trudged outside.

In my car, I punched the steering wheel. "Stupid. Why did you say that? *Why* did you talk to him at all?"

Someone pounded on my window. I didn't look because I knew it was Parker. I sighed and prepared myself.

"Are you going to roll down the window or what, weirdo?" Carly asked.

Immediately, I started to cry.

She came around the car, opened the door, and climbed in with me. "Hey darlin', I'm sorry I was late, but don't cry about it."

"It's not about that, idiot. I ran into Parker. Then I had this weird dream last night that shook me up. And, I don't know, I'm just kind of tired of living."

Carly sat there a minute, saying nothing, which was rare for her.

"Say something," I said, I don't care what it is.

"Airport."

"What?"

"You heard me," she said. "Let's fly to Georgia and do that Usher House thing—it's only a few days away."

"But it's expensive. And I'm supposed to go alone."

"We'll figure that out when we get there. I don't know about you, but I'm ready for a goddamn vacation."

"But the *money*."

"Forget it. I've been saving to move in with you. We'll use that."

"No way. The flights, the rental car, meals, places to stay—it's too expensive."

"If you feel guilty about it, hun, you can pay me back later when you get rich."

I laughed. "Don't hold your breath." I stared out the window watching the red leaves sway in the October breeze. They looked like they were aflame. "Are you *sure* about this?"

"I'm sure," she said with a smile. "Let's do it, love, let's go."

And just like that, I was planning a trip to the Deep South.

THREE

Two days later, Carly and I hit the city limits of Barlow, Georgia before night fall.

Calling Barlow a city, of course, was like calling a mole hill a mountain. With a population of 1,280, the town in Charlton County wasn't much more than a blip on the map. We had driven southeast virtually non-stop for almost five hours from the Hartsfield-Jackson Atlanta International Airport after renting a car. The closer we got to Barlow in our borrowed black Honda Accord, the more energized I felt, if that made any sense. Each mile we traveled closer to the destination made that mysterious invitation all the more real. What was this? Why me? Why now?

We pulled into Barlow on the evening of October 12, a day before I was to go to Usher House. We rented this Airbnb on the edge of town. In fact, it was the *only* Airbnb on the edge of town. It was 32 dollars a night. Guess there wasn't exactly a large demand to stay in Barlow. As we explored the town, I could see why. Many of the downtown shops had gone out of business. The only things that were open was the local post office, a diner, and a convenience store. Since we were sick of fast food while on the highway, we decided to go into the diner, called Shirley's, to get some down-home southern cooking and hospitality. Uh, I wish that was what we actually got.

When Carly and I came through the door there was already a peculiar vibe. The place was gray and gloomy. A long, silver counter lined one wall and under it, empty stools covered in worn red leather. The black and white checkered floor looked gray from the years. The walls were painted a sickly, pale pistachio color. A line of booths stood against the windows, all empty. The waitress behind the counter, wearing a turquoise and pink outfit, appeared worn down and tired. I guessed her at about 50 or so, Peggy's age, but she seemed so much older. She seated us in a window booth. So painfully thin and frail, I worried that her arm would break off pouring us two coffees. The "coffee," for lack of a better word, tasted like warmed-over iodine.

"You two aren't from around here."

I was hesitant to speak, but then, I'm with Carly, who runs off at the mouth any opportunity she has.

"No, we're not, Faye," she said, staring at the faded pink name tag in swirly script. "We've driven down all the way from Atlanta."

"You live in A-Town?"

"No, darlin'," Carly said. "Washington."

"Y'all from D.C.?"

"Uh, no, Washington state."

The woman looked in the air, perhaps trying to figure out exactly where that was, then she cracked a faint smile that made all of her wrinkles stand up on end. "Bet you didn't come all of this way southeast to stay in Barlow. Folks don't ever stop here and stay. No reason to really. They're always passing through to go to the coast or check out Okefenokee Swamp or down to Florida or whatever there is outside of the city limits."

"We're that close to a famous swamp, huh?" Carly said with mock enthusiasm.

The waitress glared at my friend, unsure if she was serious or not.

"So you've lived here your whole life," I finally said, trying to change the subject. "Born and raised?"

"That's right. And I'll die right here too. Probably drop dead right here in Shirley's one day." She cackled. But it was a dark and sinister cackle that made my spine shiver.

"So, where's Shirley at, hun?" Carly asked.

"Died about nine years ago," Faye said in a matter-of-fact tone. "She left me to run the place. So what do y'all want to eat?"

"What's good here?"

"Well," the waitress said. "Nothing really. But if I *wanted* to eat nothing here, I'd probably order the chicken fried steak and mashed potatoes. Comes with a side of collard greens."

Carly and I looked at each other across the table. Is she for real?

"I guess we'll have that then," Carly said.

"All right," the waitress said, not writing it down. "So, where did y'all say you were headed to anyway?"

I regretted telling her. It was the first mistake of several. I pulled out the invitation and showed her. "I'm heading to a place called Usher House. Looks like it's on Route 13. Do you know it?"

Whatever friendly demeanor our waitress had suddenly slipped away. Her face hardened to stone and it was like somebody had poured cold water on her. "I'll get this order started."

She turned and strode away.

"What was *that* about?" Carly asked, stifling a giggle. She often did that as a kind of defense mechanism when stressed out I'd noticed.

"I have no idea."

"You'd think she just saw a ghost."

"Yeah, she didn't like the name Usher House."

"Yeah, or she's seriously bi-polar, like my mom," Carly laughed. "Just add a case of borderline personality disorder and they could be sisters."

"Would you shut up."

Faye returned with two waters and silverware. She squinted at us as if she had heard every word.

"So," Carly said, trying to break the tension. "What's there to do around Barlow? What kind of night life do y'all have, love?"

Faye stared at Carly for an uncomfortable moment. "It'd be best not to come out at night in Barlow."

"And why's that?"

"Be best to stay at home and mind your own business."

"Uh, OK," Carly said with faux concern. "Noted."

"You're not as smart as you think you are, little lady," Faye hissed and then walked away.

"Could you not provoke our waitress, please? No wonder Southerners are suspicious of outsiders."

"How would you know, darlin'? You've never been out of Washington."

"I've been down to Oregon. Briefly."

"If I wasn't so hungry," Carly said, "I'd get up and leave this greasy spoon shithole. I don't need this passive-aggressive bullshit. I get that at home from my mother. That's why I took this goddamn vacation from work."

"Best not use the Lord's name in vain," Faye said as she brought our dinners out to us. She set the plates down hard on the table. "Using the Lord's name in vain is a sin. Now watch those plates, they're hot." She ripped off a check, slammed it on the table, and tromped off.

The food was, shall I say, underwhelming. The potatoes were bone dry and the chicken fried steak tasted like rubber. The soggy collard greens tasted as if they were boiled with dirty socks. The gravy, which I had hoped would at least cover the underwhelming flavor of both, tasted like cardboard. As if it was a mix that sat in the package too long.

No wonder Shirley's was empty.

A customer would only patron here for Faye's charming company and the appalling food as a kind of punishment. Or if you'd lost a bet. The place was about as friendly and comforting as a cry for help.

"We're seriously GPSing a Mickey D's after this," Carly said. "'Cause I ain't eating this, hun. Our Golden Retriever, who eats *everything*, would turn his nose up to this slop."

I tried to eat as many bites of potatoes as possible and cover the steak with the rest so it looked like I had eaten it. At least I didn't shove it in a napkin and hide it under the table. That was something I had done in many foster homes. In fact, Faye and this terrible food made me feel like I was ten-years-old again and at one of the foster homes that I had ended up running away from. The only way I could find another foster home was to keep running away enough times where I would get relocated.

And every one after that would have a bland meal and a terrible host like here in Barlow.

In fact, this town had an odd feeling of familiarity. I'd never been anywhere, and yet, I felt like I'd seen this place before. Maybe it was looking at all the Airbnbs online? Lots of towns in this vicinity appeared similar. Like they were towns that were prosperous a couple of centuries ago, and then slowly died.

I grabbed the check. "I'll get this since it was my idea to come down here."

Carly smiled. "Normally, I would dispute you, love, but if you're willing to pay for this lame shit, who am I to stop you?"

The bill was thirteen dollars even. Weird. And Usher House was on Highway 13. Guess it's probably one of those weird coincidences. I pulled out my debit card, and Carly and I climbed out of our booth.

"I'll wait in the car," Carly said, making a hasty exit outside.

Faye waited at the cash register. She reminded me of a vulture perched in a tree waiting for an animal to die so it could pick their bones clean.

I glanced down not to meet her intense gaze and that's when I noticed that something was written on the back of the check. I turned it over. And in her handwriting that resembled a bunch of dead spiders all strung together, it said:

<u>STAY AWAY FROM USHER HOUSE</u>

Pretending that I didn't see her writing, I walked up to the counter and passed her my debit card. She handed it right back and pointed at the register.

In block letters on a faded 3 x 5 card it said "Cash only." I rarely carried cash, and doubted that I had any. Maybe Carly had some? I didn't want to spend another minute in this place washing dishes or mopping floors to work off the bill. The further distance I could put between Faye and myself, the better I would feel.

I dug into my wallet. I happened to have two fives and three ones —13 dollars exactly. Maybe it was a sign? No, I didn't believe in signs. A happy coincidence. I handed her the money and the check, then I turned and started for the door.

"You didn't leave a tip," Faye said.

I sucked in my breath and turned. "Sorry, maybe next time. That's all the cash I have."

Faye regarded me the way a scientist might study an ant under a microscope.

"Well," I said. "See you around."

"You saw my note, didn't you." It was more of a statement than a question.

I nodded.

"That's *my* tip to you, girl. And about the best advice I've ever given anyone. Heed it."

"Why?"

"The same reason that you don't jump off a bridge or swim in a pond filled with leeches. You just don't."

"Uh, thanks," I said, and hurried out the door.

FOUR

1

The Airbnb that Carly and I stayed in was a modest home that reminded me a lot of the Bland house. It was about the same square footage and had three small bedrooms. The décor the hosts provided was, shall we say, Generic Chic—white walls and plaques on them that stated sentiments like LIVE, LAUGH, and LOVE. Carly and I finished our burgers, fries, and sodas. We'd found a Jack in the Box about 25 miles out of town. Even though we were sick of fast food, it was worth the drive, believe me. Once we got back to the place, we sat there and reminisced about our weird Faye experience at Shirley's Diner.

"I think I should go with you, hun," Carly said. "If she's saying it's dangerous."

"Maybe we shouldn't go at all."

"But we've came all of this way—and you did RSVP. That'd be rude, right?"

The WiFi in this basic house sucked, the signal dropping in and out. I was, however, able to search for anything I could on Usher House, just as I had done back at home. There wasn't much more information though. They were a prominent aristocratic family who'd had a manor moved over from Europe stone by stone back in the late 1800s. They had been prosperous tobacco farmers, but then had fallen on hard times due to an unexplained drought in the area. The Ushers were forced to invest in other businesses to stay afloat but after some bad ventures, most of the fortune was lost. I couldn't find any relevant information on the family or the house for the last few decades.

2

The next day, Carly drove me to Usher House.

We left an hour early, five o' clock, so we had enough time to find the place and I could make an entrance. I wore the best dress I had, a black cocktail one, and a cute little matching handbag. I had hoped that there would be royalty attending and decorative lights strung in trees. Valet parking. Butlers. Handsome guests. These had been a family of aristocrats once. I couldn't have been more wrong.

"Where the fresh hell is this place, love?" Carly said.

I used Google Maps on my phone. It didn't give us a precise location to the place. The address was Route 13, Box 1839, Barlow, GA. To top it all off, it was raining hard. Like Biblical rain. The drops struck the car like bullets. It made visibility challenging. It seemed unusually dark for five o' clock in the evening.

The trees down this stretch of the highway, many covered in gray Spanish moss, seemed to lurk near the edge of the roadway almost reaching down to scratch at us with their leafy limbs. I didn't see a light or a house for miles. It's like nothing lived out here except trees and wild grass sedges. Like we had found a part of the world where two strips of concrete had been laid down for a road and then forgotten, and nature had taken over. The road was cracked in places with potholes that Carly either hit or veered to avoid.

"Obviously a well-maintained road," Carly quipped, squinting into the darkness. She turned to me. "This whole thing seems weird. I'm just getting a bad feeling about it. Maybe we should turn back. What's the harm, hun? Forget the RSVP shit."

I wanted to agree with her. It was strange, and I was nervous. The closer we came to our apparent destination, though, the more anxious I felt, and in an odd way, energized too. I had to know what this was about. I didn't care if it was raining. We'd come a long way and I wanted to find out what this Usher House business was all about.

Headlights appeared on the horizon coming from the other direction made me feel relieved. *Someone* was out here in this mess with us. Even if it was a total stranger who we would only pass in the night. It was odd that an anonymous person's headlights could be so reassuring.

The figure appeared almost out of nowhere—a person wearing a dark, hooded cloak standing in the middle of the road. The individual raised their hands, the fingers long, thin, and feminine-looking, but I couldn't see a face under the shadowy hood of the cloak.

"Don't hit them!" I screamed.

"Who?" Carly said.

She kept driving, but the person wouldn't move.

"Can't you see them?"

"See who?"

Carly was going to strike them. I don't know why she couldn't see a person in a dark cloak standing in the middle of the road like a six-foot-tall raven. Reaching over, I jerked the wheel.

"What are you doing?" she asked.

The car swerved. We missed the person who stood statue still. Our rental car hydroplaned on the slick road. All I could see was a red Tundra pick-up about to hit us. The driver swerved.

Our car slid off the side of the road and into the tall grass.

"Holy fucking shit," Carly said. "Why did you do that? You nearly killed us."

"I don't know," I said, catching my breath. A dark figure approached the car. "They're coming this way. Lock the doors."

Carly rifled into her bag, fumbling for her phone. "I'm calling the state police, Duane 'The Rock' Johnson, I don't give a shit, somebody..."

A guy wearing a tan jacket knocked on my window. It wasn't the cloaked figure. It must've been the driver of the Tundra. This guy wore a green and white cap that said DELANEY FARMS across it, water dripping off the brim. He wore jeans, work boots, and a tan jacket. He had a handsome, kind face and the rain didn't seem to bother him much. He said something but I couldn't hear him. I rolled down my window a couple of inches, trying not to let the rain in.

"Are you all right in there?" he asked. "I nearly hit you."

"We…there was this person in the road…almost hit them," my voice was shaking.

The driver searched around.

"What person?"

I peered out into the storm. The cloaked figure that bore a resemblance to raven's wings was gone. "Well, they *were* there." I know what I saw even if I sounded crazy.

"OK," the guy said. "I'll take your word for it."

"I didn't see anyone, darlin'," Carly said. "I think she's off her meds."

I punched her in the arm. "I don't take meds."

"Then maybe you should. Why would you grab the wheel like that?"

The guy regarded us like we were deranged. "So, do you think y'all can pull out of this ditch?"

"Of course," Carly said. She threw the car into reverse. We didn't go anywhere. The motor revved as the tire in the ditch spun in the wet grass and the red clay.

"Try putting it into drive, coming forward, and then rocking it back into reverse."

Carly did that. A few times. We were stuck. I looked at my watch. It was 5:45. I was going to be late to the mysterious Usher House. A knot formed in the pit of my stomach. Was that kind of a bad omen? First Faye in Shirley's Diner and now this cloaked person out in the rain in the middle of nowhere who was there one minute and gone the next. I *saw* them. I may be a little tired and anxiety-ridden at the moment, but I'm not prone to hallucinations.

"I'll give you a tow," the guy said. "Don't go anyplace." He disappeared. I rolled the window back up as the rain was pouring in.

"Don't go anyplace?" Carly said. "Wow, he's a laugh riot."

I shrugged. "Well, at least he's nice-looking."

"Yeah, great."

The back-up lights of the red Tundra came on. The driver backed up to our car. He hit the hazard flashers on his truck. Then he jumped out and grabbed a chain from the bed. He hooked it onto the bottom of his truck and then the bottom of our car. He ran back through the rain to Carly's side and knocked on the window. She rolled it down again.

"Throw your car into neutral," he said. "I'll do the rest."

"Gotcha, hun," Carly said.

And she did.

The driver jumped back into the truck and pulled forward. After the chain's slack was taken up, our car shuddered backward out of the red mud and wet grass, and back onto the road.

The guy jumped back out and started to unhook his chains.

"Do you think he knows where this place is?" I asked Carly.

"Wouldn't hurt to ask."

I waved to the guy. Hopefully he could see me through the rain. He threw the chain back into the bed of his truck and scrambled over to my window, which I lowered again. He leaned in closer this time. His face was angular with high cheekbones and a pronounced chin. He had sparkling blue eyes and an even tan.

"Hey," I said. His handsomeness made me forget the question I was going to ask.

"Hey," he said back and seemed amused.

"I, uh, I'm Mads." I reached out a finger. He touched his finger to mine and pretended to shake it.

"Ahem," my friend said.

"And this is Carly."

Carly nodded. Even though he was wet from the rain, he smelled good. Like ozone from the outdoors and a hint of fresh pine.

"Glad to meet you Mads and Carly," he said, shouting over the rain. "I'm Liam. Liam Delaney. Of Delaney Farms. We're just down the road apiece." He pointed. "And I'm glad I didn't run into y'all. That would've been bad."

"Yeah," I said. "So, Liam, we're trying to find this place called Usher House. Can you help us?"

Liam's friendly countenance shifted to a grave expression, and I was reminded a little of Faye back at the diner when the mention of the same place was put to her.

"Why on God's green earth would you want to go there?"

I unearthed my invitation and pressed it to the window. He studied it. "An invitation?" he said, shaking his head. "Well, if you really want to go to that place, you're in luck. You just head down this road another half mile and you're there. It's on the left. You have to look for the gate though. The place just kinda creeps up on you."

"Thank you, Liam," I said.

He gave me an intense look. "You be careful there, Mads. I mean it." Then he reached in his pocket and pulled out a business card. He slipped it through the gap in the window. "And if anything, I don't know, weird, should happen, you give me a call." He gave a faint smile. "I'll see if I can tow you out again."

He sauntered back to his Tundra. Though it was hard to see outside in all the rain, I watched him go in the side view mirror. The Levi's he was wearing fit snugly against his well-formed buttocks and strong-looking legs. Not a bad view for such a rainy evening.

"Are you ready?" Carly asked.

"Yeah," I said, remembering that I had a date with this place. "We'd better go or we're going to be late." I slipped Liam's card into my purse.

3

Five minutes later, we found ourselves in front of a gate. It had a large padlock on it. Over the top arched an iron U. Rusted metal numbers in the stone gate pillar read 1839. Beyond the gate though the trees were so thick, that I couldn't see a house. Only a lane that disappeared into the darkness.

"This has to be it. Just like Liam said."

"What?"

"See," I said, pointing to the tell-tale letter U on the metal archway.

"But there's a huge lock on the gate. They're obviously *not* expecting company."

I couldn't exactly tell Carly how I was feeling, and why I was feeling this way, but I felt like two witching rods that had found a well. The skin on my arms stood on end. My spine tingled. Every part of me felt alive like an electrical surge had jolted my body. This *was* the place. This was Usher House.

"This. Is. It."

"OK, fine. How are you even going to get in, hun? What, did you bring a pair of bolt cutters to chop that lock and then you're going to stroll out into the storm? Or should we call lover boy back there to come and bail us out?"

"What do you mean, lover boy?"

"I saw the way you were looking at him, Captain Obvious."

"I was not," I lied. She did have a point. This place looked as foreboding as it did unwelcoming.

We sat there for several moments, not speaking.

"What do you want to do, darlin'?" she finally asked.

What should we do? We were on time but nobody to greet us.

At that moment, a face appeared in our headlights. He stood there, holding an umbrella, behind the fence. He was a gaunt man with a milky complexion, and his grizzled, thin, white-whiskered face made it clear he was old enough to collect social security. He wore a dark woolen flat cap, grimy khaki dungarees, and a ratty tweed jacket. He didn't resemble the person in the road who was there and then vanished. But who could tell? That person was wearing a dark, hooded cloak. The man reached up and with a long black skeleton key, unlocked the gate.

Carly inched the black car forward through the tall, wrought-iron gate. The man left barely enough room for us to navigate the car through. He skulked on my side of the car, solemnly, not moving. Only looking at me with his one dark eye. The other eye had a thin coating over it that reminded me of a spider's egg.

I buzzed the window down a couple of inches.

"Is this Usher House?"

He nodded.

"I have an invitation." I held it up.

The one-eyed man nodded again, and then peered at Carly through the glass. It was obvious from his stone-faced gaze that he didn't approve of her.

"Yeah," I said, "the invitation said I wasn't supposed to bring a guest. This is my driver. I, uh, *need* my driver."

Carly gave a big smile and wave. "Some weather, huh, hun?"

The thin old man said nothing. Was he purposely saying nothing or could he not speak?

"Do you want a ride?" I said

The gatekeeper stood there, the rain pelting down on his umbrella like a drum, and then he motioned us on.

"Proceed, James," I said, rolling up the window.

"What's up with Stoney McStonerFace?" Carly asked.

"Would *you* be happy standing out in the rain?"

Carly drove slowly up the narrow lane. The one-eyed man shut the gate behind us and locked it. Carly and I took note. He trailed us.

"This place is like Red Flag City," she said.

"It will be fine."

"Oh, great. And what happens if they axe murder us up into tiny bits? Will that be 'fine' too?"

"Why would that happen?"

The trees were thick on either side. We crawled along the lane in silence. In the headlights, I noticed pale, wiggly things that slithered on the cracked pavement. Thousands of them.

"Worms," I said and pointed.

"Oh, hun, that's some nasty-ass shit right there."

"Avoid them," I said.

"How can I, love? They're all over the damned road."

"Well, try, 'love.' Poor things."

Carly slowed down and tried to avoid as many earthworms as she could. Still, I could hear them under the tires popping, their little bodies exploding, and it made me cringe. I stole a glance in the side view mirror. The silent man in the tweed coat shuffled behind us under the umbrella.

Up ahead—Usher House appeared.

FIVE

The massive beast of a house lurked in a clearing. More than a mansion but not quite a palace. I guess it was what you'd call a manor. Its stone walls reached up into the dark sky. Several chimneys spouted off the roof, each one resembling cylindrical tombstones. A single tower spiraled upwards, capped with a flat roof and a widow's walk surrounded by a steel bar railing. Copper lightning rods, many ornate in design with scarab beetles and stars and moons, were interspersed on the roof's spine like spindly insect legs. Stone gargoyles peered down from the roof's cornices. The Gothic arched windows all appeared like eyes. It was a dreary house that was visibly unhappy, a mansion of gloom. The web had said that Usher House was brought over stone by stone from someplace in Europe. It seemed out of place here in rural southeastern Georgia.

Another thing that I thought peculiar was the trees around the place were dead. Leading up to the house, they were very much alive and teeming with green foliage. But at almost a perfect circle around the place, all of the trees were naked of vegetation with dark, twisted trunks. Trees long dead. What appeared as if it was once a lake in front of the towering house was now black and stagnant, a swampy marsh. It seemed as if nothing had lived in it for a long time.

"Hashtag Count Dracula," Carly said, slowing the car down to a creep.

"No shit," I agreed.

We inched up to the house. Most of the windows were dark and the house seemed empty, but at the same time, I felt like a thousand eyes were watching us.

In front of the house stood a gargoyle fountain. The winged, stone demon with pointed horns rested its massive head on its hands. It gurgled dingy liquid from its fixed, gaping mouth into a pool filled with brackish water. The gargoyle peered at Carly and me with fixed, lifeless eyes.

The vibrations on my skin felt electric as if my outer layer might crawl off my body on its own. Carly parked. The one-eyed man strolled up to my side of the car and waited for me to open the door. He gestured, wanting to walk me to the front door, which were two tall and sturdy doors made of what looked like oak with heavy iron hinges.

I rolled down my window a few inches. "What about my driver?"

The silent gatekeeper motioned to "stay."

"Can you wait here a few minutes? Just so I can find out what they want?"

"I will be waiting by the phone. Call me or text if it gets weird. And if you're not back outside in fifteen minutes to tell me what's going on, hun, I'm driving off."

"You'd leave me?"

"You're my best friend and I love you, but I love myself more." She kissed the air.

"I'll be right back."

"Huh," Carly said. "Don't you know that in a horror movie you're not supposed to say that."

"This *isn't* a horror movie." I rolled my eyes, grabbed my purse, and climbed out of the car into the pouring rain. I put my bag over my head to protect my hair the best I could. I didn't want to walk into this creepy mansion looking like a drowned rat. But, who knows, maybe that would be a perk considering the state of the place.

Clutching the umbrella, the gatekeeper ushered me up to the colossal oak doors. He grasped one of the iron knockers with a dirty, bony hand and struck it three times. We waited. The man cocked his one good eye at me. I turned away, still marveling at the antiquated architecture of this astonishing and yet foreboding mansion. With its dark chimneys jutting up from its arched, gothic gables, it's the sort of place that you've seen in every old scary movie. Now here I was, every fiber of my being on edge, hopefully not starring my own horror story. What the hell was I doing here? Why did I need to find out what was behind these towering doors so badly?

One tall door creaked open. The quiet man with one milky eye gestured for me to enter. The foyer was dark. It took my eyes a moment to adjust. As they did, I noticed a figure standing in front of me—a woman who was anemic-looking with high cheekbones, an aquiline nose, and intense gray eyes wearing a long, black dress frocked with a white collar. A style of dress out of date about 100 years ago. Maybe longer. Her hair, charcoal-colored with traces of silver lightning bolt strands, was pulled back into a severe bun. She stood there, thin-lipped. After a moment, she cracked the faintest of smiles, one that made it seem like it damaged her face to do so.

"You are one Madeline Bland?"

"Uh, Maddy, or, you know, Mads, if you really get to know me."

The woman seemed unamused at my attempt of humor.

"You've been expected," she said. Then she looked at the man. "You can go."

The man nodded. She shut the large door in his face.

"He, uh, doesn't say much."

"That is because he cannot. He's mute and stupid. But he does serve a purpose. He's the groundskeeper."

Groundskeeper, really? I have news for you—everything around the circumference of the house that I saw was dead and decayed. What was the alleged groundskeeper doing, napping?

"Does he have a name?"

"You can call him Knapp."

Oh, yeah, appropriate name.

The tall, dark woman led me from the foyer into the entry way of the manor. The ceilings were cathedral tall. A winding staircase covered in red carpet on one side led up to the second floor. The walls were lined with dark wood wainscoting. A huge glass chandelier stood in the center of the room. Though it was lit, it didn't seem to lighten up the impenetrable gloom. The place seemed like it had been sealed up since the early twentieth century. Nothing modern was around. No TV, no computer, no telephone. It's like I'd stepped into another century when I crossed the doorway threshold.

"I am Dietrich," the woman said. "Mrs. Ingrid Dietrich. Let me take your wet purse."

"It's fine," I said, keeping my purse close to me, my phone inside. Carly was a press of the button away, though I couldn't imagine running back out into the storm. Knapp had locked the gate behind us, after all. "My, uh, driver is waiting outside in the car," I added. "Is this going to take long so I can let her know?"

"We are expecting more visitors," Mrs. Dietrich said. "However, because of the storm, they seem to be late. You're the first to arrive."

"I see."

"The invitation also said no guests."

"Yeah, like I said, Ms. Mackenzie's not a guest. Just, a, uh, driver that I hired. But I don't want her to be uncomfortable."

Mrs. Dietrich turned away from me. Obviously she didn't care about my friend waiting in the car during a storm. Poor Carly.

"You brought no bags," the housekeeper said, peering at my tiny purse.

"Why would I do that?" I said. "I didn't know this was an overnight thing."

The housekeeper gawked. She motioned to the door of another room. Inside it glowed with firelight. Walking in, a long table was elegantly set with food—red wine, a roast bird of some kind, and about every variety of cuisine imaginable. A crackling fire roared. The Usher crest loomed in the back of the fireplace. The antique wallpaper was crimson, casting the room in a blood-red tint.

My stomach rumbled. I hadn't eaten much since we had arrived in Barlow. But I also felt guilty possibly eating anything while my friend was outside in the car. I strolled over and searched for a water pitcher.

"Is there, um, any water?"

"The water here is foul," Mrs. Dietrich said, not offering any more information.

Wine it is, I guess. So I poured a glass. Partially to take what was offered, and partly to calm my frayed nerves. Now that I was in Usher House, anxiety had gripped me again. So many shadows stood here. So many dark corners. Though the place did have some dim electric lights on, it was mostly lit by candlelight. Candelabras were on the table and sconces with candles glowed on the scarlet walls. It gave the place a warm glow, but also a menacing feeling too. Trophy animal heads hung on the wall—deer, antelope, wild boar, and even a lion. One of the Ushers, it seemed, was a sportsman and liked to hunt big game. I detested dead animals hanging on walls with their dead, glassy eyes staring at me. It always made me feel uneasy, and in a foreboding house like Usher, this was no exception.

When Mrs. Dietrich left me alone, I sauntered over to the fire, set my blood-colored wine on the hearth, and then pulled out my phone. I texted Carly that there's food and wine inside. She texted back that she's bored, there's no WiFi signal, and she's thinking about leaving me in here if I don't invite her in. I told her I would think of something.

As I waited for Mrs. Dietrich to appear again, I wandered out of the dining room and back into the entryway. Along the staircase leading up to the second floor were portrait paintings. I thought I would look at those while I waited. And I was also trying to figure out a way to get Carly in the manor without upsetting anyone.

The first painting was Lenore Usher, according to the gold plate at the bottom of the frame. She was young and beautiful, looking like she was about twenty or so when the painting was done. The next portrait up was Vincent Usher, who wore an intense gaze and a shock of white hair, though he didn't appear that old in the picture. The next painting up from Vincent was Sebastian Usher, another intense -looking gentleman with a sheaf of dark hair and bushy eyebrows. One thing I noticed was the clothing that they wore in the paintings. Lenore, at the first landing of the stairs, wore more modern-looking clothes, where the other Ushers, the further up the stairs you ventured, wore more old-fashioned clothing. It seemed that the lineage of Ushers hung on the wall was in an ascending order down the stairs. At the top of the stairs stood a painting of Eva Usher. She was a ravishing beauty with midnight hair and fierce green eyes. The same color as mine. The painting was more mesmerizing than the others, at least to me. Unlike the others, Eva's eyes seemed alive and constantly staring at you no matter what angle you looked at the portrait. Whomever this particular Usher was, she seemed a bright one. Next to her was a dapper and refined Corbin Usher, and—

"You found the family portraits," Mrs. Dietrich said from the shadows of the second-floor hallway. When I left her, she had been downstairs. She travelled fast—and silent.

"Um, yeah," I said, trying to not look unnerved. "Some interesting-looking people."

"They were all colorful and unique in their own ways."

"Did you know them?"

"I have been in the service of the Usher family since nineteen-sixty-six," she said. "I only knew Ms. Lenore, Sir Vincent, and earlier, Sir Sebastian and Lady Virginia. The rest, I am afraid, are before my time."

My phone buzzed with a fresh text from Carly.

"Ah," I said. "My, uh, driver, Ms. Mackenzie has a bladder condition and needs to use the bathroom. Do you think it would be all right for her to come in and do so?"

"It seems you don't have a very efficient driver."

I shrugged. "What can I say? She came cheap."

Mrs. Dietrich glided past me. "Now that you're on the second floor, I will show you to your room."

"Uh, like I said earlier, I wasn't expecting to stay."

Strike two for Carly. I'm going to have to think of something else.

Mrs. Dietrich ushered me to a room at the end of the hall. It had a roaring fireplace, a four-poster canopy bed with red velvet curtains. A beautiful vanity with a silver hairbrush and mirror. An oak writing desk. A huge oak wardrobe. And two French doors that led out to what I presumed was a balcony. It's the kind of room I'd seen in old movies, but this was the real deal. It was gorgeous.

"This was Ms. Eva's room, I have been told," she said. "It has remained exactly the way she left it the day she died over a century ago."

"You mean nobody's came in here in all this time?"

"Naturally. The linens need to be changed, the windows opened to freshen up the room, and the usual dusting of furniture. It was selected only for you as it's one of the most hospitable rooms in Usher House. We don't receive visitors otherwise, and haven't for many decades. I freshened it up personally this afternoon in preparation for your arrival."

Wow, it's a pity that this Usher House was so creepy because this was the most charming room that I'd ever seen. Over the fireplace was another portrait of Eva Usher. The bewitching eyes that seemed to follow you wherever you went in the room appeared in this painting, too. Eva seemed to stare at me from across the room with those emerald eyes in silent judgement. If I stayed, I didn't know if I could take her peering at me like that all night. I was glad that the old canopy bed had red velvet curtains.

"Is, there, a uh, little girl's room?" I asked.

"There's a common lavatory at the end of the hall. When the house was shipped over from Europe and reconstructed nearly one-hundred and fifty years ago, such conveniences in each room were not commonplace, I'm afraid."

"That's fine," I said. "Can you point the way?"

She escorted me back out into the hallway and pointed to the room at one end. At least I had the room that was closest to the bathroom. Another room stood directly across the hall. The door was closed, but underneath the crack, light flickered. Evidentially, that room had been freshened up by Mrs. Dietrich this afternoon, too.

Excusing myself, I sidled into the bathroom, shutting the door. The knob was a beautiful cut glass. The floor was a black and white honeycomb tile. It was one of those old-fashioned toilets I'd seen in photographs where the water reservoir was kept above the toilet bowl, and it had a pull chain instead of a handle. I sat on the pot, relieved my full bladder of some burdening fluids, and flushed. Ugh, the fresh water rolling into the toilet reeked like rotten eggs. That meant a high sulphur content according to my science classes. The water was foul indeed. Glad I'd drank the wine instead.

After that, I checked my hair and make-up in the mirror. I resembled a drowned rat—*great.* I didn't bring much but lipstick in my bag. Pretty sure Carly had some though.

Oh, damn, poor Carly. I called her.

"Branson speaking," she said as she answered the phone. "He's about to call the chauffer's union and let them know that he's being abused and neglected by his thoughtless client at motherfucking *Downton Abbey.*"

"I'm trying to get you into the house, 'Branson'. You should see this place, it's incredible."

"Well, I wouldn't know."

"I'm working on it, Jesus. I'll think of something."

"Have you found out what they want?"

"No. Some other guests are supposed to show up but they haven't arrived yet. And, uh, there's another catch too."

"Thrill me."

"They want me to stay the night."

She sighed. "I'm not staying in the car all damned night, darlin'. I'm your best friend but that does have its limits."

"Well, I'm guessing that they'll either let you stay or they'll send you home."

"Right now, I'm game for either, but I want out of this damned rental car."

"OK."

"Hey, wait a sec. There's something out here. It moved near a tree."

"Don't you mean someone? It was probably that Knapp guy who showed us in."

"I don't know. It didn't look like a person. It was kind of hunched over." She started to whisper. "Get me out of here. I don't have a good feeling about this."

"Don't get out of the car," I whispered back. "I'll come get you now."

SIX

1

Hurrying out of the bathroom, I expected Mrs. Dietrich to be waiting for me. She wasn't. I glanced in the room I was to stay in. She wasn't there either. The lady had vanished.

I rushed down the hall, past the banister, around the newel post and down the stairs. Maybe I could just let Carly in. You know—don't ask for permission and beg for forgiveness. I was getting tired of this game anyway. I was tired of being in the dark, literally—I wanted my friend.

When I reached the front door, I turned the knob. It wouldn't move. It had several bolts in place. Odd that it was locked so tightly. I shoved the bolts open, at first trying to be quiet as to not make Mrs. Dietrich aware of what I was doing, but then I didn't care.

I threw open the last bolt, opened the door, and burst out into the storm. The rain hadn't let up at all. A flash of lightning blinded me for a moment, and deafening thunder rolled through the dark sky a moment following—the storm was close.

Reaching the car, I pounded on the window, motioning Carly to come into the house.

She climbed out of the car, clutching her bag close to her.

The blackness beyond the driveway was as murky as mud. I could only see the outlines of the trees and the swamp from the brief but brilliant flashes of lightning. Another bolt flashed. At the edge of the swamp, I saw something. It crouched near a bush—and the eyes lit up yellow in a flash of lightning. The thing didn't move. I couldn't tell if it was a man crouched down or an animal. But it didn't give me a good feeling. When the lightning flashed again, the thing had moved. Closer. It was stalking us.

"Come on, Carly," I said. "Move."

Carly didn't look behind her. She slipped—and fell on the wet tiles out in front of the house.

I picked her up.

When the lightning flashed again. The thing had moved. It wasn't where it was previously. It lurked near the car. It was coming closer—and it moved inhumanly fast.

"Let's go."

Rushing Carly inside, I slammed the door against the storm and whatever that thing was stalking around outside. I threw a deadbolt across the heavy door.

"What in the blue blazes are you doing?" Mrs. Dietrich stood in the hall with her arms crossed.

"There's something outside," I said. "It was *stalking* us."

"The only thing outside is Mr. Knapp making sure that everything is in order."

"It wasn't Mr. Knapp. And I hope he's safe somewhere. Whatever it was seemed to want…"

"Want what?"

"I don't know."

"The storm plays strange tricks with the light. I have seen many strange things in all of my years here, but they turned out to be nothing. It is only an old house and old grounds, nothing more. The imagination can conjure phantoms, but they exist only there."

My imagination didn't conjure this phantom, my eyes did, because it was *there.* Carly didn't see the cloaked person in the road, but she saw this. That means I wasn't imagining it.

Mrs. Dietrich stared at Carly with an icy gaze that would freeze a glass of water.

"This is my driver, Ms. Mackenzie. I was concerned for her safety."

Carly waived. "Hey ya. Just call me Carly, darlin'."

The housekeeper wrinkled her nose at my friend. "We have servant's quarters. I can show you where they are. You will need to freshen up." She looked over at me. "Both of you."

"Servant's quarters? Seriously?"

"If it's all the same to you, Mrs. Dietrich, I'd rather that Ms. Mackenzie stay in my room with me."

"That is not permitted."

"Why not?"

Mrs. Dietrich evaluated both of us. "Because no illicit behavior is allowed in this house."

"We're not, like, a couple or anything."

"Uh, no," Carly said. "I like guys. Like, a lot. Probably too much. I mean, if I were into girls, I could do worse than shit-for-brains here. But yeah, I'm all about the hotdog in the bun, the beef in the taco, the sausage in the Kaiser roll, if you know what I mean." She winked at the housekeeper.

I kicked Carly's foot and whispered. "Don't do this. Please."

Mrs. Dietrich glared.

"Very well, I will prepare another room on the second floor. Which means much more work for me."

"I am terribly sorry, Mrs. Dietrich," I said." I can help you with that."

"The tidiness of the rooms in Usher House is my sole responsibility," she said. "In the interim, you may utilize the lavatory to freshen up. You know where it is." She spun around on her heel and was off.

"Wow, who's Nurse Ratchet?"

"That's Mrs. Dietrich."

"No, not Nurse Ratchet," Carly whispered. "Remember that movie where the four kids were forced to live in the attic of that creepy old house? *That* lady. She reminds me of the *Flowers in the Attic* lady."

"Come on," I said. "I'll show you to the bathroom. 'Sausage in the Kaiser roll.' You embarrassing asshole."

"Hey," Carly said. "I am endowed with my gifts."

2

Once I was freshened up, I went into my room. I peered outside through the lace curtains. The storm was passing on the other side of the house. The lightning and thunder subsiding. In the darkness, and the brief flashes of light, I couldn't see any trace of the person or thing that had stalked us. Nothing at all but the swaying trees and blackness.

Then something sliced through the trees—headlights. They slashed through the night and the rain. I watched as the car pulled up behind our rented black Honda Accord. It was a late-model car, also black. It looked regal and expensive.

A man climbed out of the car. An older gentleman from what I could tell. And then a younger man, slender and good-looking, climbed out of the passenger seat. He peered up at the house. I stood absolutely still. And yet, he scanned over in my direction and held his gaze there for a moment. Staring directly at me, I was certain he couldn't see me through the lacy curtains, but I could have been wrong. He turned away and the two disappeared under the eaves of the porch.

Though the room was more comfortable than the rest of Usher House, I was here to meet whomever those people were; might as well get this over with and find out why I was invited here.

I sat down at the vanity. I was hesitant to use the silver-plated hairbrush there, which looked a couple of centuries old, but I didn't really have anything else. I brushed my hair, which had dried some. Not much I could do without a blow dryer and a curling iron. Carly, who was staying in the room down the hall, had some make-up in her purse. Later, I would touch myself up with that. I startled a moment, catching somebody watching me in the mirror. That's when I realized that it was Eva Usher. The painting over the fireplace. Her feline eyes seemed to peer right into mine.

"Sorry, Ms. Eva," I said to the mirror. "But I had to use your hairbrush." The bristles still had strands of her midnight black hair. It's the darkest hair I'd ever seen, even darker than mine, which was about the color of dark-roast coffee.

I set the brush down and climbed off the chair.

Then I crept down the hall and knocked on Carly's door. She opened it. I checked out her room. It was similar to mine with a canopy bed with red velvet curtains and a fireplace. Comfortable, but not as cozy as my room, I mean *Eva's* room. Mrs. Dietrich had prepared it in a hurry. She seemed to have superhuman abilities of speed. Though I guess since that was her sole job, as she said, she was efficient at her duties.

"Can you believe this place?" Carly said. "I swear to god I died and became a Disney Princess in her own castle."

"Well, don't get too used to it, Belle," I said. "We're out of here in the morning. Back to Barlow."

Carly made a pouty face.

"I'm going downstairs. Some more guests have arrived. I'm guessing this is it."

"They're like, almost an hour late."

"Yeah."

"Give me a sec, I just need to do a touch up and we'll go down together."

I shook my head. "You're my driver, remember? You stay put. I'll report back with everything soon. Just, I don't know, do whatever a Disney Princess does when they're alone."

"Sing to bluebirds and squirrels and shit?"

"Yeah, that." We both laughed.

I walked down the hall. It was odd—I'd been here for nearly an hour and I was starting to feel comfortable. Despite, of course, whatever the hell was stalking around outside. It would be a shame to leave this place in the morning. But, it would also be nice to get back to familiar surroundings. Pickman Flats wasn't exactly heaven, but it's the only heaven I knew.

Strolling along the hallway, I glided my hand along the smooth banister. The grainy wood was well worn, as if a dozen Ushers had done that exact thing over the centuries. Peering over the banister, the men who had come in were nowhere in sight, neither was Mrs. Dietrich. That's odd. I thought that for sure there would be pleasantries and all of that.

Heading to the staircase, I descended, gazing at the Usher portraits along the wall. They all seemed to watch me. I kind of remembered a few of them looking in opposite directions, but maybe I was wrong. It was easy to be disoriented in Usher House—like the law of physics didn't quite operate the same here. Like as soon as you stepped on the grounds, you were swallowed up into a world that existed within the shadow of our own. A dark, remote island lost among the sea of trees.

Voices chattered from the dining hall, so I followed them. The older gentleman was helping himself to a heaping plate of food where the younger gentleman was sipping wine by the fireplace, exactly as I had done. He had a familiarity about him that I couldn't quite pinpoint.

Mrs. Dietrich, as usual, appeared out of nowhere to my left. I hadn't noticed her there a moment before.

"Miss Madeline," she said, in a tone much softer and kinder than it had been previously. "I want you to meet Mr. Ernest Walsh and Mr. Roderick Smith."

The men each turned to me. Mr. Walsh, the older one, had thinning auburn hair, wore a tan herringbone jacket, and had a handlebar mustache with flecks of gray in it. He looked very old-fashioned. He extended his waxy pink hand.

"It's a pleasure to finally meet you," he said. "It was quite a devil tracking you down."

"It was?"

"Why yes. I'm the one who sent you the invitation."

Yeah, a guy who sends an invitation to a party and shows up an hour late.

"The terrible weather delayed us from the airport, unfortunately. Apologies to keep you waiting."

"It's all right," I said, forcing a smile. "I've been making myself as comfortable as possible here."

The younger man rounded the table. He was dressed like midnight —a black blazer over a black shirt and slacks. His dark shoes gleamed in the firelight. He extended his hand. Though he was slender and looked even a tad delicate, his grip was bony and strong.

"A pleasure to finally meet you. I've heard so much about you."

"You have?"

"Of course," he said. "Don't you know?"

"Know what?"

He looked over at Mr. Walsh, who shrugged, and then to Mrs. Dietrich, who turned away.

The young man smiled. "I'm your brother."

<h1 style="text-align:center">SEVEN</h1>

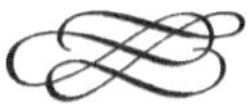

*P*ardon me if I catch my breath. It's not every day you find out that you have a sibling. I mean, it could be a mistake. But studying him, we had so similar of features. The same quaint nose, the sharp eyes, the high forehead, the pointed chin, and almost the same color hair, though his was much fairer than mine, and shorter, but as equally wavy. Our eyes were also a creamy emerald.

"Your mother," Mr. Walsh interrupted, "was Lenore Usher. After she gave birth to you, she gave you each up for adoption. It was a complete nightmare to track her down, and the records, in fact, it took me years, but, well, here you are. Brother and sister. The next line of Ushers."

"You mean I'm an Usher?" I asked.

"Why yes," Mr. Walsh said. "Being an Usher is your birthright. And since you two are the last remaining Ushers—this house, and all it contains, are yours equally."

My knees felt weak and I thought I would fall over. I grabbed the edge of the table.

"Would you like to sit down?" my "brother" asked me.

"I'll be OK," I said. I grabbed a silver goblet and poured myself a cup of wine to the brim. I drank it down, then poured another. Drank half of that.

Mr. Walsh, Mrs. Dietrich, and Roderick all looked at me like I had climbed out of a spaceship.

"This is, uh, a lot for me to handle right now," I said, the wine already loosening my lips. "I mean, you know, I go from one foster home to another, just bam, bam, bam, and then I get with a family I really like. They even adopt me. Yeah, the adopted dad takes off but the adopted mom's cool. And then, just when I'm feeling comfortable and in a good, safe place, said adopted mom goes and drops dead. And then, my boyfriend, he decides to break up with me too and date a cheerleader. And so I'm living this shitty little existence working at a grocery store. And now you're telling me I've inherited a mansion and have a long, lost sibling?" I shook my head. "Sorry, but that's a call for a few more drinks."

"Oh," Mr. Walsh said. "This is all completely understandable. And I do apologize for the secrecy. In fact, I wasn't even sure you would come if I gave you all the details in the invitation—it is quite unbelievable. But I had to try. I've been handling the Usher House family affairs for years."

"So, are you saying like, I am now I'm rich and live in a mansion?"

"Well, it's not quite that cut and dry. I've managed to keep Usher House, financially speaking, above water. With a modest income from land assets and some business investments, and the yearly taxes and upkeep, it has been a struggle."

"So why do you do it?"

"Because your father, Vincent Usher, was good to me. I was born and raised in Barlow. My parents died when I was ten. He raised me as one of his own children. I've spent many years running up and down these halls. I feel, I suppose, indebted to the Ushers that way, being an orphan. And so I've always tried to give something back."

"Ernest gave me all the excruciating specifics in the car ride on the way up here," Roderick said. "Rather earnestly." He winked.

Mr. Walsh pointed to his attaché case. "I do have the deed to the house, as well as the last will and testament of your mother and father. It was your father's wish that you carry on the Usher line."

"And my mother?"

"We will go into more specifics about that in the morning," Mr. Walsh said. "I apologize, but I am absolutely bushed and this will take some time to go through thoroughly."

"Uh, OK," I said.

"In the meantime," Mr. Walsh said, "perhaps you two should become more acquainted. Good night."

Mr. Walsh whispered something to Mrs. Dietrich. She led him out of the room.

"Well," Roderick said. "That was quite a mouthful."

"Yeah," I said. "Wait until morning."

"No," he said. "About your life story. I could completely picture it."

"Oh, yeah, that was kind of an inappropriate outburst. It's not every day you're summoned to some country manor and told that you're not only the legal inheritor of it, but that you also have a twin brother."

"Right," he said. "Ernest located me living in Massachusetts. He spends his time between New York and Georgia, so after we met during a luncheon, he told me everything. I was floored. Then he'd said he had found you and sent you the invitation. Even though you sent back an RSVP, we weren't sure that you would show up for it. I thought maybe you would cancel at the last minute considering the confidentiality of details."

"What if I did?"

Roderick shrugged. "Well, I would've hopped a flight to Washington State personally and introduced myself."

"Oh, yeah, that would have been awkward."

"Yeah."

"So, tell me about yourself. Tell me how you grew up."

Roderick told me. He was adopted eighteen years ago from a wealthy family in Boston, Massachusetts named the Smiths, who owned a software company. He grew up attending all of the best schools, and he excelled in education and sports, especially swimming, though he downplayed his physical prowess as "jockish." He also grew up similar to me. He had a mother who died, though his had died when he was 6, and then he was raised by a nanny while his father worked and traveled. Roderick, it seemed, never had a secure, emotional bonding with anyone. Something I could relate to. With his handsomeness and upper-crust privilege, he was popular with girls, but he found most of them silly and immature. He connected with women who were older. He had courted one woman, about ten years older than him, but she had left him for another man her own age. It crushed Roderick and he swore off romance forever. I could relate to that, too. Roderick was in line to take over his adopted father's company. Warren Smith had emotionally and psychologically abused his adopted son. When Warren died, Roderick learned that he was cut out of the will and left penniless. When Mr. Walsh found Roderick, he had started his own software company, Axis Security Systems, which was now worth millions.

I could get a sense of Roderick that he was extremely intelligent and compassionate, based on what he told me, but he was also emotionally frail and sensitive. This broke my heart. Roderick and I were so similar and so different. He held my hand reassuringly the entire time he told me his story and I let him, it seemed so natural.

"So, that's about all there is to know about me up to the present moment," he said with a smile. "What about you?"

I told him about my financial troubles with the Bland house and my current job. Normally, I am reserved, but I felt like sharing with him. It may have been the wine that had made me open up, or the fact that he looked so much like me, but I felt at ease with him. He listened quietly and nodded, never interrupting—I really felt heard for the first time in a long time.

After I finished, he nodded. "We have lived such different lives, and yet, they were the same in many ways."

"Oh, right," I said, "Like me being enrolled in all the finest schools and having the financially supportive adopted parents. Yes, it's like I'm gazing into a parallel universe at you."

"Wow, your sarcasm is on point," Roderick said. "You'd do well in a place like Boston. No, I just meant, we grew up without a lot of love, and the love that we did have, well, it didn't last. Those people died. It kind of messes with you. I've read many psychology books to try to figure myself out. In those types of situations, people tend to have bond issues with other people. Because they're afraid that they're going to lose them, too."

I nodded. "Yeah, I can see that," and smiled. "It's also good to have friends. My best friend Carly helps keep me sane and steady."

"Yeah, but where is she now?" he laughed.

"Actually, she's upstairs lounging in her room."

"Oh," Roderick said. "Mr. Walsh was specific about no guests. He didn't want any distractions from the legal matters and the specifics therein."

"Well," I said, "she's not really a guest. She's my, uh, Emotional-Support Driver. She just forgot to wear the fluorescent yellow vest that says so."

Roderick laughed. "Oh, I love your sense of humor. It's so sharp."

"Yeah," I said. "I try."

"And it's also an incredible mask and coping mechanism."

"Excuse me?"

"In the psychology books I've read, and living in a city like Boston, people often use humor, especially the sarcastic or self-deprecating kind, to cover a deeper emotional hurt. It's kind of a defense mechanism. You know, you make light of things and that makes you detached from them."

I took a beat to say something, and then: "You do see a lot."

He shrugged. "Yeah, I try."

I don't know if it was the wine or the stress of coming here, but I felt completely exhausted. I thought I might fall asleep right in front of that crackling fireplace if I stayed down there much longer. I told Roderick so.

"Oh," he said. "I didn't mean to chatter on incessantly. Let me know if you ever find my company an absolute bore."

"Not at all," I said. "In fact, even if you weren't my brother, if that's actually the case, I would still find you one of the most fascinating people I've met."

"Well," he said with a laugh, "you must not meet many new people then."

"I work in a grocery store—I meet new people every single day and most of them are either boring, annoying, or both."

"Oscar Wilde once said there are only two types of people—charming or tedious."

"You're definitely the former."

He smiled. "Well, I'm happy I'm more charming to you than your typical grocery store shopper, thank you."

I rose. "And now I'm off to bed. It's been a long, difficult day."

"I'll join you," he said, rising.

Uh, what?

"What I meant was, I'll go to sleep too. In my *own* room."

He gave a nervous laugh. I did too.

"I knew what you meant."

"Oh, good," he said. "I didn't want you to think I'm some kind of weird sicko or something who wants to sleep with his sister. I mean, yuck, right?"

"Uh, yeah."

I gazed at all of the food on the dining room table. I wished I could eat but my stomach was tied in knots. Instead, I grabbed my wine glass and a bottle. I hoped this trip wouldn't turn me into an alcoholic. But I needed to sleep. This would help.

"Having a little nightcap, are you?"

"Yeah, seems appropriate."

Roderick smiled. He grabbed a glass and another bottle. "Like brother, like sister, right?"

"Right."

We walked into the entrance hall. We stopped at our mother's painting. Lenore Usher's bright, angelic expression seemed to gaze down on both of us. In fact, her painting was brighter and more posi-tive than the other Usher paintings. It was like she wasn't a part of them. Maybe that's why Roderick and I had been spirited away from the house. Maybe she didn't want to be a part of all this. I wondered if that was the case. Or if it was something else. I made a mental note of it to ask Mr. Walsh tomorrow morning. Though he might not know or might not want to answer. I had to be prepared for that and to phrase my question tactfully. If I even was an Usher. I wonder if there was like, I don't know, a blood test or something. Yeah, I definitely had a resemblance to these people in the paintings, especially this person beside me and the woman in the portrait. But that also could be coincidence. Who knew for sure? Maybe some answers would appear in the light of day. I awaited that. The house may seem less gloomy and creepy with fresh morning sunlight pouring in.

"So that's her," Roderick said. "That's our mother."

"It appears so," I said. "But who can really be sure."

Roderick turned to me. "What do you mean?"

I shrugged. "Well, I mean, sure, she could be. But Mr. Walsh could have made a mistake. I might just be Plain Jane off the street and not Madeline Usher, inheritor of the family fortune."

"Of course this is your mother. And I am your brother. Mr. Walsh is very thorough." Roderick seemed to get angrier as he spoke. "Do you think he would invite complete strangers into the house? He's been a sentinel of the Usher name for decades. He wouldn't do that. I *know* him. He wouldn't throw caution to the wind like that. If he says you're an Usher, then like me, you're an Usher."

Roderick was red-faced and wide-eyed. He had quite the explosive temper. And I'm guessing he noticed that I had taken a step back and was regarding him with dismay. I gripped the wine bottle in my hand in case I had to use it.

EIGHT

1

After his explosive tirade, Roderick's countenance softened. "I'm sorry. I kind of flew off the handle, didn't I?" He smiled and gave a nervous laugh. "I really apologize. I'm just kind of passionate about this whole affair. And though I've only been acquainted him for a short time, I know that every word Mr. Walsh said is genuine. He's not a man who likes to waste his time."

"Right," I said.

Roderick reached out to touch my hands. I shrank back. He noticed.

"Again, I am sorry for that outburst. Can we start over?"

"In the morning," I said. "I'm very tired."

"Yes. Of course. I'll walk you to your room. If that's acceptable with you, of course."

I wanted to decline the invitation, but I didn't want to upset him. Not to see his pale face be flushed red again. "Sure."

We walked up the stairs in silence. Once we reached the landing and were overlooking the banister to the entrance hall below, he said, "I want to apologize again. That was uncalled for."

"Apology accepted," I said. "We all have our moments of madness, I guess."

"Thank you." He smiled. "I am an Usher—and I know you are an Usher. I feel it in my bones. Don't you? I also felt it coming here. Like how a magnet attracts another magnet."

Yes, Roderick, I felt it too. In fact, I almost felt like I could find the house without looking for it. Simply going by feeling. But I didn't want to tell him all of this. "Kind of, yeah."

"Things will be better in the light of day," he said. "After a good sleep."

"I hope so."

At the doorway to my room, I wished him a good night. His room was right across the hall from mine. I guess that room belonged to our father, Vincent Usher. When I was sure that Roderick was in his room with the door closed, I slunk down to Carly's room and knocked.

She didn't answer.

Huh.

I opened the door quietly.

She laid passed out across her bed. Still in her clothes. I guess she had a long day, too.

I snuck over and pulled off her shoes. She stirred. I pulled back the covers and tucked her into bed. In a sleepy daze, she complied. Then I kissed her on the forehead and crept out of the room.

"Good night," a voice said in the darkness. It was Roderick standing in his doorway.

"Huh, oh, goodnight."

He gave me a conspiratorial look like Carly and I were scheming something. "I was just checking on my Emotional-Support Driver."

"And how is she?"

"Dead to the world."

"Ah," Roderick said.

"Well," I said. "Good night."

I vanished into my room and shut the door. There was a lock on it. I slid across the bolt as quietly as possible. I would sleep better with a locked door. Outside, the storm had long passed and a bright yellow moon had settled over the landscape. The wet tops of the trees glistening in the moonlight. The silvery light was so bright it almost looked like the noonday sun. I thought about peering out the window to see if that thing was prowling around outside. I closed the drapery instead, which were thick, red velvet drapes that covered the gossamer lace curtains over the French doors, the only window into the room.

Then I poured another glass of wine and drank it down. Now I felt good and tired. In my daze, I accidentally knocked my purse on the floor. It spilled open and the business card tumbled out. It read: LIAM DELANEY – DELANEY FARMS – Route 13 Box 1976, Barlow, GA. There was a phone number. Should I? Maybe it was the wine, but I sent a text to the number. THANK YOU FOR PULLING US OUT OF THE DITCH. I AM MOST GRATEFUL.

The second after I sent the text, I regretted it. Text regret. Why did I do that? Stupid.

I sat my phone down on the edge of the walnut vanity table, but in my inebriated state, it fell off the edge. Leaning over, I picked it up and accidentally scraped my index finger against one of the ornate metal drawer handles. Thankfully, the scrape wasn't deep, but a drop of blood welled up from the pink wound. I grabbed some tissues to stop the bleeding. The blood dripped onto the carpet, which was a deep wine color.

What was strange was that the blood had vanished.

I attempted to swipe it up with a clean tissue, but there was nothing. Maybe the carpet was super absorbent? I held the tissue against my finger. Then I started getting sleepy again. The blood had coagulated, so I didn't think I'd need a bandage. I slipped off my dress and draped it over the chair. I'd have to sleep in my underwear tonight.

Climbing into the feather bed, my body weight sank me into it. It felt like I was drifting on a cloud, it felt like heaven. As I closed my eyes, I sensed that someone was watching me—the Eva Usher painting. Her fixed expression seemed like she was angry I was lying in her bed. Ugh, I wouldn't sleep with those painted green eyes glaring at me through the night. I pulled the dark velvet curtains of the canopy bed closed on that side. Hell, why not close them all? I did. Now I was in this cozy cube of warmth and silence. This was the first time I'd felt comfortable since touching down in the South. Maybe it was the wine, the curtained featherbed, or maybe it was because I was dead tired. As I started to drift off to sleep, I thought I heard a howl. I couldn't be sure. But it sounded like an animal baying. Not like the yips of coyotes I sometimes hear back home, or the howls of wolves I've heard in videos, but almost like a scream. My flesh prickled.

2

The dream returned. The bald man from before, and the other vicious men. They grabbed and tossed me against the spidery oak tree, webs of Spanish moss dangling from its branches. A man tied my hands behind me with a strand of leather. I was wearing a dark, hooded cloak. A veil of low fog levitated off the muddy earth.

"Hang the witch!" the bald man shouted, spitting on me.

A man in black appeared out of the fog. As he walked closer, I could see his collar—he was a priest holding a Bible. He regarded me with disdain. He wore circular spectacles that made his eyes appear too large on his face. The effect would have been comical if I wasn't in such a dire state. I was aware that this was a dream, and I tried to wake myself from it, but I couldn't. It was like I was being shown this dream, like it belonged to someone else.

"Eva Usher, you are charged with witchcraft, conspiracy, adultery, and consorting with the devil. By the powers within the church, you are hereby condemned to hang until dead." He smiled. "We've hanged a lot of undesirables in Charlton County. You're just richer than most."

"You will not get away with this," I said. "I will see to it that every one of you is punished for this outrageousness. For this heresy and this hypocrisy. And that the name of Eva Usher will flourish long after you are all dust in your graves."

The priest regarded me with a sidelong gaze. Then he motioned to a man. "Commit the sentence."

The man marched up with a rope and unceremoniously tossed it around a tree branch. He then collared the noose around my pale neck. "The winds of wrath will rise up against all of you."

Another man stuffed a rag in my mouth and then tied it in place around my head with a length of rope. He stood back. "Commence."

Some men pulled on the rope. My feet raised off the ground. My cloak fluttered like dark wings. I tried to scream through the gag but the rope pulled tight against my neck.

3

A cry from somewhere outside of the bed curtains awakened me. Ugh, what a dream. I was so disturbed by it, I was afraid to go back to sleep. The faint cry continued.

Parting the thick bed curtains, I stuck my head out. The clock on the mantle read 3:13 in the morning. The cry came from the behind the balcony doors. Stalking over to them, I peered through the velvet curtains. A dark shape stood outside the glass doors. Small with long ears. I parted the gossamer blinds. Outside, mewing to get in, was a shadowy shape with two intense green eyes that sparkled in the moonlight—a black cat. I wondered who it belonged to? Was it a stray? How did it get up here on the second floor? Seeing me, the cat stood on its hind legs and scratched at the glass—a strong and spirited thing. I unlocked one of the French doors. The cat weaved its way in. The October night air chilled my face. Soothing. I thought about leaving the door open for some fresh air, but remembered that stalking thing from earlier. I quickly closed the door against the dark and shut the curtains.

The black cat, which appeared like a shadow cut out of the night, threaded around my feet with the loudest purr I'd ever heard.

"Where did you come from?"

The cat peered up at me with its emerald green eyes, which were intensely green even in the darkness. They resembled two emeralds suspended in the night.

"I don't have anything for you to eat," I said. "But if you behave yourself the rest of the night, I can let you stay."

As I tiptoed back over to the bed, the cat trotted along with me. It leapt up onto the bed and immediately stalked over and laid on my pillow.

"Uh, no," I said, picking up the warm, purring fur ball, "you have to lay over here." I set the cat down near the pillow. Then I tucked myself back in. I closed the bed curtains again. I was afraid I'd have that stupid dream again.

The cat licked herself next to me, performing a thorough self-washing. I must admit the gentle sounds of the animal, the purring, and the warmth of a living thing next to me, had put me back at ease. Sometime during the long night I fell asleep again and had a restful, dreamless sleep.

NINE

1

$\mathscr{A}$ sliver of morning light peeked through the bed curtains. The cat had moved sometime during the night and now laid on my belly, rising up and down with my breath. She stared at me with unblinking eyes.

"Hello again, cat," I said with a yawn. "I see you finally settled down."

I laid in the bed for a minute, not wanting to disturb her. However, the sable feline jumped down off me and escaped through the curtains slit. So, I was inclined to get up.

The clock on the wall read 7:55. I felt rested. Really rested. The scrape on my finger didn't look as bad in the daylight. I wouldn't need a bandage at all. When I picked up my phone that lay face down on the vanity, I noticed I had a message from a number I didn't recognize. HAPPY TO OBLIGE. IF YOU WANT TO GO OUT FOR A SWEET TEA OR SOMETHING, LET ME KNOW. And then there was a smiley face emoji. That could only be Liam. I added him to New Contacts in my phone so his number wouldn't be a stranger anymore. I texted back. I DON'T KNOW HOW LONG I'LL BE IN

TOWN, BUT I WOULD LIKE TO SEE YOU AGAIN IF THERE'S TIME.

I wished I had some other clothes to slip into, but I didn't, so I climbed back into my black cocktail dress draped over the chair. "You stay here," I told the cat. "I'm not even sure you're supposed to be in here—so stay so I don't get in trouble from that creepy Mrs. Dietrich."

Entering the bathroom, I locked the door and stripped down. Turning on the shower, the milky water that vomited from the nozzle had that tell-tale rotten egg smell. How long had the water been bad here and why hadn't anything been done about it? I was hesitant to take a shower, but I really wanted to clean up. I slipped in and did a quick wash, and then stepped out. I would have to go to Carly's room to get made-up again. And I'd have to towel my hair dry since I didn't have a blow drier. It would not look great, but I'd have to manage. Slipping back into my dress, I stalked down the hall past Roderick's room to Carly's chamber. I rapped on the door.

She didn't answer, and I found the door unlocked, so I slipped in.

She laid in a bundle of sheets snoring. I didn't want to wake her, so I grabbed a few make-up items from her purse. As I was rifling around, her snores slipped into gasps as she woke up.

"What are you doing, darlin'?"

"Just getting some make-up."

She yawned. "What the hell time is it?"

"It's just a little after eight."

"Ugh, I feel like I was drugged," she said, rubbing her tired eyes. "I slept so hard."

"Did you, uh, did you have any dreams?"

"No," she said. "None that I can remember. Why?"

"No reason," I said, which was a lie.

"I wonder what time breakfast is—I'm completely starving."

"Uh, let me go downstairs and see what's going on," I said. "Then I'll come up and get you."

"If I don't get a venti triple-shot mocha latte and a banana nut muffin soon," she said, "someone is going to die." She yawned. "Or at least get seriously maimed."

"Let me check things out," I said. *"Please* wait up here."

"Hurry," she said, throwing a pillow at me. "Pronto—or your 'driver' mutinies."

As I headed downstairs, I hoped that I was the only one up, but I found Roderick and Mr. Walsh in the dining room. Another buffet of sweet rolls, tea, and coffee had been set out. (Hopefully made with another water source than the house tap.) The assortment wasn't exactly the mocha latte and banana nut muffin that Carly was looking for but they'd have to do. I stocked up with what I could. I smelled the fresh brew. It had the rich aroma of coffee, not the eggy stench of sulphur. Apparently it was made with another water source?

"Ah," Mr. Walsh said. "Ms. Madeline. How did you sleep?"

He caught me as I was pouring two coffees and grabbing a handful of sweet rolls. "Uh, excellent. Like a rock."

"Looks like you have quite the appetite," he said, smiling. After you, uh, dine, we'll go over the details of your father's will."

"Uh, this isn't all for me. For my driver."

"Her 'Emotional-Support Driver,'" Roderick said with a chuckle.

"She's welcome to come down and dine," the elder gentleman said, "as long as she's not present during our proceedings."

Oh, yeah, I could imagine Carly down here with everyone. Being the center of attention with all of her catty witticisms. No thanks. I could not handle that right now.

"I'll just take these up to her," I said. "And then I'll join you."

2

After I delivered the food to a thankful Carly, I returned to Mr. Walsh and Roderick.

"Before we begin," Mr. Walsh said, "I want to give you a proper tour of the place. Just so you can see the entire scope of the estate. I must admit, she's in a bad state of repair. With the dwindling remainder of the fortune going for property taxes and what not, little was left over for maintenance. Mrs. Dietrich and Mr. Knapp did what they could to keep the house and grounds tidy, but I fear it wasn't enough. At one time, Usher House had an entire staff of maids and groundskeepers. In its heyday, it was a place of beauty. People from miles around came to visit. In fact, during their visits to the area, a couple of former American presidents even stayed on the grounds, Rutherford Hayes and Benjamin Harrison, I believe."

One of the first things I marveled at was the great glass skylight in the entrance hall. I hadn't noticed it last night. But as the morning sun shone through, it resembled a great orb spider's web—a black iron structure with a mosaic of blue, red, and yellow glass creating a kaleidoscopic pattern. A hypnotic sight to gaze upon.

"Lovely, isn't it," Mr. Walsh said. "It's a nine-foot circumference, I believe. Part of the original house that was designed to bring in some much-needed cheer to the entryway."

"Yes," I said. "It's so lovely."

"Shall I escort you through the rest of the house?"

Mr. Walsh showed us the ground floor first. It consisted of a ballroom, a library, a billiard room, and a conservatory. The latter was in a terrible state of disrepair. It was one of the old conservatories that had the paned glass and the vaulted ceiling with an iron framework. Many of the glass panels were broken. The only thing that grew now were weeds. Birds had nested in the metal eaves; their ancient white droppings lay everywhere. A brightly colored coral snake slithered past my feet on the stone.

"At one time," Mr. Walsh said, "this was a tropical paradise filled with some of the most exotic plants imaginable. Your great-great-great grandfather, Edgar Usher, was a world traveler and had quite an interest in botany. He had this built and maintained. In my youth, I played among the greenery. In his autumn years, the eldest Mr. Usher could be found here, I was told, the heat and humidity agreeing with his arthritic aches and pains."

I could almost picture it. The lush tropical vegetation and the bright yellow sunlight glistening through the verdant leaves. How beautiful it must have been. Now it looked like it had been bombed. A complete mess. Just like most of the house.

The other rooms hadn't fared much better. The ballroom had mold growing down one wall of faded yellow wallpaper. The billiard room had a broken-down pool table. The library was dusty and forgotten like the other rooms. Mrs. Dietrich, I supposed, had closed them off so she would not have to deal with them. Mr. Walsh revealed to us that the rooms "fell out of favor" with each generation of the Usher family.

"What about this room," I said, pointing to a steel door.

"Ah," Mr. Walsh said. "That goes down to the cellar."

"Shall we check it out then," Roderick said. "It *is* part of the house."

Mr. Walsh was hesitant. "Well, perhaps another time." He seemed a little, pensive, I don't know, maybe even scared. He licked his thin lips.

"No time like the present," I said.

"That's right, sis," Roderick said, and slapped the back of Mr. Walsh. "They call it the present because it's a gift." He chuckled at his humor.

"Did you really just say that?" I asked, rolling my eyes.

Roderick grinned. "Banalities are friends of mine."

"It's a dirty and filthy place down there," Mr. Walsh said. "Not very agreeable."

Roderick grabbed the doorknob. "I insist, good sir." He found it locked. "What are you hiding down there, a pit and a pendulum?"

"There's only one key to the door, I'm afraid."

Roderick and I both waited. Mr. Walsh reluctantly fished a ring of keys from his jacket pocket. He singled out one long, black, old-fashioned skeleton key not made in a hundred years. He slipped it into the lock and rotated it. As it connected with all of the tumblers inside, the entire door shook. A door, I guessed, that wasn't opened too often. Mr. Walsh regarded Roderick and I as if to say "are you sure that this is what you want?" When we urged him on with our silent but eager faces, he sucked in a breath and opened the door.

The odor immediately assailed my nostrils. The ponderous smell of dampness and decay. And a smell under it, I'm not sure, maybe rotten, moldering meat. I covered my nose with a hand to ward off the stench.

Mr. Walsh watched me. "As I said, it's not very agreeable down there."

Roderick didn't seem to mind the vile smell. "Let us be the judge of that." He motioned. "Onward, brave Christian soldier."

Mr. Walsh smiled.

He grabbed a torch off the wall and then pulled out a silver Zippo lighter engraved with ERW, which I presumed were his initials. He lit the torch and immediately it bloomed into a bouquet of flame.

Roderick's face lit up from the light show. "Wow, a torch, how medieval."

"I'm afraid that under the house was never wired for electricity," Mr. Walsh said. "It is, in many ways, like stepping into a time capsule. The original Usher house as it existed one hundred and forty-years ago."

"It certainly smells that way," I said.

"Yes," Mr. Walsh said. "As you may suspect, this area is not used much."

Mr. Walsh led us down the winding stone stairs. The walls were rounded brick with many pillars, which I guessed assisted to the structural integrity of Usher House.

A solid foundation, I thought.

As he passed the unlit torches on the wall, Mr. Walsh would kiss his cone of flame to each, igniting them. Shadows danced around the place from the flames casting all kind of shivering phantasms on the walls and ceiling. This was definitely not a place you would want to visit often. Between the smell and the creepiness, this was a part of the house that I would avoid.

On the stone landing at the bottom of the cellar, we approached an iron gate. Somewhere was the *drip, drip, drip* of water, which I found appropriate for the murky atmosphere of the subterranean apartment. Mr. Walsh produced the keys again. The same black skeleton key.

He regarded Roderick and I again as if to warn us off from going through this locked gate.

"What are we waiting for?" Roderick said. "I'm guessing something astonishing lies beyond this."

"I'm not sure 'astonishing' is a word I would be comfortable to use for what lies beyond this point."

I shuddered in the chill.

Not only in the gradual drop in temperature as we had descended the stairs, but the uneasiness that this place gave me. Closed, dark places terrified me.

When I was young, I imagine about six years old, I had been living with a foster family, the Geddys. They had a son, age 12, Daryll Geddy, who was one of the cruelest of people I had ever known. He would do things to neighborhood cats like tie ropes around their necks, attempting to strangle them to death.

In a few cases, he was successful.

And when I had seen him do it one time, he'd grabbed me and locked me in an old steamer trunk that they had in their fruit cellar. It had smelled of old and decayed wood and then he'd sit upon it. I'd struggled and cried, trying to break free.

Daryll told me he'd would leave me in there forever if I ever told anyone what he'd done to Mrs. Radcliffe's cat, Pluto.

I told him I would not, and I would have told him anything in order to get out of that box, which I found suffocating. I'd screamed and cried and pleaded, but no matter what I said, he would not open the box.

And I suspected he never would have if Mrs. Geddy hadn't found us "playing" down there.

I'd wanted to tell her what her son had done, but he shot a cold and chilling look in my direction. A look I knew meant I would end up in that cold and lonely and suffocating box again if I said anything.

So, I'd had to calm myself down, wipe my eyes, and agree with Daryll that we were "playing a game," and days later, when poor Mrs. Radcliffe couldn't find her cat, I'd had to agree with Daryll that I hadn't seen it. Even though I knew it was buried in Mrs. Geddy's flower bed under her begonias, undoubtedly fertilizing them.

After that, as you can imagine, I've been terrified of tight spaces.

And whenever I was in one, I'd remember that time when I was six years old, screaming and clawing at the steamer trunk lid to get free, and that feeling that I would die inside. A six-year-old is too young to understand the concept of death, but that day, I learned it.

Soon after that, I ran away from the Geddys. That had been my first time running away from a foster home. And I kept doing it again and again until I had gotten a new foster family. I don't know what ever became of Daryll Geddy, who would no doubt be around 24-years-old now. Most likely he was either a lawyer, a politician, or a serial killer.

"Are you doing all right, Ms. Madeleine?" Mr. Walsh asked. "You look so pale."

I nodded. "I'm fine. Can we get this over with?"

Mr. Walsh opened the gate and it shuddered with a creak. "Since you are the last two remaining Ushers, I want you to meet all of the previous ones. A family reunion of sorts."

"What do you mean?"

Mr. Walsh gave a macabre smile. "This is the family crypt, of course."

TEN

1

ith torch in hand, Mr. Walsh shepherded us into the mausoleum of Usher House. It was a room about twenty feet by twenty feet square. In the flickering fire light, bronze plates along the stone wall glistened. They began with Edgar Usher, the original founder of the house, (1860-1922) and his wife, Trippetta Usher (1869-1925). Then there were their children, Eva (1899-1920), and her brother Corbin, (1895-1921). From there, Corbin had a wife, Annabel Usher (1897-1951), and two children, Theodore Usher (1919-1970) and Myra Usher (1920-1958).

Mr. Walsh worked his way across the mausoleum. "Here all of the Ushers lie in their peaceful, final rest. The casket is interred in the wall and then bricked up. The engraved, bronze plate is then placed."

The rest of the family included Theodore Usher (1919-1970), his wife, Eliza Usher (1932-1972), and their son, Sebastian Usher (1952-1992), his wife, Virginia Usher (1955-1997), and their son, Vincent Usher (1969-2020). My mother, Lenore Usher (1979-2003), was interred next to him.

"They can bury their dead down here?" I asked.

"If this were modern times," Mr. Walsh said, "no, I don't believe so. But the many old families have their crypts on the premises." He brought his torch closer to my parents.

"As you can see with your mother and father, the order is different. Typically, the widow outlives the husband. But in the case of your mother, she was found in the Mystic River in East Boston not long after you were given up for adoption. It was during the summer, so it's not sure if she merely drowned while swimming or committed suicide. Some I've spoken with believe that she leapt off the Mystic River Bridge. The death records state 'death by misadventure,' which, of course, leaves a lot for interpretation. But, of course, that is the Usher way. Your father here, Vincent Usher, was interred here only weeks ago."

"How did he die?" I asked.

Mr. Walsh smiled. "Natural causes. He was 51. Heart attack."

"That's pretty young to die of a heart attack."

"He did love his smoke and drink and rich desserts," Mr. Walsh said. "So it was a natural death for him. I'm afraid that after your mother left with his children, and then she later turned up dead and the children were unable to be located, that he became an unhappy man. He spent long days in his room, smoking and drinking mostly. When he did eat, it was only cakes and puddings. He didn't take much exercise, unless you count moping around the house from room to room. If you had known him before, he was a funny and vivacious man. But he grew sad, withdrawn, and bitter. I would visit him with news that I had tracked you down. But it was in vain. He altered his will to account for his children if they were ever found. They were to inherit the house, as you were the last of the Ushers. I, of course, being the benefactor of the estate. I can't tell you how overjoyed I am that you both are standing here now. If there is a God, and the Ushers are with Him, then God bless their poor, wretched souls. They would be at peace knowing that the house would fall into the hands of their, I am sure, capable descendants."

Why did he say poor, wretched souls? That seemed like an odd choice of words.

"Maybe we can discuss this some other place," I said. "Like in the warmth and light of upstairs."

Mr. Walsh smiled. "Of course."

Next to our parents' graves stood two empty holes. They were vacancies about four-foot-high by four-foot-wide and about seven feet deep in the stone. The plates above them read: Roderick Usher (2002-) and Madeleine Usher (2002-). A dusty, cherry-wood coffin with gold handles sat on a dais near the holes.

My flesh crawled on the back of my neck and I couldn't get any oxygen.

"Hey," Roderick said, "are you all right?"

"Do I look all right? *Why* do we have our names down here?"

Mr. Walsh shrugged. "It's nothing to be alarmed about, it's simply tradition."

"I don't like this. And why is there a coffin sitting out?"

"You don't look well, sis. Maybe we should go back up?"

Mr. Walsh grinned. "I can explain. The coffin is empty. Vincent Usher had chosen two before his death—the cherry and a mahogany. He couldn't decide. After his death, we chose to put him in the mahogany. We never returned the other." He sighed. "As I said, there's nothing astonishing about this place. Let's venture back up, shall we?"

As we walked out of the mausoleum, I couldn't help but glance back at the empty spaces where my alleged brother and I were to spend our final resting days. The idea of being locked down here for an eternity made my heart skip a beat. And I couldn't help but think of that goddamned steamer trunk down in the Geddy fruit cellar. This wasn't much different.

2

"We haven't seen the entire house," Roderick said after we explored the second floor, which was primarily bedrooms. "I saw a tower when we were outside."

"Oh, that," Mr. Walsh said. "That's primarily attic storage. It's ravaged by time and rodents. It's not a place that you want to see. Not at this time anyway."

"I insist," Roderick said.

"Very well."

At the end of the hall was a door. It appeared as part of the wall, part of the dark ebony wainscoting. Had Mr. Walsh not shown us where it was, I would have never known. Only upon closer examination, after he touched the wood, I could see where it was smoother than the rest of the wood, where others had pushed there to gain entrance. He shoved a key into a hole that I hadn't notice at first, and the hidden door creaked open.

He ushered us up a narrow flight of stairs. The walls were papered with the most hideous green wallpaper I had ever seen—the floral patterns, typical of Victorian décor, resembled tortured souls screaming for release from their papery prison.

"I bet there's lot of secret passages and maybe a hidden fortune buried in this house," Roderick said.

"Afraid not, son," Walsh said. "You'd be chasing leprechaun pots of gold to the ends of rainbows. This is the only 'secret passage' in the house. And as far as a fortune, well, any financial reserve was exhausted long ago to maintain the house and property taxes."

At the end of the stairs stood a door. A heavy door. Mr. Walsh fumbled for the keys and tried several, but he didn't have one that fit.

"Uh, sorry about that," he said. "Afraid I don't have a key for this one."

I pressed my ear against the door—I didn't know—why and I tried to listen. I thought I heard something. A scraping sound. Methodical. Something was living on the other side of that door; I was sure of it. I told Mr. Walsh so.

"Raccoons, I'm afraid," he said. "They've gained entrance through a hole in the roof. And they've made quite a home in there."

"But if you don't have a key, how do you know?"

"Because I've seen them coming and going from the outside," he said. "Perhaps someday a locksmith will have to see to the door. And then have someone come from animal control to see to the invading vermin."

"Not kill them," I said.

"Of course not," he said. "We'd have them humanely relocated. Back into the wild where they belong."

"Such a humanitarian, sis," Roderick said. "I'd poison the filthy bastards where they stood."

"You're a cruel person then."

He laughed. "Kidding—I wanted to see your expression change."

"Cruelty isn't a joke," I said. "I don't appreciate it."

"Oh, man, so serious. I'm sorry."

"Shall we go back down?" Mr. Walsh asked.

3

Mr. Walsh had his office set up in the library which had a crackling fire and two wingback chairs. It was a rather cozy room. Dusty books lined the walls.

"Quite a nice collection of tomes," I said, noting the books.

"There certainly are some rare editions," Mr. Walsh said. "You might have them evaluated." He looked at Roderick. "You mentioned a fortune, there may be some volumes you could sell to rare book collectors that might fetch a rewarding price."

"I would want to keep Usher house whole," Roderick said. "The way it was intended."

"Oh, well, good," Mr. Walsh said.

HE SERVED US THE LAST WILL AND TESTAMENT OF VINCENT USHER. THE gist of it was that Roderick and I were to split the house and everything in it equally. We were encouraged to keep what integrity of the house was possible with no major renovations, only enough to maintain the house and the grounds. And the remains of the fortune, which unfortunately was only forty thousand dollars.

"If you both sign your lives away here," Mr. Walsh said, "it will be official."

"But how do you know that we're Ushers?" I asked him. "I mean, you could've made a mistake. Don't you need to do like, I don't know, a blood test or something."

Mr. Walsh sighed. "I conducted an exhaustive search. I am very thorough, Ms. Madeleine. Besides, one only need to look at the portraits. Roderick is a spitting image of his father. And while you don't exactly look like either your mother or father, there's a family resemblance that is unmistakable. It's as if, in your own way, you resemble the entire Usher line. Particularly Eva Usher. I'm sure you've noticed the similarities."

I had. Enough to make me uncomfortable.

"But after we sign it," I said. "*If* I sign it. Am I just supposed to uproot my life and live here? I don't think I can."

"Nobody is asking you to," the attorney said. "You can have the place bulldozed if you want. Or you can sell it. Nobody said you had to live in it. Those were Vincent Usher's wishes, but not his orders. The dead can't complain, even in a house steeped in such history."

"I will like to know more of that history," I said. "I feel like we've barely scratched the surface."

"Oh, you will, you will." He handed me the pen.

I didn't have to sign. I could, technically, give everything to Roderick by not signing. He'd inherit by default. But that didn't seem right. If Vincent Usher *was* my father, this was *his* wish. I never really had a father, or father figure I could put my faith in. The last one, Jeff Bland, said he was going out for a pack of cigarettes and never returned. He left Peggy and me in a tough spot. At least this father, the father I never knew, was trying to take care of me, even while lying in his grave somewhere beneath my feet. Taking a breath, I placed the black tip of the pen to the paper. "Do I sign in Maddy Bland or Madeline Usher?"

"The latter."

"But that's not my legal name."

"But you are an Usher. That is your birthright."

And so, after Roderick signed his name, I, for the first time, signed the name of my birth, Madeline Usher. It was a strange experience. It was as if, overnight, I had become a completely different person. I guess I had. Now I was Madeline Usher of Usher House. Maybe I would make Mrs. Dietrich call me Lady Usher—simply to annoy her now that she was my employee.

"Well," Mr. Walsh said. "That makes it all official. I will submit these papers to the probate court and have them notarized. You are now each co-owners of this house and everything in it."

I regarded Roderick; he regarded me back.

"What are you going to do with your half, sis?" he asked with a conspiratorial smile.

"I don't know," I said. I could only answer him honestly.

I excused myself and headed upstairs. I told Mr. Walsh I would be down later to see him off. I needed to talk to someone. Someone who knew me. For at this moment, I didn't feel like I knew myself. I had roamed the earth for eighteen years thinking I was somebody else. Just mild-mannered Maddy. I'd taken the last name Bland because they had adopted me, and I loved the family. They were now gone. And I was an Usher, truly an Usher, though I hadn't known that 24 hours ago. My head swam and I felt dizzy. Confused.

I knocked on Carly's door and went in. I told her everything that had transpired since I had brought her breakfast.

"What are you going to do?" she asked.

"I was hoping you could help me with that?"

"You can't live in this creepy old house in southeast Georgia," she said. "You belong back in Pickman Flats with me, darlin'."

"Yes," I said. "I could go back. But to what? I'm up to my eyes in debt with a job at a grocery store. I'm going to have to move soon. You're the only thing that makes living there worth it."

"Exactly," she said. "You have to come back with me. Let this Rod guy take care of the place. Sell your half. Live off what you can get for it. I bet you could buy a nice house with your chunk of the proceedings, right? We could move in together. I'd love to get away from mom. She's driving me crazy. I'm serious. You know that expression 'driving you to drink.' Yeah, that's her, right?"

"That sounds tempting. I don't know." I looked around the room. This house was huge and creepy and decaying, but there was something about it. And the more time I spent here, the less I wanted to leave it. I felt like it could be something great and beautiful. I imagined it was once. It could be again. I revealed this to Carly.

"Yeah," she said. "Maybe so. But that will take cash. You said there's only forty thousand dollars, right?"

"Yeah."

"Tell you what. You fly back home, think about it, and decide what's next."

"Yeah," I said. "That makes the most sense."

"I've gotta go back. Harrington's is going crazy without me."

I laughed. "You should be managing that store, not your 'manager.'"

"Yeah, love," she said. "But who takes a teenager seriously?"

ELEVEN

As I entered the room I was staying in, I didn't have anything to pack, I needed only to grab my purse. The black cat greeted me. I brought her a little saucer of creamer from the coffee station downstairs. The cat lapped it up greedily. After she was done, she stared up at me with those impossibly bright eyes.

"You're sure a pretty girl," I said. "Where do you come from?"

The cat purred and rubbed at my ankles. I picked her up. "If you were mine, I'd call you Esmerelda, because of those eyes. But you're not."

I hated to put her back outside, but I couldn't leave her locked in the room either. Mrs. Dietrich would no doubt discover her, and I couldn't trust that stone-faced, callous woman to treat the cat well. So, I opened up the French doors and put the cat back on the balcony where I found her.

The day was glorious and bright, a light October breeze in the air. The grounds didn't appear any better than they did under the moonlight. The swamp, which was likely a lake once, stood blackish and stagnant. Cattails surrounding it swayed in the breeze. The trees around the house looked like pale skeletons, which was odd considering everything had "died" surrounding the house. It's as if the land immediately attached to the house went "foul," as the water had. Maybe that was it. The water was poisoned in some way. I guess that could make sense.

"You stay out here, Esmerelda," I said. She leaped up onto the stone balcony ledge and crept along its lichen-littered surface, and then vaulted up onto the roof of the house. It made me dizzy, and a little worried, watching her. If she slipped, she'd fall two stories and land on the cobblestone driveway below. But the velvet-footed cat slunk like an able gymnast across the gray, mossy shingles of the house and disappeared.

OK, then, cat, goodbye. I guess she'd only used me for a warm place to sleep and a saucer of fresh cream. So be it.

Walking back inside the room, I closed and locked the French doors, then peered into the vanity mirror again. Once we returned to the Barlow Airbnb where all of my make-up supplies were waiting for me, I could clean up. Eva Usher watched me from the reflection in her painted silence with what appeared to be intense disapproval.

"You can have your room back now, great-great-great aunt," I said to her oily reflection. "You have a cozy room."

Glancing down at the carpet where my blood had dropped, I couldn't find a sign of it. Well, that was good. No more disapproving looks from Mrs. Dietrich were in order. Grabbing my purse, I strolled out the door and closed it. I needed to tell Roderick what I was doing, and to say goodbye; Mr. Walsh, too. Ambling across the hall, I knocked on Roderick's door.

"Come in."

Opening the door, Roderick sat in a wingback chair strumming a 12-string guitar. He was in his velvety red bathrobe, which hung open, revealing his ashen chest and defined stomach muscles. I recognized the song he was playing—"Black Hole Sun" by Soundgarden. He appeared at home in Usher House, as if he'd lived here all his eighteen years.

He stopped playing. "Oh," he said. "Excuse me."

"You play very well."

"I ought to. I've had lessons for about the last decade."

"Do you play anything else?"

"Uh, the piano, a little, but the guitar is mostly 'my jam.' I don't go anywhere without it." He noticed me holding my purse. "Planning on going somewhere?"

"Well, yeah," I said. "Back home. I have a job, a house, a life, you know, the usual."

"You have a house and a life here now, Mads," he said. "And you don't need a job. That is, unless you *want* one."

Mads. That's the first time he's addressed me by my nickname. I don't remember saying it around him. How did he know?

"I can't let all that stuff go—I have to work to pay the mortgage on that place. I'm kind of stuck with it. It's not like I was adopted by a wealthy family like you were."

"Oh," he said. "I see." He set the guitar down and rose, tying his robe tighter, hiding his naked flesh. He went over to his phone. "What's your number and your email?"

"Oh, yes, so we can keep in contact."

"Well, yes, that too, but I'm going to Venmo you the money."

"The money? For the mortgage?"

"Only for a few months," he said. "Until you can find a buyer for the house."

"That's very generous, Roderick," I said. "But I can't accept that."

"So formal. Call me Roddy. All my friends do. We're kind of related, if you hadn't noticed."

"That's really kind and thoughtful, uh, Roddy, but I can't accept your money."

"It's not my money, sis, it's *our* money. What's mine is yours. We're the last Ushers in the world. We need to take care of each other now."

Mr. Walsh gave a light tap on the open door, and wandered in. "Excuse me, the door was ajar and so..." He saw my purse. "Planning on going somewhere?"

"Yes," I said, extending my hand. "It was a pleasure meeting you, sir. I need to go back to Washington State. For a little while, at least."

"Oh," he said. "I see."

Carly barged in. "So, are we ready to hit the road or what?"

Roderick narrowed his eyes at Mr. Walsh and Carly, his pale face growing flush.

"Everything all right?" Carly asked.

"We were having a private conversation," Roderick said.

I smiled at him. "Thank you for your generous offer, Roddy. But I just can't agree to it."

"Generous offer," Carly said. "What generous offer?"

"It's nothing," I said. "Are you ready to go?"

"You know I am—I'm bored out of my mind. There's no WiFi and the books in the room are at least one-hundred years old. Hasn't anyone heard of Danielle Steel or James Patterson, hello?"

"This is the Emotional-Support Driver, I take it," Roderick said.

Carly turned to him. "In person, darlin'."

Roderick stepped toward her and like some old aristocrat, reached out for her hand, and kissed it. "Charmed," he said.

"Carly, this is my twin brother, Roderick Usher."

"Sis, so formal. I told you to call me Roddy."

She smiled back at him. Not a casual smile. Her coy, flirty kind of smile that I'd seen her do a million times at bars. The kind of smile she did when she liked a guy. *He's my brother, Carly, are you serious right now?*

"I can see who got the looks in the family," she said to him and chuckled. "Nice to meet you, Roddy."

Bitch.

"Are you sure there's no way I can convince you both to stay?" my brother asked.

"Wait," Carly said. "I didn't know that staying here longer was part of the invitation."

I grabbed her arm. "Text me your number, Roddy. I'll call you when I get back to the PNW." I told him my number. He picked up his phone and added it. "Now, let's go, Carly."

"You're so abrupt and rude, love," Carly said. "You could use a lesson in refinement from Roddy here."

"Shut up."

Carly and I headed downstairs. As if she knew we were leaving,

Mrs. Dietrich was hovering by the front door. With her pallid, bony hand, she opened it. The heavy door groaned on its rusty hinges. "It's a shame you must leave, Ms. Madeline. We were getting so comfortable having you here with us."

"I'll most likely be back," I said.

"I have no doubt," the housekeeper said. "Safe travels, Ms. Usher."

She opened the door for us, and for the second time today, the bright October sun blinded me. My phone vibrated—I had a text. It was from Liam. CAN I INTEREST YOU IN DINNER TONIGHT?

I was about to respond when Esmerelda sprang from a nearby hickory tree onto our rental car. Limbs from a dead tree stretched over the house. It was from there where she had scaled up, skirted across the rooftop, and over to my room on the south side. She meowed and purred, an emissary from somewhere unknown that relentlessly sought my affections.

"Oh, it looks like we're under attack," Carly said. "But I don't think that was the thing stalking us last night."

I picked up the warm mass of black fur. "No, this is Esmerelda." She climbed on my shoulder and nuzzled into my hair. It made me laugh.

"Well, she seems very comfortable with you. Let's jam."

The cat nuzzled close to my ear. If she could speak, I'm pretty sure she was saying *stay with me stay with me stay with me* in a kind of frenzied proclamation as she nudged me.

I couldn't leave. In that moment, I can't tell you why, but everything inside me was telling me not to go. Screaming at me. *Stay with me.* "I can't go," I heard myself blurt out.

"Excuse me?"

Yes, *stay*.

"I'm going to stay. Only for a week or so. Get all of this business sorted out."

"Are you insane? What about your job? The house?"

I shrugged. "I'll figure something out."

"You're seriously going to stay while I have to drive back to Atlanta and fly back alone?"

"I'm sorry," I said. "I'd go with you, but I now want to stay. It seems like the right thing to do."

"It's that guy, isn't it? That guy we met on the road."

"Liam."

"No," I said. "But he does want to have dinner."

"I knew it," she said. "I fucking knew it. You little bitch."

"It's only dinner."

"What about your stuff at the Airbnb?"

"I'll pick it up tonight. Maybe Mr. Walsh will give me a ride into town."

"Are you sure you know what you're doing, love?"

"No. But, I don't know, it just kind of feels appropriate. For right now."

"But ten seconds ago you were ready to leave."

"Yeah, but I was seriously fighting the urge to stay. It just got worse when I stepped out the door."

Carly looked around. "But this place is so…strange."

"I know. And maybe that's it. With Peggy dying and Parker's bullshit…it feels like my soul is dying. I can't describe it."

"Soul dying. Very poetic, Shakespeare," she said. "And I know that expression. I can't convince you." She sighed. "Fine, asshole, come give me a hug." I did. "I'll call you before I board the flight. To check in on you."

"Yeah," I said. "OK."

"If things get too weird, darlin', you come home to me."

"I'm going back to Washington anyway, silly, just not today."

Carly nodded.

Knapp appeared from around the corner of the house. He was carrying a rake. I wondered if he'd been standing there the entire time listening to us. He peered at us with his one good eye.

"She'll need the gate opened, Knapp."

I had an odd sense of déjà vu saying that. That feeling like I had told him that before.

He nodded, set the rake against the side of the house, and then started ambling down the tree-lined lane toward the gate.

Carly gave me a hug, then climbed into the rental car. She started it up, waved, and then followed behind the groundskeeper slowly.

I watched as the man and the car vanished behind the bend in the lane, swallowed up by the swaying brush of pines.

Turning back to the house, its vacant eye windows all seemed to stare at me. I texted back Liam. HOW ABOUT SEVEN?

GREAT, he texted back. I'LL PICK YOU UP AT THE GATE. And then: I DIDN'T MEAN FOR THAT TO RHYME.

I sent him back three laughing emojis.

Then went back into the house. My house.

Mrs. Dietrich was waiting for me. "Back so soon, Ms. Usher?"

"I'm going to need my two bags from the Barlow Airbnb." I told her the address.

"I will have Knapp retrieve them. Anything else?"

"Not right now."

"Very good," the housekeeper said. "Enjoy your stay."

TWELVE

1

I met Liam outside the gate promptly at seven o' clock. He pulled up in a black Volvo. Like a gentleman, he climbed out of the car, came around, and opened my door.

"I should be back before midnight, Knapp."

The groundskeeper nodded. He shut the gate behind me and locked it.

I smiled at Liam, feeling comfortable. Knapp had retrieved all of my things at the Airbnb and I had time to freshen up. Mrs. Dietrich pressed all of my clothes. Roderick was in a bit of a mood that I was going out for the evening and not spending my time with him, but I promised we would have breakfast tomorrow and catch up. That felt like the right compromise. I also had to call my manager at Williamson's Market and let them know I wouldn't be back for at least another week, as I had "out of town family business." They weren't too happy as I was one of the best bulk container fillers that they had, but they excused me.

Liam wore a gray, pressed, button-down shirt and dark slacks. He looked much less rustic than he had pulling Carly and I out of the ditch. With the Volvo and the new clothes, he cleaned up like a different person.

"This is a lot fancier than your truck," I said.

"Well, we could go back to the farm and take the dusty Tundra if that's more to your liking."

I shook my head. "The Volvo is the finer choice I think."

"Agreed. This also gives me a great excuse to drive her. She mostly sits in the garage covered by a tarp."

"I really want to thank you again for helping us."

He smiled. "It was the least I could do. After all, you did veer right in front of me."

"Yeah, to avoid hitting the person standing in the middle of the road."

"I didn't see anyone."

I *know* I saw someone draped in a midnight black cloak, and I wasn't prone to hallucinations. But how could somebody be there one minute and disappear the next? Unless they were a ghost. The thought chilled me and made the flesh on my skin crawl. Time to change the subject. "Where are we going?"

"A quiet little place I know."

"Hopefully not Shirley's Diner."

His face dropped. "You ruined the surprise."

"I am absolutely not eating there. The food tastes like rubber dog biscuits and you get treated like a prisoner in the Spanish Inquisition."

"When did you eat rubber dog biscuits?"

"Uh, never. But if you've had the chicken fried steak there, you'd have a pretty good idea."

"Oh, no worries," he said. "That place used to be really good once. My mom used to take me there all of the time. I'd get a chocolate shake and they'd not only bring out a big tall glass full of milkshake but the tin tumbler they blended it in, so you had extra. Places like Shirley's don't really do that anymore. Including Shirley's."

"Are you close to your mom?"

"I was," he said. "She passed a number of years ago. It's only Pops and me now. And a couple of sisters. Except they live out of town. The Volvo belonged to her."

The night was still and I watched the trees whiz past. I hoped that the cloaked figure wouldn't appear again. I don't think I could handle that right now. If they were even there to begin with. Of course they were. "So where are we going?" I said, trying to stay on topic. "There can't be anyplace good out here."

"Oh," he said. "You'd be surprised."

2

We ended up in a little town not far from Barlow called Wilsonville. It was a lot like Barlow, except this rural town was warmer and friendlier with a downtown of open shops and colorful facades. They had this French bistro called Le Petit Maison. It was a cozy little place. Carly and I had eaten at the Jack in the Box here. The place was once an old farmhouse, but refurbished as a restaurant. It was painted ivory white with green trim and had amber lights strung around it.

The waiter, a pleasant-looking man, seated us inside. We sat at a table for two. With a candle on the fresh white tablecloth, the lighting was cozy. I had seen two other well-dressed couples dining, but we were seated away from them. It felt like we had the intimate French bistro to ourselves.

"How do you know about this place?"

"This was my mother's favorite restaurant. We used to eat here often. I know everyone here."

They brought out a bottle of French wine. The waiter, wearing a black tuxedo and who sported a pencil-thin mustache, uncorked the bottle and poured. Liam sniffed the wine, approved, gave a nod, and then the waiter poured us two glasses. He then excused himself and walked off.

"He didn't even card me," I said. "I'm not 21."

Liam smiled. "I told you I have a lot of pull here. We sell them their produce and I'm good friends with the manager, Pierre. Don't worry about it."

He raised his glass. We toasted.

"So," he said. "I'm dying to ask. What business did you have at the Usher House?"

I drank. The wine was sweet and good.

"I, uh, I'm an Usher."

I thought Liam was going to choke on his wine.

"You're an Usher?"

"Yeah, imagine that—I'm shocked myself. They kind of have a weird family history."

"Kind of?"

"Yeah," I said. "A little eccentric, I guess."

"Well, 'eccentric' being a euphemism for insane, then yeah, I guess that about sums it up."

My face flushed and felt hot. I couldn't tell if it was from the wine or what Liam said suddenly made me angry. He seemed to notice.

"I didn't mean to offend you or anything," he said. "I didn't know that there was any family left after Vincent died."

"He was my father. Did you know him?"

"Well, the Ushers and the Delaneys share a property line. We've been farming that land for generations, though not as long as the Ushers. There were lots of wild stories." I could tell Liam was choosing his words carefully and trying not to offend me. "But, you know, small farming community. I'm pretty sure that's all they were, wild stories. People like to talk about other people, especially when they're eccentric, er, different."

I was about to ask him about some of the "wild stories" when the waiter showed up. Liam spoke to him in French with what sounded like a well-practiced delivery. He cocked an eyebrow at me. "Do you have any kind of food allergies?"

I shook my head "no." Then he continued to order. The waiter nodded to me, turned, and left.

"I took the liberty of ordering for us. I hope you don't mind. It's kind of a custom for the host to do so."

"As long as you didn't get anything too extravagant. Or raw."

"Pretty sure you're going to love it."

"You know," I said, remembering the unshaven guy in the Carhartt jacket, dirty jeans, and work boots who'd previously driven a farm truck, "you don't seem like the kind of guy who eats in snug French bistros and speaks the language perfectly."

"Oh," Liam said. "It's all from my mother's side. She was French. And, at one time, a well-known concert pianist. She met my father at a Farm Aid charity event, married him after six months of a whirlwind romance, and he took her back to the farm." He stopped himself. "You know what, it's a long boring story that you probably don't really want to hear. And it's rude for me to be talking about myself when I don't know anything about you except that you're an Usher and you see strangers standing in the middle of the road."

"Fine," I said. "You asked for it." So, I told him about growing up in Pickman Flats and being bounced around from foster home to foster home. My time with the Blands, and then my invitation to Usher House. Dinner arrived during all of this, which made the expositional information dump more pleasant. I don't know if he was bored or not, but he seemed to hang on my every word. This could make him nice, or he could be a desperate loner acting interested so there might be a chance of some after-dinner romance. *Ah, no, Mads, don't go there. Not everyone's like Parker.*

Liam had the beef bourguignon, which smelled mouthwatering, and I had the Salade niçoise, which was made with tuna, greens, anchovies, red potatoes, and shallots. It was incredible. We traded bites. His bourguignon was a beef stewed in red burgundy and had carrots, onions, garlic, and bacon. It was sensational.

"Next time," I said between bites, "I want what *you're* having."

He smiled, and his cheeks turned the color of the wine.

"What?"

"You said 'next time.' I hope there is one."

Keep being a decent and generous guy, Liam Delaney, and there will be.

Later, the pleasant fellow in the tuxedo brought us dessert and espresso.

"Wow," Liam said, taking a bite of the sugary crème brûlée. "What you said earlier. I feel like you've lived about five lives compared to me."

"Your mother sounds fascinating," I said between bites of the rich and creamy concoction. "Tell me more about her."

His mother had been a concert pianist who had been raised in Lyon, France, and then moved to America. She had been playing at an Atlanta concert which Liam's father had been attending for a charity. They'd met backstage and started dating. Liam's mother had grown up on a farm in France, and so they had a lot in common. Once married, they'd moved back to Delaney Farms and she'd helped him run the business of growing and selling fruits and vegetables. Having an artistic temperament, though, his mother, Marie Roget, had become disillusioned with farm life. She had three kids—two daughters and one boy. She'd instilled the love of the arts in them. One of Liam's sisters had moved to Atlanta to start a media company, his other sister curated a museum in Chicago. His mother had died of breast cancer and due to his father's ill health, Liam couldn't finish his university business studies and had had to return home to help run the farm. He'd started a charity in his mother's name though, The Art Foundation of Marie Roget Delaney. So, we had a lot in common with lost mothers.

"Boring story?" he asked after he finished.

"Not at all," I said. "And I love that you have an arts program in your mother's name. That's about the sweetest thing I've ever heard."

"It's the least I could do," he said. "Mom would have liked that, I think. Her last days weren't great. She became so secretive and was drinking a lot. It felt like she'd kind of lost her way."

"I'm sorry to hear that."

3

It was nearly eleven o'clock when we left the Le Petite Maison. We'd been talking for over three hours at dinner. I'm sure our waiters wanted to kill us for keeping them so late.

Liam opened the car door for me and let me in. He came around the Volvo and climbed inside.

"I had a nice time with you," I said, leaning in close.

He leaned in close, too. "It's one of the best times I've ever had."

My stomach turned knots in that way that I knew we were probably going to kiss, but I held back. It was too soon. Parker was a shit, but I still was conflicted about my feelings. "I probably should get back."

Liam pulled away. He almost seemed embarrassed. "Yeah, that's probably a good idea."

"I got out of a painful relationship recently. Thank you for understanding."

He smiled. "I get it. It's OK."

On the dark drive back, we spoke more, mostly about the future. He had dreams to leave the farm at some point and start his own business as possibly a restaurateur, but that all depended on his father. For me, I didn't have a plan. I'd thought my future was set making ends meet back in Pickman Flats, but now it seemed wide open. I didn't know what tomorrow would bring.

When we pulled up to the gate, I noticed that it was chained but not locked.

"I wonder if Knapp forgot to lock it?"

"Either that or he didn't want to wait around all night for us," he said. "Want me to open it?"

"No, I got it."

I climbed out of the car and strolled up to the gate, pulling the heavy chain aside, and opened it. It seemed odd that a little over 24 hours ago I had been visiting here for the first time, and now I was opening the gate for a guest. Talk about not knowing what would happen from one day to the next. I felt like I was living someone else's life. It sounds crazy, but that's about the best way I could describe it.

I motioned Liam to drive through. I closed the gate behind me but didn't lock it so Liam could leave, and then climbed back into the car. The night air was cool and calm, the moon full and bright. Such a sharp contrast from last night's storm. As we were driving in, I was relieved that the driveway wasn't covered in earthworms. One less creepy thing that might not scare off this kind, inquisitive guy.

He turned to me. "The suspense is kind of killing me about this place."

As he turned, something bolted across the lane in a blur, lit for a moment by the headlights.

"What was that?"

He turned, facing the driveway.

"What?"

"Something ran across the road?"

"The stranger from yesterday you claimed to see?"

"No," I said. "An animal of some kind."

"It was probably a deer. The woods around here are full of them."

"I know what a deer looks like," I said, frustrated.

We drove in silence. When the house appeared, I waited to hear Liam's response.

"Are your sure your last name isn't Addams and not Usher?"

"Huh?"

He laughed. "You know, like *The Addams Family*—Gomez and Morticia."

"Are you making fun of my family?"

"Not at all—I love those movies."

I punched him in the arm. "Don't be a jerk."

He smiled. "I'm just kidding. It, uh, looked like it was a nice place… at one time."

"It needs a lot of work, and a buttload of gardening."

"Guess you have your work cut out for you for the next decade."

"Better be careful," I said. "I bet Knapp needs an assistant gardener —I'll put your smug ass to work."

He raised up a hand in mock surrender. "Hey, I was just kidding. It's a nice place, really."

The tires of the Volvo clicked on the cobblestone driveway in front of the house. He pulled up to close the door. The house looked asleep but at the same time, ready to awaken and pounce. There was that awkward moment of a goodnight kiss. Instead, I extended my hand.

He shook it. Yeah, weird and awkward. So what. I'm an Usher after all, it's kind of our *modus operandi,* or so I'm told.

"See you again soon?" he said.

"I don't know, do you feel like dating Wednesday Addams?"

"Are you kidding, Christina Ricci is totally hot."

"She was like a ten-year-old kid in those movies, sick-o."

"No," he said with a laugh. "I mean now."

"Yeah, right," I said. "I'll text you."

"OK," I'll make sure to close and lock the gate. Also, say hello to Cousin It," he said, and then drove off.

I flipped him the bird. I considered that a good sign. If I flip you the bird, that means I probably like you. Otherwise, you'd get nothing from me but ice.

The moon was yellow and glorious and cast the woods beyond in a pale glow. Then some dry twigs snapped out beyond the perimeter of the house. Time to go.

I went to the front door and tried the knob. Locked.

Whatever it was was coming closer.

I pounded on the door. Hard. I needed to get a goddamn key if I'm going to live here.

The door creaked open and I pushed my way in.

Mrs. Dietrich closed the door behind me. She was holding a candle.

"I must remember to give you a key if you're going to keep such odd hours, miss."

"Odd hours," I said. "It's not even midnight yet."

"Some of us have long days ahead of us and don't like their sleep disturbed."

"Right."

"Will there be anything else?"

"I think I can handle it. Sorry for waking you up."

"Good night," Mrs. Dietrich said, and then vanished into the shadows.

Oh, Mrs. Dietrich, what would I do without your stone-faced, passive-aggressive ass?

I made my way up the stairs. The air in the house felt heavy like a thick fog. Much heavier than the night before. The portraits on the wall all seemed to look at me in disapproval in the darkness.

"It was a first date," I told their painted faces. "We didn't even kiss. Give me a break."

I sauntered down the dark hallway to my room. I really missed Carly. I would love to give her a recap of the entire night, which was one of the best dates I'd been on in a long time. Guess I could. It was three hours behind in Washington State. She'd be home from her flight most likely. No, I'd talk to her tomorrow.

The light under Roderick's door burned bright. I was not the only one up burning the midnight oil it seemed. I thought about knocking on his door and wishing him a good night, but I thought better of it. Time to just go to bed.

As I entered my room, well, great-great-great aunt Eva's room, I saw a familiar feline shadow waiting at the French doors. So, I let in the cat. I called her Esmerelda and she seemed to respond to the name, wriggling around my ankles. "Guess you're my cat now," I said. "I mean, you came with the house, right?"

She only purred at me.

In the night were howls and strange sounds outside Usher House. I ignored them the best I could, distracting myself with warm thoughts of Liam. It would have been nice to kiss him, and maybe I should have, but we had time. If he was really the kind of guy he seemed, there would be lots of time for that. And more.

THIRTEEN

The next morning, I made the most incredible discovery!

It started when I woke up early—earlier than I wanted to, so I got up. Nothing drives me crazier than lying in bed awake. Esmerelda was purring, gazing at me with those beautiful green eyes.

"I'm up already, I'm up."

Mrs. Dietrich had pressed all of my clothes and put them in the oak wardrobe. It was rather unusual to open the ornate door and discover all of my things inside. I climbed into my robe and slid my feet into my fuzzy slippers. Carly wouldn't be up this early to call her, and I didn't want to bother Roderick in case he was sleeping, so I crept downstairs to take a look at the rooms again, primarily the library. I must admit, I wasn't as much of a book reader as I'd have liked to be, but maybe now was a good time to get into the habit again. When I was in grade school, I would check out the maximum number of books at the library and wade through them. Mostly because books transformed me to another place—a magical land far away from grim reality of foster homes. I could be anyone I wished and live any place I wanted between the covers of a novel. That was what made them enchanting. However, when I entered high school and had to start reading books for English classes and writing reports and all that, some of the joys of reading took a back seat. Then after I met Parker, I'd all but forgotten about reading. So, maybe, I could find a nice volume downstairs. Who knew, there might be some first edition Jane Austen or Emily and Charlotte Brontë books on those dusty, forgotten shelves.

The library was behind two tall, thin oak doors. Leather-bound books stacked as high as the ceiling stood on dark Cherrywood shelves. The fireplace was unlit but the two wingback chairs in front of it looked cozy enough. I could have some coffee down here and enjoy the morning. In fact, if I wanted to, I suppose I could make a habit of it.

Esmerelda trailed me down the stairs. I thought about keeping her hidden in my room, but why? If I co-owned the house, that meant I had a say in what pet I could keep. Mrs. Dietrich would have to deal with it if she didn't approve. Although I did find myself rehearsing my "responses" if she wanted to get passive-aggressive with me again. I'd dealt with plenty of cranky old ladies at my store, so I could handle her. She did, after all, work for me now.

So many books lined the shelves that I didn't know where to begin. I discovered an assortment of fiction and non-fiction books. The non-fiction books were mostly travelogues, so that didn't interest me too much. I decided I'd go with fiction. I unearthed a leatherbound copy of *Wuthering Heights*. It wasn't a first edition, but it was old. This one had been published in 1915—over 100 years ago. The book was a little dusty, but other than that, it was completely pristine. It even creaked open. I doubted it had ever been read until I gazed at the front page—PROPERTY OF EVA USHER. Ah, so this had been her book. She'd died in 1920 according to her epitaph in the family crypt. I wondered how many other books belonged to her? I searched through the fiction, many of which had her name inscribed on the opening page. The travelogue books belonged to Edgar Usher, as his name was inscribed in the front of them. Mr. Walsh had mentioned that he had been the one into traveling. Made sense. There were other novels from other Ushers. I recognized their names from the gold-plated placards on the paintings and their epitaphs down in the family crypt. However, Eva seemed to be one of the most avid readers of the family.

As I combed through the books, Esmerelda sprang up onto the hand-carved oak table. The table sat behind a loveseat upholstered in tufted red velvet. I snapped on the stained glass lamps at the table. The black cat pawed at the table's drawer. I hoped that a mouse hadn't made a home in there. Opening it, I found a stack of framed photos. They were faded, but the images were still clear. On the walls of the library, in the spots with no shelves, there were perfect squares of discolored yellow wallpaper where the pictures had once been hanging apparently. Why had someone taken them down? They were lovely, revealing photos.

All of them were of Usher House and at the same angle. They were taken in the middle of the lake, which meant I guessed, someone had rowed a boat out there. Or perhaps there was a small island. The angle captured the water and a specific angle of the house. The first photo was silver in color. The quality of it reminded me of photos of the Civil War and the Industrial Revolution that I had seen in high school textbooks. Grainy black and white photos with a hint of brown. Sepia, I believe it's called. Usher House looked new. In fact, on the side of the photo, just at the edge of the frame, I could see some scaffolding. The date was July 23, 1880. It was incredible how well-kept up the house was. And all of the full trees around the place. The next photo was dated fifteen years later. It was also sepia toned. The house had a more lived-in look, and the grounds were more developed with blooming flowers and trees. It was dated August 13, 1895.

I went through many of the photos. Each from the same angle. Each about 15 to 20 years apart. There wasn't anybody in the photos, only the same image at the same angle. As the decades progressed, the quality of the photos improved. Sepia turned to black and white turned to full color. The house and the lake still looked mostly the same. It wasn't until after the 1970s when the house and the grounds started to look, well, bad. The lake started to take on a swampier-looking appearance and the house started taking on a forlorn countenance. Yes, I say countenance because Usher House seemed to have a face. It was like the windows were eyes. Vacant and staring out into the middle distance, but aware. It was in the later photographs, too, that I started to notice a crack at the base of the house. And every few years, the crack increased.

Funny, I hadn't noticed it when I arrived or was outside when it was full daylight.

Then the photographs abruptly stopped. The last one was June 23, 2000—110 years after the first one. The house pretty much looked the way it did now. Well, besides the twenty years of extra wear and tear. It seemed that any attempt to improve Usher House had been abandoned. I wondered if that was when all of the photos were pulled down off the walls. Maybe my father had gotten tired of seeing the place that Usher used to be. I couldn't imagine Mrs. Dietrich pulling these photos down unless she was asked to do so. Maybe my mother had done that. It had also been a year or so before Roderick and I were born. Mr. Walsh had mentioned that my father was heartbroken after our mother had taken us from Usher House. Maybe that had been the straw that broke the proverbial camel's back. Maybe he couldn't stand to look at Usher House any longer and demanded that these photos be taken down and stuffed unceremoniously in the drawer.

"What's the story behind all this?" I asked the cat who only stared at me with those warm, emerald eyes.

I shoved the photos back in the drawer. Except for one. The original one taken. I'd hang that up in my room as there was something cozy about it. Over in one corner of the library was an old phonograph. Some music would lighten the somber mood hanging over the house. Looking through all of the records was like looking through the photographs—each a snapshot in time. The earliest records were some old 78 RPMs of classical music, some jazz compositions, and then some delta blues. Later record albums were from artists like Benny Goodman and Glenn Miller. Lots of lounge-type music. Some records that piqued my interest weren't labeled, except for a date. One said October 13, 1935. They were heavy. I placed one on the turntable, cranked the handle until the record spun, and dropped the heavy phonograph needle on it. As the record popped and crackled from the dust and scratches on its shiny black surface, the voice of a man came on. It was a clear, intelligent-sounding voice. Like the kind you might hear on the radio or a documentary. He identified himself as Edgar Usher and he went into the family history of the Usher family. Oh, this was like a recorded journal. How fascinating. I would definitely like to listen later—and tell Roderick about it.

As I was putting the record away, Esmerelda was playing with something. At first I thought it was an insect, like a cricket. But then I realized that it was a key. A black key about two inches long. A skeleton key of some kind.

"What do you have there, little one?"

I picked it up and looked at it. Maybe it belonged in here. Perhaps it opened a desk or a drawer. I dropped it in my robe pocket for safe-keeping.

"I thought I heard voices."

The sound startled me.

Mrs. Dietrich stood in the doorway of the library.

"Oh, I was just talking to myself."

The housekeeper narrowed her eyes. "A *man's* voice."

"Uh, and I was playing some records."

Esmerelda jumped up and attacked the ends of my robe belt.

"Where did that *thing* come from?" Mrs. Dietrich hissed.

"She, uh, visited here the other night. I brought her in from the cold."

"I have seen that cat around for decades and it's never been allowed in the house. Black cats are bad luck. Mr. Usher never allowed pets in the house."

I considered her statements. First, Ezzy was *not* decades old, she was young and spritely, so that was impossible. Next, black cats being bad luck was an outdated superstition. And finally, who cared? Scooping up the cat, I held her to my breast like a baby. "Mr. Usher doesn't live here anymore."

"You should probably respect your father's final wishes."

"I will not turn away this poor sweet animal. Esmerelda will live here with us. My 'father' will have to deal with it. May he rest in peace."

"Esmerelda," the housekeeper said with some perceptible dissatisfaction.

"It's a great name," I said. "Don't you like it?"

"Now that you're up, miss, I will see to preparing breakfast. It will be ready in 20 minutes." Mrs. Dietrich turned and marched out of the library, and without another word or glance at the purring black cat, she slammed the door.

Well, the score was now Madeline Usher 1 – Mrs. Dietrich 0.

FOURTEEN

1

"I hope that I'm not allergic to cats."

Roderick sipped his coffee. Esmerelda lapped up cream from a saucer under my feet. We sat in the dining room. A high-spirited fire crackled on the hearth. I had been enjoying my coffee alone with my new cat until my brother had come shuffling in wearing his red silk robe and leather slippers, his disheveled hair like a dark bird's nest.

"You don't know if you're allergic to cats or not?" I said, not really wanting to talk about this right now. Instead, I was contemplating the tiny key in my robe pocket, which I planned to unlock *something* with it later, whatever that something may be.

"I'm allergic to practically everything—hay, dust, mold. I'm pretty sure I keep Sudafed in business."

"Well, there's quite a bit of dust and mold here."

"Yeah, and since it's an old house, I've been prepared or I'd be sneezing my head off." He looked at me. "You look kind of tired."

"Uh, thanks. I woke up early; I couldn't stay asleep."

"I did notice that you got in kind of late, too."

"Well, it was before midnight. That's actually not *that* late."

"Guess that means that your 'date' was a success."

OK, I really don't want to talk about this with a brother I just met. One with a slight twinge of jealousy in his voice.

"I like him. He's nice."

"Oh," Roderick said. "That's a relief I thought girls mostly liked jerks."

"That's not true at all." Well, except for Parker. I definitely still liked that jerk. But that feeling was slipping away each day, especially being here and not having anything to remind me of him. Time to change the subject. "You know, I was in the library this morning and there's the most remarkable collection of books."

"Yeah, Mrs. Dietrich told me that you were rifling around in there at the butt-crack of dawn."

"I wasn't rifling around, I was just bored and wanting to know more about this place. And since when does Mrs. Dietrich report to you about my actions?"

Roderick shrugged. "I don't know. I guess she simply likes me better than she likes you."

"Oh, and you hate that, right?"

"Well, no. She does make it nice here for us."

"Yeah, maybe between the cold looks and snotty comments," I said. "Or do you not get those?"

"She's pretty on the level with me. I can speak with her if you want."

"Uh, no thank you. I can handle her."

"She also mentioned that she spoke to you about the cat and of father's wishes about not having house pets."

Seriously? This again?

"I'll paraphrase what I told her—our father is dead and I'm keeping the cat. End of discussion."

"Oh, that's fine. Like I said, I hope I'm not allergic. But, you know, if I am, I will gladly sacrifice my comfort for your desire to own a four-legged fur ball with a heartbeat if that's what makes you happy."

OK, I'm tired of this conversation. Obviously Mrs. Dietrich *and* Roderick woke up on the wrong side of the bed today.

"I'm going to go freshen up and begin the day," I said, picking up the cat. "I'll see you around."

"Oh, what are your plans today?"

"I'll let you know."

"Because, I had hoped to spend some time with you. You know, getting to know the house and one other. Like maybe going for a walk and talk or something."

"That sounds nice. We'll definitely do that sometime."

I gathered up the cat and started to withdraw from the dining room. "Oh, and if Mrs. Dietrich has anymore concerns about me, please let me know."

2

I called Carly. She was getting up. I was telling her all about my great date with Liam the night before. I left out all of the Mrs. Dietrich stuff and Roderick being slightly pissy this morning. I didn't want her to worry.

"Well," she said, still sounding tired. "I'm fucking envious. I have to open the store every day this week. The manager texted me in the middle of the night and said she was sick again. All this after flying back all day yesterday. The district manager left a message that she's probably going to let her go. She asked if I wanted to be the manager instead. I'll probably call her back and say yes, because I'm a sucker for self-punishment."

"That's terrific," I said. "Congratulations."

"Are you serious? You get the steamy romance with the hunky country guy with the southern drawl and I get to manage retail clothing. Life isn't fair."

"It's not a steamy romance, jeez. We're just kind of friends."

"I saw the way he looked at you. He doesn't want to be your friend."

"He's not like that at all. He was a perfect gentleman."

"Oh, I've known plenty of 'perfect gentlemen.' They're gentlemen until they get a little taste of your fine, pink flesh—and then they turn into goddamn werewolves."

Ugh, *why* was everyone trying to annoy me that morning?

"Well, Liam isn't this way. He's sweet and he's educated. Do you know that he even started a charity in his mother's name? Is that the sweetest thing you ever heard or what?"

"It's always the quiet ones," she said. "They love their mothers and then they turn out to be psychos like Norman Bates."

"All right," I said. "I'm sorry you're tired. I'll let you go."

"Hey, I was just kidding around. I'm happy for you. I really am. I'm being jealous and a tad bitchy."

A tad?

I nodded. "Yeah, OK. Try to stay sane as the new manager of Harrington's."

"Yeah, I'll probably go full Harley Quinn on customers when we run this early Christmas sale the day after Halloween."

We both laughed, said our goodbyes, and hung up.

I noticed I had a text from Liam. I'M FREE TODAY. WANNA HANG OUT?

Before I even knew what I was doing, I had already texted back. YES. HOW SOON?

I didn't want to sound desperate, but after this morning, I needed a new change of scenery.

I fished out the mysterious key from my pocket, and plunked it down on the vanity. Someday I'd solve the secret and uncover what it went to. It was probably some lock box full of old cancelled checks or something boring.

HOW ABOUT NOON? he texted back.

PERFECT, I texted back. Who cared if I sounded desperate?

1

After getting a passive-aggressive guilt trip from Roderick about leaving again, I slipped out of the house. It was clear and bright, a beautiful day. I would stroll up the lane and meet Liam at the gate. Remembering the crack in the house from the photographs, I wandered around to the front. Yes, there it was—a barely-noticeable fissure along the wall about a quarter-inch wide that zigzagged from the roof down to the foundation. It almost resembled a bolt of lightning. Strange. I wondered if an earthquake had caused it or a general settling of the house over one-hundred and forty years. Hopefully, the whole house wouldn't split in two someday.

The winged, horned, stone gargoyle gurgled green water from its gaping mouth into the briny fountain. Though its eyes were sightless, it seemed to peer at me and laugh with its watery words. "You're certainly a charmer," I said to the concrete demon.

As I clicked over the cobblestones of the driveway, I noticed Knapp was burning some leaves around the side of the house. He wore the same baggy dungarees and tweed coat as before. He raked leaves into the smoldering smoke. I walked up to him before he noticed me. Either he was engrossed in his work or hard of hearing.

"I'm leaving for the day, Mr. Knapp, and I don't want to trouble you opening and shutting the gate behind me. Would you happened to have a spare gate key?"

The man gazed at me as if trying to comprehend the meaning of my simple words. Then he groped into the pocket of his oily tweed jacket and produced a key with a grimy hand like a half-rate magician. He handed it to me and nodded as if to say, *you keep it.*

I nodded and smiled, holding up the key. "Thank you." I guess I did all the added gestures as I wasn't sure he could really hear or understand me.

Knapp returned to his work as if I wasn't standing there. Fine.

I strolled down the driveway and toward the gate, skirting as close to the swamp as I could. Then I stopped, turned, and gazed back. I was remembering the photos that I studied this morning. Hard to believe how much this place had changed. It was like they had given up.

Inspecting closer, I could see a little dock in the reedy weeds. I guessed that was where a boat was tied up. The wood was old and weathered and many of the boards had fallen through. I imagined the whole thing would collapse under the weight of me if I stood on it. Beyond the reeds and the stagnant water stood a tiny island out in the middle with a lone dead tree in the center of it. That was where the photos were taken, I was sure of it. I visualized the photographer, whomever that was, loading up his old-fashioned box camera into a rowboat on a warm summer day and paddling out into the middle of the lake to the island with fish jumping in the clear blue waters, ducks swimming and quacking, and butterflies dancing on the warm breeze. All of that gone. You would never have known that it resembled paradise, Eden, without having seen all of those grainy, sun-faded photos.

As I looked back up at the house, I had the distinct feeling of being watched. I quickly scanned all of the windows, but I didn't see anyone at them or any of the curtains move, as if they had seen me looking, and then tried to hide. I peered up at the tower window. I had thought that I had seen movement there, but the dark window stood untenanted like a dead eye. I shivered, getting the creeps.

Turning, I ambled away from the lake and headed down the driveway. Then I quickly turned again, hoping to see whoever was spying on me, but the house appeared still and empty. Oh well. I wandered along the lane. One thing I noticed was that no birds perched in the dead trees around Usher House, they only perched in the live ones. Somewhere up above in a fir tree a murder of crows peppered the late morning air with their collective caws.

I walked to the gate and opened it. That's when I noticed some alarming markings on the brick pillar that supported the gate. It had some scratches on the sides of the bricks as if something had grabbed the top of the pillar and then pulled itself upward, kicking with its clawed feet, scratching the bricks. I don't know if that's what happened, but that's the way it looked. If this gate had been designed to keep something in, then it wasn't doing that good of a job.

But what kind of animal made marks like that? It'd have to been something like a bear. But what I'd seen over the last two nights hadn't been a bear. It had appeared more human in shape. But who could it have been? Could Knapp be turning into a werewolf in the night hours and running around under the light of the moon? What a stupid thing to think. Mythical beasts like werewolves didn't exist.

Going through the gate, I locked it behind me with the spare key. Then, I waited for Liam.

We would later have a perfect day together.

Except for one tiny thing.

2

"I've got the perfect day planned for us," Liam said when he was driving me back in his truck to his house. "Have you ever ridden a horse?"

"Uh, no."

We traveled down a dirt road for about a quarter mile off the highway and pulled up at his house. It was a gorgeous Victorian-style farmhouse that appeared to have been built early last century. It was painted sage green with an ochre trim. Beyond the house was a big red barn and beyond that, green fields. It was almost a picture-perfect postcard of what you'd imagine a farm to be. I told Liam so.

"Thanks," he said. "It's been in the Delaney family for generations. Like your house."

"I wish my family's house looked like this. It's gorgeous."

"Thanks."

He drove past the home. I stole a look in the windows but I couldn't see much, only dark windows lined with curtains. No occupants inside. We drove past another building that had tractors. A middle-aged man wearing faded bib overalls and a blue t-shirt was working on one. Liam beeped his horn and the man waved and gave a big smile.

"That's Herb Legrand," Liam said. "He fixes all of the Delaney farm equipment. Herb's like a sorcerer with a spanner set—he keeps everything running smooth. We don't pay him enough."

"He seems agreeable."

"Yeah, I've known him my whole life. He's like family."

"I'd love to meet your family sometime."

Liam gave me a look. "My sisters occasionally come home for the holidays. You just saw Herb. Pops is probably plunking around in town somewhere. I don't like him driving but he's too ornery to let me take the keys from him."

"He sounds…spirited."

"Yeah, I love Pops but he can be a pain in the butt sometimes too. But I live in his house, so what am I going to do?"

We drove up to the barn. It was probably the biggest I'd ever seen, painted a wine-colored red with cream trim. The roof was completely round and sloped. It had two large barn doors in front and two smaller doors on the side. Liam came around the truck and opened my door.

"You don't have to keep doing that," I said. "It's a nice gesture, don't get me wrong, but I can manage."

He gave me a formal bow and pulled off his hat. "As you insist, ma'am."

We both laughed.

He opened one of the smaller doors. My nostrils were assailed with the stench of dust, stale hay, and horse manure.

A row of stables lined one wall. Across the hall was the larger part of the barn. It had a well-trodden sawdust floor and three colorful barrels in the middle spread out in a triangle.

"That's the riding arena," Liam said. "I'm going to get you warmed up here."

"I've only seen horses at the fair that we have every summer. That's about it."

"They're like driving a motorcycle. Super easy."

"Can't say that I've ever been on one of those either."

"A bike?"

"Of course."

"Just as easy."

I stared at two horses in their stalls. Both of them were big, beautiful animals. They examined me to see if this stranger was some kind of threat to them. Liam handed me some green cubes that smelled grassy. "Here," he said. "Feed them those, that will make them like you."

I fed them each a cube and they munched them, eagerly wanting more. I offered more, petting their heads. They didn't seem to mind.

"See," Liam said. "They adore you already."

"Because I'm giving them something that they like."

"Well, isn't that the basis of any successful relationship?"

"Yeah, I suppose it is." I petted the horses more. "Do they have to stay in these cramped little stalls all day and night?"

"No," he said. "Not at all. Normally they're grazing in the back fields getting fat. I caught them earlier so it'd be easier to saddle them up. They haven't been ridden in a while. I don't do much riding myself. They were my sister's. Pops used to ride, but he's too crippled up to do it now. I take them out every blue moon to try to give them some exercise. And to clear my head."

"I'm not going to get bucked off or anything, am I?"

"No," Liam said. "These here are Tennessee Walkers. They're about one of the most docile and agreeable horses around." Liam looked at me and got serious. "I'd never do anything to put you in danger, Mads. Not willfully."

"Uh, thank you," I said. "I appreciate that."

He led the first horse out of the stall by a lead rope, the horse wearing a blue nylon halter. Liam tied him to an O ring in the side of the wall. "This here is Ranger, he's a good boy. And as gentle as a summer stream." He took a brush and combed through the dark, short coat. Dust matted up in the brush. "Just brush him easy like this, going with the grain. He'll like that." He handed me the brush and I did as instructed.

As I did that, Liam opened the second stall and walked the other horse out wearing a violet nylon halter and tied her up. "This is Willow. She's another saint on four legs." Liam pulled out a brush and started to run it across the gray animal.

"So, how do you like being in the country, City Mouse?" Liam asked.

"Well, Pickman Flats isn't much a city, Country Mouse. It's kind of a big town. There's only, like, twenty-thousand people or so. It's not huge or teeming with skyscrapers or anything."

"Sounds like a city to me."

"Well," I said. "It's nice to get away. I'm enjoying my time with you right now."

"Happy to hear it," he said.

Liam unlocked a wooden locker against the wall and opened it. He pulled out a leather western saddle and set it on its face. Then he pulled out a blanket and set it on the back of Ranger. "So," he said, "we start with a saddle blanket, like so." Then he plopped the saddle on top. "And then this." He started strapping the chest belt and the belly straps. It all looked complex. I told him so.

"It's about the easiest thing in the world once you do it a few times. You'll see."

I had to smile. He seemed to believe that we had a future together. I liked that.

Liam saddled his own horse, and then bridled them each up.

He handed me the reins to Ranger. "Here, we'll lead them out to the arena so you can get a little riding practice first."

Liam grabbed the reins of his own horse and he led me into the arena.

It was big and wide and smelled of damp wood from the sawdust floor. Light streamed in from skylight windows. Doves cooed from their rafter nests. It was a gentle sound.

Liam gazed up to where I was looking. "You like them, City Mouse? I call doves country pigeons."

I laughed. "You're quite the wit, Country Mouse."

Liam led me over to a yellow bucket. He tipped it upside down, stood on it, slipped a toe of his boot in, grabbed the saddle horn, and then swung his leg over. Then he sat high up in the saddle. "You see. Those are the steps to climbing on a horse."

He climbed off. It took me a few times to get up there. Liam standing behind me and showing me. We were close with my back to him. He grabbed my hand and showed me where to place it. It felt nice. I had such a feeling of security around him and didn't feel weird or threatened in any way. He had such a quiet, gentle nature about him. Almost like a Zen-ness. Parker was a little high strung and anxious. And he often made me anxious. He'd tap his leg, or drum with his hands, or be in a hurry, so it would stress me out. Liam seemed to take everything in stride. Yeah, it was only our second date and third time meeting. But that first time on the road, he was so calm and cool when he didn't even know me. He wasn't trying to impress me; he was just being who he was. And I liked that.

I climbed up onto the horse. The saddle seat felt hard against my butt. I adjusted myself a little. Liam adjusted the stirrups so the saddle fit me a little better. Then he climbed onto his own horse.

"We're gonna have a little lesson of 'Follow the Leader,'" he said. "You turn with the reins like so, left and right." He pulled back on the reins. "Here's how you stop." Then he made a clicking noise and tapped his stirrups on the side of the horse. "And here's how you go."

"Try it."

I did, and to my amazement, the horse underneath me knew exactly what I wanted him to do. We rode around in the dusty arena for a few laps with Liam showing me how to ride. We even took slow turns around the three barrels in the middle of the arena, which Liam told me were for barrel racing, but I wasn't ready for that at full speed anytime soon.

Then, as we came around the track again, near Liam's truck, a black and white blur bolted into the barn. He ran around looking at me.

"Snooker," Liam said. "Take a chill pill, buddy."

Snooker was a black and white Border Collie had some of the most distinctive face patterns that I'd ever seen. Gray hair salted his muzzle. Though a senior dog, he acted much younger.

"He's about the oldest puppy that you'll ever know," Liam said. "He still thinks that he is one."

"Hi, Snooker," I said. "You're so cute."

A man appeared in the doorway. He was walking with a silver cane. Wearing jeans, cowboy boots, and a rust-colored Carhartt jacket. He was gray haired and ruggedly handsome. He resembled an older version of Liam.

"Hey, Pops," Liam said.

"See you're busy," he said.

"This is my friend, Mads. Madeline."

"Hello," I said. I would have tried to shake his hand or something but I was afraid of bending down. I still didn't feel like I had the whole riding thing down yet. "A pleasure to meet you."

"You look pretty good on a horse," he said.

"Thanks," I said. "It's my first time."

"Well, you take to it like a fish does to water."

"Where were you at, Pops?"

"Went into town for some parts to that tractor that Herb is fixing. Can you believe they raised the prices again? Damn inflation."

"Yeah, Pops, that sucks."

"So where are you from, Madeline?"

"I'm from Washington."

"Oh, all the way up in D.C. with all of those crooked politicians?"

"No, Washington State. On the other side of the map."

"Oh, then you're a girl made out of mountains and rainwater then. What brings you down this way?"

"Well, I got called here on some family business."

"Oh, yeah, anyone I'd know?" the old man asked.

"Well," I said, "I am your new neighbor down the road."

The wide smile that Mr. Delaney was wearing slipped away. His entire gesture changed. He became colder and more reserved. "You don't mean the Ushers."

"Yeah, Pops," Liam said. "It's totally fine."

"What's an Usher doing here on my property?"

Now he wasn't acknowledging me anymore. He was talking to Liam about me as if I had left the arena.

"She inherited the place. I met her a couple of days ago. I took her to the restaurant."

He looked at me like one might look at a flat tire. "I see." Then he started to turn and walk away. "Goodbye."

Great, I was pretty sure Liam's father hated me.

SIXTEEN

1

"I'm so sorry about that," Liam said. "I'll have a talk with him later about his rude manners."

"Please don't," I said. "I don't want him to hate me any more than he already does."

"He doesn't hate you. He doesn't even know you."

"He knows my family. He reacted to the name."

"All will be fine. Pops is a little set in his ways."

"Maybe it was a bad idea. This whole thing. Maybe I should go."

"Go?" Liam said. "No way. Don't let him bother you. There's something I wanted to show you."

"What?"

"Well," he said. "If I tell you then it won't be a surprise."

I peered down at Snooker, who was gazing up at me. "I don't know if I'm up for any surprises. Meeting your father was enough."

"No, this is good, trust me. You'll love it."

We rode along a field. Rows of broken yellow corn stalks stood about a foot off the round. Birds chirped in the trees from the surrounding woods of oaks and pines mingled together. I was starting to get the hang of this riding thing. Ranger wanted to be close to Willow, so I didn't have to do anything, really. The Tennessee Walker led the way on his own. This way I could enjoy Liam.

"You're a corn farmer?"

"Mostly corn. We harvested in September."

"From farm to table, that kind of thing? Hopefully it's not GMO."

"Our corn is mainly used for livestock feed and ethanol production. Not people. And before you ask, it's non-GMO corn. My idea to switch to that a few years ago." He shrugged. "Wish you could have seen all of the corn rows then—it was much more impressive."

"There are lots of corn fields back home. I can picture it. Do you ever do Halloween corn mazes or anything like that?"

Liam laughed. "I wanted to. I thought it'd bring in some good revenue for the off-season, but Pops vetoed that idea right out of the gate."

"Oh. I love going to corn mazes on Halloween night. So much fun."

"Hey, I'm sorry again about my pops," Liam said. "I really don't know what got into him."

"It's all right," I said. "You don't have to apologize for him."

"But I do. I want him to like you. At least as much as I am liking you."

"Uh, that would be weird."

"You know what I mean."

"So you do like me?"

Liam nodded. "Can I tell you something?"

"Of course."

"Well, it's kind of personal and it's about another girl, would that be all right?"

"Why wouldn't it be?"

"When you're with a girl and you talk about another girl, it uh, sometimes gets awkward. But I only want to make a point."

"Go ahead," I laughed. "I think I can handle it."

"So, I was actually engaged to be married. Uh, maybe engaged isn't the right word. Promised. Yeah, that's it. I had a girlfriend all through high school, Christina. I had lots of girls interested in me. And I'm not saying that to sound like I'm some kind of player. But, I guess, girls liked me for some reason."

"Well, you are pretty cute and kind, so I can imagine."

Liam blushed and looked the color of a honeycrisp apple.

"Anyway," he continued. "Christina was everything to me. We studied together. Hung out all of the time. Her family has a farm down the road, too, Van Burens. Her pops and my pops were friends, good friends, they liked to drink sweet tea and play pinochle together. You know, wild and crazy stuff." He laughed. "It was pretty much assured that Christina and I would get married, and that our fathers would give us some land and we'd start our own farm. It was kind of like our futures were laid out. Our moms were already counting their grandchildren." He laughed again. "So I felt like we were like, royalty or something. That I was a prince and Christina was a princess, and we were getting married to bond our kingdoms. That's what it felt like. Then, after a while, it started to get to be too much. The pressure. Christina kind of told me that she wanted to see other people. She didn't want to only be with the first person she'd dated. That kind of hurt, but I understood. I didn't have my eye on anyone else, but the parental pressures had started to make me resent the whole thing. Part of me wanted to break up, and part of me wanted to drive her as far away from Barlow as possible and start a new life together alone—without our families."

"So what happened?"

"Well, Christina started seeing this guy, Kyle Withers. They're uh, engaged to be married. His family doesn't have a farm. He plays sports and has a scholarship to college."

Wow, I could kind of relate with what happened with Parker.

"Pops was mad about it. But he blamed me for not being assertive enough in the relationship. He told me that I was too wishy-washy with Christina. That I let her make her own decisions. And I was like, 'Pops, of course I'm going to let her make her own decisions.

She's her own person.' He didn't like that. Mom died shortly after. She told me that Christina didn't have the love for me that I did for her. She could see that. And the last thing she told me was to follow my heart and do what makes me happy. Not for her, not for Pops. For me."

"Oh, I see."

"So, I'm guessing that has a lot to do with why Pops was a little, uh hostile with you."

"No," I said. "He was kind to me until the name Usher was mentioned. Then it's like a light switch was flipped."

"Yeah, I guess you're right."

"I've been delving into the family history a little bit. There's something strange and unusual about the Usher family. And I'm guessing that 'strange and unusual' isn't exactly a welcome set of adjectives in Charlton county."

"Yeah, you're right. I didn't want to say anything, but the Ushers aren't thought of with any great love. Pops has a personal vendetta against them."

"Why? What did they do to him?"

Liam shrugged. "I don't know. He would never tell me. Honestly, I was kind of hoping that he wouldn't know that you were an Usher until he got to know you a little better. You know, so he could let his wall of prejudice down."

Something angered me about that. "Well, sorry to spoil your plans. I am who I am. I can't help it. I've only known about this whole crazy thing for a couple of days—and now I'm being *judged* for it. By your father, by a woman I don't even know in a restaurant. And I'm sure by plenty of other people if they knew."

"No, I didn't mean it that way. Do you think I would be out here if I didn't like you? Since the first time I saw you, I couldn't stop thinking about you. It's like a light switch was flipped. I'd honestly given up on relationships and love after Christina. I was discouraged and afraid. Then, bam, seeing you made me forget all that. You don't think I gave you my card for nothing, right? I kind of hoped you would call."

"That's pretty smooth, Mr. Delany. I bet you do that to all the girls you meet."

"Actually, you were my first."

"Yeah, right, sure."

He smiled. His eyes were so bright. The sunlight glistened off his teeth. He looked like Dionysus on horseback. Normally, I went for niceness and decency over looks, but I must admit, Mr. Liam Delany wasn't hard on the eyes. He seemed in his element in the country riding a horse. This was the happiest I'd ever seen him.

"Up here another quarter mile, we can stop for lunch," he said. "I packed an entire picnic for an army. Hope you're hungry."

"Let me guess—peanut butter and jelly sandwiches on white bread with juice boxes."

"Oh, man, you spoiled the surprise." He laughed.

An antiquated, wrought-iron fence came into view. It snaked along the field. Within it were acres upon acres of trees. It was as if they were all being contained. That kind of seemed like the general mission of Usher house—put a fence around everything and contain it. Don't let anything in or out. Stumbling upon the fence in this otherwise wild place gave me a sinking feeling.

The smell hit me before seeing the corpse.

"Oh, what *is* that?"

Near the fence laid the bloated corpse of a buck. Something had ripped his throat out. He looked at us with dead, pale marble eyes and an open mouth, his puffy, leaden tongue out. His stomach bloated in the sun. His expression seemed to be that of shock and horror, the last moments of him being alive.

I couldn't help it. With the smell and the sight of dried blood and rotting flesh, and the thousands of maggots boiling on it all, a wave of nausea overtook me and I threw up breakfast. The vomit burned my throat. The sour stench of my vomit made me want to puke again. Instead, I dry heaved.

"Oh, hey," Liam said. He jumped off his horse, ran over to me, and helped me off. "Here, walk over here, upwind, away from that awful smell."

My knees buckled and I felt like I was going to fall over. The smell was so atrocious and heavy in the warm autumn air. I couldn't get it out of my nose.

"Are you all right?"

"I will be once we get away," I said. And then I remembered how we got here. "The horses—they're going to run."

Liam smiled and pointed. "No, they're trained to stay put even if you don't tie them up." He was right, Ranger and Willow just stood there, pawing the ground, nosing each other. Apparently the sight and stench of a dead, rotting deer corpse didn't bother them in the least.

"Sorry," I said. "I'm not usually such a baby. It's just the stink overtook me. Not exactly what I was expecting.

"No," he said. "It's OK."

Behind the fence, some sticks cracked. Something was lurking on the other side, a dark shape. Liam and I fell silent. What if that thing was back? What if it was stalking me the entire time? Maybe it had killed the deer? Maybe it was planning to kill us too.

"We should get out of here," I said. "It doesn't feel safe."

"Wait," Liam said. "I want to see what it is. Don't worry. We're safe. It's on the other side of the fence."

"That's what worries me," I said.

Then the figure came into view. And I wasn't any more relieved. It seemed like an odd coincidence that he would just happen to be out here. But here he was.

"Troubles on the trail?" Roderick said.

<h1 style="text-align:center">SEVENTEEN</h1>

oderick clutched a wooden walking stick. He was dressed in a long dark wool coat and had a gray cashmere houndstooth scarf wrapped around his neck. He looked like someone from the Edwardian times. My brother peered at us from behind the fence.

"Roderick," I said. "What are you doing here?"

He shrugged. "Since I was all by my lonesome, I decided to walk the perimeter of the property and get to know it." He shifted his stick. "I was hoping you'd join me so we could make it a family affair, but you made other commitments." He nodded to the rotting animal corpse. "Naturally, I smelled the corpse and tracked it here."

Liam walked over to the deer. With a boot, he kicked up some loose dirt to cover the deer's head and the maggots. The smell dissipated a bit. And it was easier to look at by not seeing the head.

"Something killed it," I said.

"Obviously," Roderick said. "There are predators in the area. Maybe a mountain lion or some wild dogs."

"It could have come from our side of the fence," I said, thinking about those claw marks on the gate posts I saw earlier.

"Impossible," Roderick said. "This fence was designed for maximum security."

One of the rungs in the fence was broken and pushed to one side. I showed him. "Not necessarily," I said.

"We'll have to mend that," Roderick said. "And that doesn't prove anything."

"There's something wandering around the grounds. Carly saw it too. I have a feeling that it may have done this."

Roderick didn't say anything, he kept staring at Liam. "Are you going to introduce me to your little friend?"

Little friend, really?

"Liam, this is Roderick, my brother."

Roderick extended a hand through the fence a little too willingly. "Any friend of my sister's is a friend of mine."

"Uh, yeah, nice to meet you, Roderick. My pleasure."

"Oh, Roddy, please," my brother said. "Roderick is just so formal. All my friends call me Roddy."

"Well, my name's really William, but I go by Liam. I'm a junior, so Liam kind of gives me my own name."

"Yes," Roderick said. "My sister and I come from a long line of family names."

OK, this whole thing was weird and awkward. I still didn't buy that Roderick happened to be here at the same time as us. Maybe I was being paranoid and suspicious, but it didn't add up. Was he tracking us? Was it really a coincidence? I tried to keep smiling.

"Hey, Roddy," Liam said, "we were just about to have lunch. Maybe you want to join us?"

No, not today. Please.

"That sounds lovely," Roderick said. And then he peered at me. He *knew* what I was thinking. "But I don't want to spoil your plans."

"Heck, Roddy," Liam said, "you wouldn't be spoiling anything."

I could kiss him for being so kind but please, shut up.

"It's all right," my brother said. "Perhaps another time. Mrs. Dietrich is no doubt preparing something right now. I wouldn't like to disappoint her." He kept looking at me when he said that as if that's what I'm doing, disappointing everyone by running off with Liam for the afternoon.

"I'll see you later, Rod," I said. And gave him a big wave. If he wanted to be micro-aggressive with his trivial barbs, well, I could do the same thing.

"Have a lovely afternoon," my brother said, and then strolled off.

"Wow," Liam said. "He seemed nice. That's crazy that he was out here at the same time we were." He said this without the slightest hint of irony or accusation. It was good-natured Liam being Liam. I had my doubts to Roderick's innocence.

"Yeah, crazy," I said and forced a smile. "He's pretty dedicated to the family."

Liam and I climbed back on our Tennessee Walkers and rode another quarter mile away. We arrived at a grassy meadow near the trees. Liam climbed off his horse and pulled out a red and white gingham picnic tablecloth from a saddle bag, unfolded it, and laid it on the ground. Then, like a magician doing a trick, he made Tupperware dishes filled with potato salad, macaroni salad, and rotisserie chicken appear from another saddle bag. He'd packed them in cold packs to keep everything fresh.

"Wow," I said. "You cooked this all yourself?"

He smiled. "Well, the market in Folkston surely did."

"Where's Folkston?"

"It's about ten miles from here in the opposite direction of Barlow and Wilsonville."

He did most of the eating. Every time I tried to take a bite of chicken, I remembered the deer. That decayed face boiling with maggots was frozen in my memories. That face of rotting terror. And that smell. I tried instead to eat some potato salad just to be kind. But I couldn't eat the meat. Not without thinking about that parasite-ridden flesh.

"You all right?"

"Yeah," I said, telling a little white lie. But I didn't want to ruin the picnic that my generous and handsome host had provided. I touched his hand. He seemed surprised by the gesture. Then I moved in closer. I could tell he was waiting for me to make the first move. So I did. I kissed him. It helped get the thought of the deer out of my head. He kissed me back and immediately I felt dizzy. I don't know how many minutes that we kissed but if felt like the sun had changed direction by the time we were done.

"OK," Liam said. "I didn't exactly have that planned."

After putting the food away, we laid on the picnic table covering and looked up at the clouds. They were ripe and full. Holding each other, we did some "cloud busting," figuring out what each cloud looked like. This was something I hadn't done since I was a kid. Doing this now, it felt like I'd known Liam my entire life. Like he was a childhood friend. It's odd to go through life and then learn that you have this other life that falls into your lap and kind of takes you over. Earlier this week, if you'd told me that I was heiress to a creaky old mansion, had a twin brother, and would be laying in the afternoon sun with a handsome boy, I would have said you had the wrong girl.

But apparently, I was the right girl.

And all the while, I still could feel the yearnings of Usher House not far away in the pit of my belly, calling to me in my thoughts.

EIGHTEEN

1

After spending the afternoon with Liam, we said our goodbyes and planned to see each other again. I couldn't help but think of him as he dropped me off at the gates of Usher House. Using my spare key that Mr. Knapp had given me, I unlocked the chain on the gate, opened it, and re-locked it. It's odd, but when you have a key, you have a small sense of power. Here I was holding an important key to the house. And why not? Usher House was half mine.

I strolled up the drive, taking my time. The sun had vanished in the trees and a golden pink glow cast all over everything. It gave this place a beauty that I had not seen yet. Frogs croaked and crickets sang. Fireflies danced under the shadows of trees. It was almost magical. And a side of Usher House that I had not seen before.

As I ambled, I did some thinking about goals. My next one was to get my car. I'd always been a person who'd never had to rely on anyone for much, and constantly having to get rides from Liam wasn't going to work. Because of Roderick, I had him let me off at the gates instead of driving me up. My brother acted weird seeing us together, so I didn't want him to possibly cause another awkward scene. I was aware that the house seemed to have eyes and knew my every movement, whether Mr. Knapp or Mrs. Dietrich or Roderick conferred with each other or observed individually. Everyone always seemed to know what I was up to, so I didn't want to submit Liam to that, too. My plan was to have a long talk with Roderick tonight at dinner and lay it out there. If I was an Usher and this was my house that I coowned with my twin brother, then some changes needed to be made. I wanted to feel like I had an equal share in things. It didn't feel like that now. I mentally prepared myself for Roderick. I felt like he would try to possess me. Don't ask me why, but that's what I felt. It was like I was a piece of property to him.

As I rounded the corner to the lane, an unfamiliar car stood out front. It was a shiny black Audi.

I wondered who was here. Could it be Mr. Walsh? Had he come back?

Striding up to the car, which shimmered in the dying light, I saw the sticker on the window. It was brand new. It didn't even have license plates on it, only the sticker in the window with a temporary one. Knapp was sweeping the cobblestones near the car. I regarded him for an explanation, which obviously wasn't all that effective considering he was mute.

"Isn't she a beauty?"

Roderick sauntered out of the house all smiles. This was the widest smile I'd ever seen.

"Whose car is it?" I asked.

"Well," he said. "It's yours, of course. It's a brand-new Audi TT Roadster."

"Mine?"

"Yes," he said. "It's about time you had your own set of wheels. Had it shipped from Atlanta. It arrived only a few hours ago."

"But how?"

"Funds from my software security business. It's OK, I logged it as a business expense. It's a tax write off, which made the price all the more affordable." He smiled. "It belongs to Usher Enterprises, which Ernest set up, and you and I are each an equal member. I ordered another car for myself, but I had some customizing done, so it will be here later in the week. Perhaps you'll let me borrow your Roadster as needed until then."

I must admit that flashy cars were not my style. Not saying that I didn't like it, but it probably cost fifty-grand easy.

He saw me admiring it. "Do you like it?"

"Uh, yeah," I said, not sure of what to say.

Roderick pulled out a set of keys and handed them to me. "She's all yours."

The keys felt heavy as they jingled in my hand. They also had a key for the house and the gate. In a way, it was like I was being handed an equal share. I now had freedom to enter and leave the grounds as I pleased. It was like my brother could read my thoughts or something.

"Shall we go for a spin?"

"Yeah," I said.

2

We drove for a few minutes in silence. The sun had set and the sky had taken on a bloody hue. The Audi Roadster hummed along the highway. The wheel felt good in my hands, and the leather seats comfortable, fitting my form. And of course, that intoxicating new car smell. I felt like I was rich and could do anything. This shiny new car really was a remarkable gift. It purred along the highway like a certain black cat back home.

"I gave Mrs. Dietrich the night off from making dinner," Roderick said, gazing out at the blur of trees whizzing past his window. "So it's up to you what you want us to do about dinner?"

Dinner? Oh, I hadn't even thought about it.

Well, Shirley's Diner was definitely out. I could take him to Wilsonville, The Petite Maison, but that kind of felt like Liam's place. We ended up going to another place outside Folkston called The Pleasant Pheasant, right off the highway. It was a quaint little family-style diner that had a cute ring-necked pheasant on the sign flourishing a top hat, spats, a monocle, and resembling Mr. Peanut as a mascot. We were seated by a friendly, smiling waitress named Shelly.

"Kind of a rustic choice, sis," Roderick said, looking around at all of the locals eating and chatting with their families. One family of three, a mom, son and daughter, all looked at their phones instead of each other. I found that kind of sad that they weren't enjoying each other's company. It made me not want to check my phone, even though I knew I probably had about 20 texts from Carly that I hadn't read yet.

"So," I said. "Did you have a good walk today?"

"Yes," he said. "Very revealing. You have no idea the wealth of land that we're living on. And it's never been used to its full potential. At least, not in a long time."

"What kind of potential do you mean?"

"Oh, I don't know. We could use it for agriculture. Build some rental cabins on it, lease them out, who knows?"

"But we're not farmers. Not like the Delaneys."

Roderick stirred at the name. "True," he chuckled, "but maybe they could give us some pointers about getting our fingernails dirty. I mean, how hard can playing in the dirt be, right?"

"Actually, it's very hard. My hometown of Pickman Flats is an agricultural town and farmers labor long hours and have to deal with the weather. It's super-hard work."

"Oh," he said. "I didn't mean to offend. I was merely thinking out loud."

Shelly returned for our orders. I didn't eat much for lunch thanks to that rotting deer carcass, but I still didn't feel like eating. I ordered cherry pie ala mode with a cup of coffee. Roderick ordered a chicken-fried steak, baked potato, a Coke, and a chocolate milk shake. He often ate big meals. For a guy so thin, I wondered where he kept all of that food. I wished I could eat like that and not gain a pound. Guess the Usher genetics gave him the skinny gene. I supposed I got the tact gene, where I didn't blurt out passive-aggressive things that bordered on rudeness. Thank God for small miracles, right?

"And I wanted to say I was sorry for how I acted today."

I acted like I didn't know what he was talking about. Part of me wanted to get more information than that, because if I accepted his apology right away, I would be acknowledging that. But if I played dumb, he'd most likely elaborate and I could, hopefully, make him squirm a bit for being such a jerk. Was this why he bought me the car? Was that a part of his apology? If so, I appreciated the gesture, but I wasn't going to be bought off to allow someone to be a rude asshole to me. Not going to happen. "How *were* you acting today?"

He laughed. "I thought it was obvious, but maybe not. I was being a standoffish asshole."

"Oh," I said. "I guess I didn't notice because that's how you always are."

"Burn," Roderick said. "Touché."

Well, at least he seemed to have a sense of humor about it.

"But, no, really. I guess I feel, you know, protective toward you. I simply want the best for you. The absolute best."

"You don't even know me though, really. How could you know what's best for me?"

"I don't," he said. "Though I am trying to learn. If you help me with that. Let me in a little bit. And I'll try to do the same. I'm not the most open book, either, but it's worth it to people who are family. And you're the only family that I have, sis. So, yeah, you're kind of a diamond to me." He laughed. "I just don't want to be like that creepy dude in *Lord of the Rings* that keeps talking about 'My Precious.'"

"That's Gollum," I said.

"Culture nerd."

"Proud of it," I said. "Though being in software development, I'm a little shocked that you didn't know Gollum's name. It seems like that kind of culture would be ripe for geeks."

"Oh, it is," Roderick said. "But I didn't pay much attention. I don't do much fiction. Mostly I read non-fiction and watch documentaries and the news. I don't get too wrapped up in fantasy. I like to know the reality of things. What's real and what's not."

I felt like he was digging at something there. Like he still wasn't ready to put aside that he saw Liam and I together, and that we were happy.

"I get that," I said, and to subtly make my own point. "But did you know that stories, and fiction, actually help readers to learn and grow empathy?"

"Oh, yeah? How's that?"

"Because you live the lives of hundreds of characters, thousands, you can understand their thoughts and feelings. Hell, I've been more upset with characters dying in stories than I have real people. Messed up, I know. But true."

"Yeah," he said. "That makes sense, I guess, if you're crazy." He laughed.

"You should try it. You know, the empathy part. It really can help give you an understanding and appreciation of other people. You know, their wants and needs, why they do the things that they do. Whom they choose to spend their time with and who they want to love."

Roderick nodded. "I get where you're going with this. I don't need to read *Jane Eyre*, *Pride and Prejudice*, or goddamn *Twilight* to figure that one out." He reached out and held my hand. "I care about you, deeply. Please use your empathy to understand that. We're the only family that each other has. We need to be strong."

I pulled my hand away. "We are. We can be strong. But not forceful. I have my own wants and needs. And if I choose to spend time with Liam, that is my decision and I need for you to respect that."

"I *do* respect that. He seems like a swell guy and from an affluent family. Dating him could help our bottom line and our future."

"We're not dating, we're just kind of spending time together and seeing where it goes. I'm not doing this to help the family or for some kind of financial gain. I like him."

"Like him," he said, considering. "But not love?"

Did I really have to have this conversation with my jealous brother in the middle of a family-style restaurant named after a game bird that's dressed like an aristocrat?

"It's too early in the cards to say," I said. "I am fond of him. And I think about him often."

Roderick nodded. "That's fine."

"Yes," I said. "It is. And it's my business and my business alone."

Roderick looked hurt. He drew his hands back into his lap. The food arrived. Saved by a distraction. Shelly served it to us with her trademark smile. Roddy's food looked and smelled delicious but he didn't touch it. He only stared at it with glassy, somber eyes. "I am sorry. I am a terrible person."

"No you're not. It's like you said, you're overly protective. But I don't need protecting, I can handle myself."

"I've always been a bit insecure," he said. "Even as a kid. You know, I was pretty much handed everything in life, but it still never felt like it belonged to me. I always felt like I would lose it. It probably had a lot to do with my adopted father. He was always making me feel worthless. And the way he treated my mother. He even cheated on her with several of his assistants. I guess I grew more attached to her. And then when she died, well, it kind of tore me up. I felt like everything in my life that I cared about could be taken away."

OK, now I felt like the complete jerkish asshole.

I reached over the table and touched his arm. "It's OK, Roddy. I'm not going anywhere anytime soon. We're going to work through all of this, and then decide what we're going to do about the future."

He nodded. "Thanks, I appreciate that."

"Great," I said. "Let's eat."

The cherry pie with a side of melted vanilla ice cream and coffee hit the spot, and for the second time today after seeing Liam, I felt better.

But that wouldn't last long.

e drove back late.

I didn't mind as I loved taking the Roadster out. It was a sporty little car so it handled the highway smoothly, even doing ninety-five.

"You've got some serious driving skills," Roderick said. "Watch out Indy 500."

I had to admit that being behind the wheel again and racing the engine gave me a sense of freedom that I hadn't felt before in a long time. The autumn night was clear and bright with the stars twinkling coldly in the sky. After about an hour of driving, cranking satellite radio on the alternative rock station, it was time to go home.

"I wasn't kidding about earlier, though," Roderick said. "I have some serious plans for Usher House. It can be great again. Like it was once before. Like in those photos."

"You saw them?"

"Of course," Roderick said. "I had Mrs. Dietrich rehang them back on the wall. With the exception of a missing one, though. It seems to be misplaced."

Oh, yes, the one in my room.

"I'm sure it will turn up," I said. "What kind of plans do you have?"

"I can maybe do some of my business out of the house once I get a decent WiFi system hooked up, which I'm already working on. Modernize it a bit and then maybe have a grand opening."

"I thought you didn't want to change Usher House. And what grand opening?"

"Yeah," Roderick said. "The place has been so closed off to the world. Maybe it's time that Usher Enterprises joins the twenty-first century finally."

"Usher Enterprises?"

"Pretty catchy, huh? Like it?"

"What does Usher Enterprises consist of?"

"Well, like I said, we'll be running the new company. But the sky's the limit, really. We could focus on tech, real estate, agriculture, a little of everything. I'm game for anything. Usher Enterprises will need to be profitable. And this will take time—it's not a sprint, it's a marathon. It could take a few years to hit big numbers, but you can't hit a home run if you don't go to bat, right?"

"You're really working the sports metaphors, bro."

Roderick laughed. "Yeah, it's my lame layman speak. I kind of go there when I'm trying to pitch people."

"Well, you don't have to pitch me. It all sounds fine. I mean, the house could use some help. Lots of help. And it will likely cost millions of dollars." I turned off the highway onto the long stretch of dark and twisted route that led us back to Usher House. "Mr. Walsh didn't really go into why the Usher dynasty became so broke, and I didn't ask him. Do you know?"

Roderick nodded. "Driving down from Boston, we had plenty of time to chat. The Usher fortune began as a tobacco farm. It contributed to the vast wealth of the family for about five decades. Our great-great-great grandfather moved over from Scotland with a few dollars in his pocket and built an empire. He became rich enough to buy the house and have it imported across the Atlantic, stone by stone. The Ushers were on top of the tobacco trade industry for about half a century. However, a drought, and some kind of rare plant disease, plagued the farm and the crops died off."

"Disease? What kind of disease?"

"They weren't certain. But every year, it quashed more and more of the tobacco crops and their yields dwindled. The stories that went around was that the Ushers were cursed, it was God's will, and all that tripe."

"Cursed. With what?"

He shrugged. "Who the hell knows? It was hearsay from dirt farmers and superstitious locals, which is about as reliable as a weather report. Anyway, the remainder of the tobacco profits were invested in real estate in the surrounding area, and as far away as Atlanta—enough to keep them afloat. But nothing like their glory days."

"In those photos," I said, "you could start to see the gradual decline of Usher House. It seemed to be more than some vague plant disease."

"Little by little, they had to sell off those real estate assets, too. They also made some bad investments from Ponzi scheme-types that stole a lion's share of the Usher fortune. It was a perfect storm of financial despair."

"It's too bad that there's not some buried treasure hidden in the walls, right?"

"Yeah, that'd really help with start-up costs," Roderick laughed. "We can dream."

Something didn't sit right with me. "When you say tobacco farmers... Edgar Usher didn't use slaves, right? Tell me he didn't."

Roderick shrugged. "I doubt it. The Emancipation Proclamation and the Civil War happened in the mid-1860s, and the slaves down here in the South were freed after that. This would have happened after that. The house was reconstructed in 1880. I believe it took a total of five years for a team of laborers working nearly around the clock."

"Yeah, but many of the slaves were still forced to work as indentured servants to many of the southern white landholders. I wouldn't feel good if our relatives took advantage of that. In fact, I'd feel downright sick."

"I don't know, sis. I certainly hope not. But what's in the past was in the past. You can't change it now."

Does the past stay in the past? Based on what I was experiencing at Usher House, it didn't seem so.

We drove a little longer in silence. A song was on the radio, "Burn the Witch" by Radiohead. It made me remember the dream I had of Eva Usher. Before she was hanged, she said *"You will not get away with this. I will see to it that every one of you is punished for this outrageousness. For this heresy and this hypocrisy. And that the name of Eva Usher will flourish long after you are all dust in your graves."* The images in my mind were so clear and vivid. Had Eva's untimely death in her twentieth year have something to do with the Usher family's demise?

In the headlights, the mysterious figure loomed again. The one in the black cloak. Only this time, the face was clear. It was as pale and sculpted as a classical statue. It was as if someone had shrouded a black sheet over a Greek goddess sculpture and left only the face revealed. I recognized it for it looked much like mine—Eva Usher. She seemed to mouth some words, but I couldn't tell what they were.

I immediately slammed on the brakes and pulled off the dark country road.

Roderick shook from his daze. "What, did you hit a 'possum?"

"No, I saw something."

"Something?"

"Some*one*. The one I saw earlier. Wearing the cloak. I think it was Eva." That slipped out of my mouth before I realized how insane it must have sounded.

"Eva?"

I backed the car up, looking in my rearview mirror. The cloaked woman stood there on the side of the road. She didn't move. I stopped the car and climbed out. There was no woman, no Eva. Again. Am I losing my mind or did she fly off like a giant raven?

I climbed back into the car.

"Eva as in our long dead great-great-great aunt who was hanged for witchcraft?" Roderick said. "Is that who you're seeing? If it is, then

I'd say the perchance of Usher insanity is well-seeded in your brain, sis."

"Please shut the hell up."

Roderick laughed.

"I know what I saw. Twice. And I've been having dreams about her."

"Why am I not surprised? You're staying in her room. There are two portraits to remind you of her."

"Yeah, Doctor Freud, so explain why I had a dream about her and saw her on the road *before* I came to Usher house. You got any quick, condescending comebacks for that?"

Roderick could obviously sense my anger and frustration. "Hey, I'm not the bad guy here. I was only trying to make things light. This kind of talk makes me extremely uncomfortable."

"How the fuck do you think it makes me feel? Am I seeing a dead woman on the road and in my dreams or am I losing my fucking mind? Let's talk about being extremely uncomfortable, shall we?"

"You're not losing your mind. I still think that she has some kind of influence on your perceptions. Some kind of projection on your unconscious. My best guess anyway."

"Wow, I'm saving so much money on therapy by listening to our resident expert here."

"I'm not trying to explain it away or diminish your point of view or narrative, I'm only suggesting a reasonable, rational explanation."

"Uh, Roderick?"

"Yeah."

"Do me a favor."

"What?"

"Don't offer any more 'reasonable, rational explanations,' OK?"

He sighed. "Fine."

Pulling the Roadster back onto the two-lane strip of road, I drove for another half mile. Then I pulled up the car to the house gate. The high beams cut through the iron spokes and casted long pointed shadows on the driveway beyond. I had the spare key with me, but I was a little too shaken up to get out and unlock it.

"Are you unlocking the gate?" I asked. "Or am I?" I hoped he'd volunteer as whatever stalked the Usher grounds terrified me. It seemed to come out only at night. And then Eva appearing. I *know* that was Eva.

"I'll do it," Roderick said and sat there for a moment, unmoving.

"Well," I said. "The gate isn't going to open itself."

Roderick opened up the glove box and pulled out a small, black plastic box. He pushed the single button on it. The gate, magically, opened by itself in front of us.

"Use the Force, Mr. Spock, right?" he laughed.

"When did *that* happen?"

"Well, tonight, after we left. I told Knapp to install it. It was a surprise. Honestly, I hoped it would work. He's kind of an odd one. But he's a skilled laborer who saved us a buttload in electrician and installation costs."

I drove through the gate. Once on the other side, Roderick pressed the button and the gate closed behind us. "Just like all the rich people have for their McMansions, right? Just like uptown, as they say."

If Usher House was a McMansion, then it was the McMansion from hell.

"Yeah, it's gonna be hard keeping up with the Ushers if you keep buying us all of this fancy stuff. Hopefully we won't go broke doing it."

"'Keeping Up with the Ushers' would make a killer reality show," Roderick said. "We should totally do it. I know a couple of documentary filmmakers in the Boston area I could hire."

"Uh, no thank you," I said. "The Osbornes and the Kardashians were enough. I'm not exactly star material."

"Well, you wanted to find buried treasure in the house. A successful reality show following us around day-to-day would be like printing our own money."

"Going to have to pass on that pitch, Roddy. I'm serious. Count me out."

He laughed. "I was only half serious. I just wanted to see the look on your face."

"Oh my god, have you been taking notes from Carly?"

"No," Roderick said. "But you could always invite her back down. I liked her."

"Love to—but she's kind of slammed with her new position at work."

We drove up to the house. Thankfully, nothing lunged across the lane in front of us. The last thing I wanted to do was to veer my new car into the neighboring swamp trying to avoid hitting it. Whatever *it* was. Knapp came out of the house. Apparently he had been waiting for us.

"Hand him your keys," Roderick said as we climbed out of the car.

"Huh?"

"Your keys. Meet the new valet."

"Where's he taking the car?"

"To the old carriage house around back. I had him clean it out this afternoon. It's the new garage. That outbuilding is big enough to fit a fleet of cars."

I handed the car keys to Knapp. He nodded and climbed into the car, and then quietly drove off. Roderick opened the door for me. Inside, the place was well-lit and seemed less gloomy than before. I told Roderick.

"I'm getting the place slowly up and running. Made a lot of progress while you were gone today. Some electricians will be in tomorrow to rewire the house's electricity. It's necessary for the high-speed satellite WiFi. Then we'll be in business. It's just the start of getting Usher House online. Hell, we could even start Usher House Bed and Breakfast."

"Uh, no thanks," I said. "That's not quite as bad as the reality show idea, but still bad."

"Kidding," Roderick said. "I like having all of this space just for us."

We walked up the stairs. Roderick noted the paintings. "You'll be proud of us, family, you'll see. Maddy and I will make the Usher name mean something again. Something good."

"You do realize that you're talking to inanimate objects, right?"

Roderick smiled. "They listen."

A chill ran through me. "Shut up."

He cackled with his best Vincent Price *Thriller* laugh. "Just messing with you."

When I finally retired to my room, I was too tired to text Carly back in any great detail. I told her I'd call her in the morning before she went to work. I'd been gone most of the day and so many changes happened in my absence. In front of the fire, which thankfully Mrs. Dietrich had been keeping stoked for me, I warmed myself up, then shed my clothes and climbed into my nightgown. I was absolutely beat.

A scratching at the glass doors coaxed me over. The familiar dark shape of Esmerelda waited for me. Her eyes glowed from the light inside my room, making her look a little bit like a demon. I opened the doors. She meowed at me. And that's when I noticed the dead rat.

"Hey, how did you get out, Ezzy?"

The cat stood there, purring, showing her present to me.

"You can come in but that thing is staying outside. I'll have to bury it in the morning."

I picked up the cat and started to close the door. "What kind of trouble did you get into today, Little Miss? Did Mrs. Dietrich let you out?"

The rat sprang back to life. I guess it wasn't dead after all, it was only playing so. It scurried into my room like a furry black rocket.

Esmerelda vaulted from my arms, scratching my skin with her hind claws, and took out after the rodent. I left the doors open, hoping that she would chase it back outside. I stood back. The last thing I wanted to do was for the rat to run up my leg and under my nightgown. The thought made me shudder with revulsion and panic.

Ezzy chased her quarry under the bed. The rat shrieked and ran for the wardrobe. Ezzy was quick on its tail. She stood there a minute. Then her prey scurried out from under the wardrobe, and over to the fireplace, ducking into the stack of wood on the bricks.

The black cat sprang onto the woodpile, her eyes wide and her tail twitching. She waited for the rodent to show itself. It didn't.

"I am *not* going to bed with a rat in my room."

I had an idea. Maybe if I stood on one side of the kindling pile and then made some noise, the rat might run the opposite direction toward the open doors. It was about the only thing I could do. I was dead tired but there was no way I could sleep knowing a rat was prowling around in my room. What if it decided to climb into bed with me? I didn't exactly want to see Ezzy kill it, but I didn't want it running around in my personal space either. I grabbed a piece of kindling from the stack and tapped the woodpile. Ezzy seemed to be enjoying this. She waited patiently for the rat to scurry.

But the rat never scurried.

Ugh, that meant that I'd actually have to move the wood stack to get it out. I grabbed Ezzy and set her down beside the woodpile, and then started unstacking the wood. Hopefully this would encourage the frightened rodent to seek shelter elsewhere—outside. But as I got to the bottom of the stack, I found no rat. It had vanished. Or maybe it had run somewhere else and I hadn't seen. But I watched the stack closely. And so did the predatory feline. She would have seen it. The cat's quarry had simply vanished.

Then I noticed that the grout between the bricks was cracked. And in one place, there was a small hole. Could the rat, which was much bigger than the hole, actually have squeezed itself down in there? Well, if it had, I would just stick an end of this wood in there to cork the bottle. The rat would just have to go between the floors to another part of the house. I had no doubt that Usher House was infested by rodents. How many houses had private mortuaries in their cellars? Sure, the coffins were all sealed up tight, but I was sure the darkness and dampness offered the kind of atmosphere that attracted rats. I mean, with a swamp and a private cemetery, how could you go wrong with your own private rodent colony, right?

"Well, we really did it now, Ezzy. Your rat friend has pulled a Houdini and escaped."

Ezzy meowed at me.

I grabbed a piece of kindling that was fairly narrow at one end and stuffed it into the hole. A determined rat could gnaw through the wood and scramble back up. But I doubted that it would. I was certain that the scared rat wouldn't return. As I stuck the wood into the grout, it crumbled, creating a larger hole. Shit. The grout was so fragile, like sand, it all started to crumble away. Oh great. Just what I need. Mrs. Dietrich to yell at me for defacing the house, she was already stone-cold livid about the cat. *I'll set the wood back on there and nobody will be the wiser.*

But when I started stacking the wood on the loose brick, the weight of the kindling made the brick fall into the hole. Great, now I'd not only done damage to the house, but the rat now had a huge entry way to return. Maybe he'd call back all of his rodent buddies too. Wouldn't that be a hoot? Now I'd never fall sleep thinking about it.

I moved the wood aside and pulled out the brick. There was a space down under the brick. It was about eight inches wide and the same in depth. No, the bottom wasn't the bottom. It was metal. I could see a handle. I grabbed my phone, then snapped on the flashlight. No rat, but there was a box. A large crack loomed in the side of the chamber. Evidentially, the rat must have slipped through there. I grabbed the handle of the box. It had rat turds on it. Not from our friend. These looked old and gray. I pulled the metal box out of the hole. It had the initials EU on them. The box had a thick layer of dust on it. Partially from time and partly from the fragile grout that crumbled onto it. The box had three locks on it. Damn. Wait a minute. That key.

I reached into my robe, feeling a cool, metallic shape, and pulled out the key. I tried one of the locks. Nope, it didn't fit. I tried the second lock. No such luck. Third time a charm? Yes, the lock opened. OK, well, that's cool. I had one third of the box open. *I wonder what's inside?* I wanted to find out, but I was too exhausted. Maybe I could try to pick the other two locks later with a hairpin or something. Not that I knew how to do that. Or, you know, smash them with a hammer. I'd deal with it tomorrow. I replaced the brick in the hole and covered it up with wood. Then I stuck the metal box into the bottom drawer of the vanity. Time for sleep.

I grabbed the cat, turned off the lights, and climbed into bed.

And then had a restless sleep.

TWENTY

1

$\mathcal{A}$ few days passed.

One morning, I awoke early. The sun had not risen yet. It was too early to be up, but I couldn't sleep. Thankfully, I didn't have that dream again, but I still couldn't stay asleep.

My phone indicated that it was five AM. Being two in the morning Pacific time, it was too early to call Carly. So I looked at the box in the bottom of the vanity. Again, I tried the key again for the other two locks.

The box still wouldn't open.

In the drawer, I found an old hairpin and fiddled with the other two locks, jiggling it with the piece of slender metal. Ironically, I believed the hairpin had belonged to Eva—and now I was trying to liberate the contents of her secret little metal box with her personal item. It didn't work. I returned the box back into the drawer.

The more I couldn't open it, the more I wanted to know what the contents were inside. Wanted to know. *Needed* to know.

Ezzy stayed on the bed as I slipped on my robe and headed downstairs. Since I found the key in the library, maybe I could find the other two keys. Of course, the cat had helped me find the key and the box. Maybe that was, uh, key, to locating it. Or perhaps just a coincidence.

2

As I headed down the hall with intention of visiting the library again, I noticed that Mrs. Dietrich carried a silver tray with a dinner plate. It had what looked like a slab of rare-done steak and a baked potato. After she reached the landing on the second floor, she carried it down the hall and to the door that led up into the tower.

Hiding in the corridor shadows, I listened as she ascended the stairs. She didn't make a sound but the wooden stairs creaked under her weight. Then the clack of something metallic sliding back and then snapping shut. It sounded like a lock.

A few moments later, Mrs. Dietrich came down the stairs and out the door. She turned, using her key, and locked it. I noticed that the plate was now empty. The meat and the potato that had occupied it earlier were gone. What was she feeding up there? Raccoons like Mr. Walsh had said? Steak and baked potatoes, really?

After the housekeeper strolled past me in the shadows and back down the stairs, I went to the door. As I figured, it was locked. I didn't have a key for it. And I doubted that I could pick it with a hairpin.

But something *did* live up in the attic tower.

Did Mr. Walsh lie about the raccoons? Was something else living up there? Surely it couldn't be a person, could it? I mean, how cruel it would have been to have someone locked up in the tower. The night I had arrived, though, I could've sworn I'd seen someone up there. And running around the grounds. Who or what was that, and were they connected? So many strange things existed at Usher House. I would find out. If Mrs. Dietrich didn't answer my questions, then I would order her to give me the keys and I'd look myself.

I sauntered down the stairs and headed for the library.

"Up early, ma'am?"

Mrs. Dietrich appeared from the shadows. Had she seen me

upstairs and pretended that she didn't? I would play dumb, which seemed to be my default setting when dealing with her.

"Yeah, I couldn't sleep."

"I still have some sleeping pills that your father had. He was a restless sleeper as well. They were the only thing that could keep him in bed. Might I give you some?"

"No, it's fine—I'll manage. In the meantime, I thought I'd check out the library a little bit more."

"Anything of particular interest that I can help you find?"

Sure, of course. Who or what did you feed upstairs in the tower not more than five minutes ago?

"Uh, actually, I am curious to know more about my great-greatgreat aunt, Eva Usher."

"Oh, really?"

"Yeah, well, being in her room, and seeing her portrait every day and every night, I was a little curious to know about her. Do you know anything about her?"

Mrs. Dietrich simply stood there a moment, tight lipped. "I'm afraid she was before my time. Anything I could offer might only be the result of rumors and hearsay."

"Well, at this point, I'm curious to know anything that you might know."

Mrs. Dietrich said nothing for several moments. "It's my understanding she was murdered before her twenty-first birthday."

Though I already knew this, based on what I'd seen in my dreams, I played dumb. There were advantages to playing ignorant to extract relevant information out of someone. I'd learned it as a foster kid.

"Murdered? Really? How?"

"Hanged, miss." Mrs. Dietrich crossed herself, which, I guessed, meant she was Catholic.

"What, like a lynch mob?"

"Yes, apparently some people from town had accused her of witchcraft and consorting with the devil. They made an example of her at the old hanging tree."

"But this would have happened, like, in the twentieth century, right? People didn't witch hunt anymore, and certainly not in the South."

"Apparently these self-appointed vigilantes from Barlow did."

"Well, what happened? Were these murderers charged with a crime?"

"It's my understanding that they were not," the housekeeper said. "In fact, Corbin Usher, her older brother, was so distraught after her death and the injustice that followed, he committed suicide in his room by hanging himself with his bedsheets. His wife Annabel found him."

Thank goodness I didn't sleep in Corbin's room. I wondered which room that was on the second floor.

"Now they're both buried down in the crypt?"

"That is correct, miss. I believe Mr. Walsh showed you that portion of the house."

I nodded. Then I pulled out the tiny key from my robe pocket. "You wouldn't happen to know where some keys that look like this might be, would you?"

"No."

"I see." I dropped the key back in my pocket. "Well, I have some looking around to do."

"I will leave you to it," Mrs. Dietrich said. "But be careful. Many things in this house were not meant to be disturbed."

"Disturbed? What things? What do you mean?"

But Mrs. Dietrich either didn't hear me or pretended not to and sauntered off down the hallway. I wanted to confront her about what I saw upstairs, but right now I just didn't have the emotional band-width to deal with that. I would bring it up at a later time when I felt less exhausted and a little stronger mentally.

As I entered the library though, I found that I wasn't alone. Under a stained-glass lamp, Roderick had his nose in a book and his MacBook Pro open. Next to him was a steaming cup of tea. He looked up.

"Up with the sun, I see."

"Well, not really. I couldn't sleep. I thought I'd check things out."

"Yes, the same for me. I thought I would come down here and take a look at some of these books. I've been pricing a few with book collectors online. Many of these are first editions that could bring a fortune."

"But do we want to do that?"

"We own the house and everything in it. I'd say we can do pretty much what we want."

"Yeah, I mean, I guess, if we needed money. But there's what the will said, about keeping everything whole."

"That was more of a guideline. We're the final Ushers, after all."

Yeah, I guess you do have a point, brother.

"I was reading this story and I came across the greatest idea."

"Yeah?"

"A masque. A Halloween Masque."

"A masque?"

"Yes, that's short for masquerade. You know, a costume party. What better time to celebrate our arrival than having a Halloween party right here? We could have it in the ballroom. Music. Food. And then, at midnight, an unmasking. What do you think?"

"Well, yeah, I suppose that could be pretty cool. But who would we invite?"

"Everyone," Roderick said. "I'd bring people—investors mostly. Give me a couple of weeks and I could put some mind-blowing business pitches together. We could wine and dine them, and bam, make money. Then we'd rebuild the house, and make the Usher family fortune again."

"It sounds…interesting."

Roderick pursed his lips. "You don't like it."

"No, I do, I do, I just don't know. With this house there are so many strange things."

"What do you mean, strange things?"

"Well, for example, I witnessed Mrs. Dietrich take some food upstairs to the tower."

"She's probably giving dinner scraps away to the raccoons."

"Are you serious? Steak and potatoes? Why would she do that? That makes no sense."

"I don't know. She's an odd one anyway."

"But what if there's someone living up there? What if they're keeping a prisoner?"

"Who, like the Count of Monte Cristo or Al Capone?"

"I'm serious."

"What do you think of my idea?"

He was deflecting, changing the subject. Did he not want to talk about it? Did he know something I don't? Or did he just want to play ignorant and not deal with it? Fine, I'd roll with it for now.

"I think it's great. But where is the money coming for something like that?"

"I told you I have some funds."

"Yeah, but if you blow all your funds on some end-of-the-month shindig, what are we going to do for money for the rest of the year?"

"You've gotta spend money to make money, right? And we'll have investors eating out of our palms when they see what I'm pitching them. Don't worry about it."

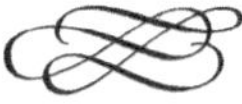

1

I found the second key.

It was while I had Esmerelda with me, and I was taking a break from collating some information for the Usher Enterprises business pitch. I looked at some possible costumes online for the upcoming Halloween Masque. I was thinking of going with a traditional harlequin costume. They were colorful and often had a mask that would cover most of my facial features.

My office was set up in the library. Roderick had bought me a MacBook Air, and we now had some killer fast WiFi in the house. In fact, he'd spent a chunk of change having electricians come in a rewire the entire house, updating it for the twenty-first century. We had a satellite dish installed on the house (but in back so that it didn't interfere with the historical ambiance of the house) and bought a flat screen for the rec room. This mansion of gloom was now homier. Our guests would feel more welcome too. Usher House carried a musty smell, and that couldn't be avoided. I suspected that smell emanated from the timbers and within the walls itself. It was a house that was nearly 150 years old after all. Time and expense might not ever get rid of the smell. I'd grown accustomed to it, but visitors might find it off-putting.

We had to impress our investors. If we could convince them to come aboard Usher Enterprises, buying shares of stocks in the company, we could make some real money. The idea of not punching a time clock every morning at Williamson's Market and instead setting my own working hours at home excited me. The money that could be made from this possible new venture was even more exciting. Sure, it'd be long hours and hard work initially, but it would pay off in the end. I had called my boss and told him I quit due to "family issues." He wasn't happy with me, but he understood.

Also, it was worth noting that Carly had also agreed to come to the Masque. Using the money from the Usher account, I sent her the funds for a round-trip airline ticket, and enough money to rent a car from the Atlanta airport and back. Being able to get her away from her busy job felt good. I almost started to feel like the Lady of the Manor.

Roderick was Lord, though, and he never let anyone forget it.

He was good for the most part, very enthusiastic, but he would fall into his murky moods occasionally where he was incorrigible. Those were times that I avoided him, and the staff did too. As terrifying as Mrs. Dietrich could be, she seemed to avoid my brother when he was "off his meds," as I liked to say. He wasn't on any kind of medication (maybe he should have been) but he would descend into these moods of relentless despair. There wasn't much anyone could do. Sometimes they would last a day or two. But then, when he snapped back, his energy was on high and he was manically happy. That was when he'd often go on spending sprees and buy me things like clothes and shoes. It was almost like he was making up for being so dour. I didn't like to accept anything from him, he'd already done so much already, but if I refused, he seemed to take it personal, so I never refused. It was best to give Roddy his way, as well as stay out of it. He was a force to be reckoned with, that was for sure. What he needed was a girlfriend to distract him from himself. He seemed to enjoy Carly, but I had serious reservations about that.

How weird would it be for my best friend to be dating my twin brother?

What was weird was Carly had this thing for Tom Hiddleston who played Loki in all of the Thor movies. Roderick looked so much like him. He often acted like Loki with his megalomaniac dreaming and maniacal scheming. So that was weird. I didn't know, we'd have to see how the Masque would go. But maybe Carly with her devil-may-care personality would keep Roderick happy and distracted. If I could have my way, I'd have Carly move in here with us. The house was certainly big enough. She had serious management skills, too, more than I did. Carly could run Usher Enterprises like a dream. Roderick might go for something like that.

Things with Liam and I were going well, though I still kept Roderick away from him. He would often take me to dinner at Le Petite Maison, which had become our place. I would have loved spending more time at his house talking and riding horses, but I hadn't been back there ever since his father had been rude and dismissive of me. It was strange, I had to deal with Roderick's disapproval and Liam had to deal with his father's—two star-crossed lovers from two warring families. We were like some fucked-up Romeo and Juliet. I could do without the final bloody act of that Shakespearian tragedy, though, thanks.

But back to the second key I found.

I was looking online for a costume. Ezzy was batting at the tassels on my slippers. Then she jumped up onto my writing desk. It was a long, wide sturdy oak writing desk. It was quite beautiful. In fact, the entire library was after it was fixed up a little bit. And I always keep a roaring fire for cheeriness, coziness, and to stave off the autumn chill. Ezzy, like any cat, wanted my attention, and started fumbling around the keyboard, trying to get me to pet her. The thing with Ezzy—she hooks her hind legs around your petting hand at the wrist so you can't take it away. She's one of the neediest cats I've ever seen, completely starved for affection. So, I didn't want to fall into her "petting trap" as she tumbled onto her back and waited for my hand to go to her soft, warm belly. It was like my hand was a fly and she was the Venus Fly

Trap just waiting for the unsuspecting insect to go after the sweet nectar and then be snatched up. Though Ezzy was midnight black, she had one spot of creamy white fur on her chest in a crescent-moon shape. She liked me to rub her there especially.

"Not now, Ezzy," I told her. "I'm trying to get stuff done."

The black cat wouldn't have it though. If my hand wasn't coming to her, she was coming to my hand. I moved it while trying to type, and was growing more frustrated.

"Is it time for you to go outside and run around for a bit?"

Ezzy purred, most likely not understanding a word I said.

I stood up and took her to the library window. All the windows had iron bars on them, which I had found a bit odd, but I could still unlatch and open the window enough to let a small black cat out onto the ledge. No doubt she would probably walk around the house, scale up the tree, saunter across the roof, and slink to the French doors of my room and yowl to be let back in. But that would be a nice distraction for her.

As I took her to the window and opened it, the sweet scent of honeysuckle from outside wafted in. I scooped up the dusky feline and set her on the ledge outside of the bars. She rubbed the metal cylinders, weaving in and out of them, no doubt thinking that this was some kind of game.

The sun was on the west side of the house, where the study window was facing, turning to an orange color as it had started to make its descent, but still warm and bright despite it being near the end of October. Something glimmered in between the ledge stones. The ledge was made up of two stone pieces. Within the space of those stones, in the Masonite, something glimmered. It was so faint, I wouldn't have noticed it before. And I certainly wouldn't have if the sun was not precisely where it was in the sky, and I had not stood here in this moment.

Using my fingernail, I tried to unearth the shimmering thing. But, unfortunately, I shoved it deeper into the trench.

I went to the drawer of the writing desk. Within it, I remembered there was a long, silver letter opener that had USHER engraved upon it. It was pure silver, not silver-plated, and was probably worth a small fortune. I grabbed it, feeling its heft in my hand, and took it over to the window.

Ezzy still waited there, rubbing around on the steel bars.

Taking the sharp end, I stuck the point down into the stone trench and dug. I felt like an archeologist who had found some missing artifact and was desperately trying to unearth it. It took several tries, but I managed to bring the thing up. By the time I had, it no longer glimmered in the light as the sun had changed positions.

It was a key. The same size and shape as the others.

I snatched up the cat, closed the window, dropped the letter opener on the desk, and escaped to my room.

2

The silver three-lock box.

I unearthed the box engraved with Eva Usher's initials from the bottom drawer of her vanity. I tried the key on one of the two unopened locks—it didn't work. Damn it. I tried the other lock and the key slid in easily. The lock snapped open with a click.

Two out of three undone.

I wondered what was so precious inside that box that three keys had to open it. Why were two of these keys in the library? Would the third one be as well? The box was hidden in the hearth of the fireplace for a century. It was odd.

Had Eva hidden the box and the keys or had someone else? And why would they do it? For fun? Was it some kind of treasure hunt or something? It didn't make sense.

Of course, little did in Usher House. What I'd learned was that insanity ran rampant in the Usher family, especially into adulthood. It was like a kind of unwritten sentence passed on from generation to generation.

It terrified me. Would I go crazy too?

My mother had given birth to Roderick and I in her twenties and then took us from here. She had given us up for adoption and then seemingly committed suicide. Roderick, with his depression, seemed to already have a touch of the mental illness gene. Did I too? I didn't suffer from depression, but here I was obsessing about a three-lock box's contents and running around looking for keys. Well, thanks to the cat, the keys kind of found me. Ezzy was responsible for finding the keys and the box. Was she helping me to find them? Am I crazy to believe that a cat was doing this willingly? Was that my mental illness gene to believe impossible fantasies like that?

I locked the box and placed it back into the bottom drawer of the vanity. Then I hid one key on the mantle of the fireplace under a Ming dynasty vase and the other under the post of the bed. Don't ask me why, but I felt like something very special was in that box and leaving it open and the keys lying around could mean anyone, like my brother or the housekeeper, could find it.

TWENTY-TWO

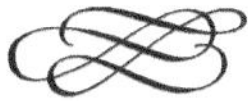

1

The Halloween Masque was supposed to bring us all together, but it turned into a disaster where people died. Had I known what was going to happen, I never would have agreed to it. Because now everything has changed.

During the week leading up to the Masque, Usher House had become busy. We had to get the place cleaned up and organized to accommodate the hordes of people that we were expecting. I was sending out invitations via Roderick's mailing list.

During that time, I saw Liam as much as I could. His duties at the farm kept him busy for the most part, but we did go out on the occasional dates, usually on the weekends. We would go bowling or to a movie, and of course, to our favorite restaurant. During that time, I started to feel like this place was now my home and that Pickman Flats was just a faded, distant memory. The only thing was the Bland house I'd left. However, Roderick said he would take care of it. I didn't like asking him to, but this Halloween Masque was an important event.

2

ALMOST THERE, DARLIN'. MEET ME DOWNSTAIRS. DON'T WANNA DEAL WITH MRS. DANVERS.

Thirty-six hours before the Halloween Masque, Carly texted me. Nice *Rebecca* reference. It made me laugh. Too true.

I texted back: LET ME KNOW WHEN YOU'RE AT THE GATE. DON'T WORRY ABOUT "DANNY."

I rushed downstairs. Fortunately, Roderick was in his room so I could greet her alone. I waited in front of the house.

AT THE GATE was the next Carly text I received.

I now had a phone app to open it.

Moments later, a sporty red Infiniti Q60 zoomed down the lane with Carly behind the wheel. She smiled when she saw me. She pulled up and climbed out. We gave each other a big, long hug.

"Oh my god, love, you look so different," she said. "You look like the Lady of the Manor or some shit."

I was wearing a new, black and white houndstooth day dress Roderick had bought me.

I shrugged. "Well, I try."

"The plane ride and drive here were boring as fuck. Help me with my bags, darlin'. I could use a drink too. How about some breakfast mimosas?"

Knapp showed up. Carly threw him the keys. "Please park it, my good sir."

The man stood there with the keys in his hand without an expression.

"Never mind, Knapp," I said. "I'll get the bags."

Carly and I packed her cumbersome suitcases in. "Are you staying for a month?"

"I couldn't decide what I wanted to wear," she said, "so I brought a little of everything,"

Inside, Mrs. Dietrich greeted us.

"Hello again," Carly said, all smiles. "How's Mr. DeWinter this morning?"

Ugh, Carly, enough with the *Rebecca* references.

"Welcome back," the housekeeper said. She might as well have said "walk off a pier" with all the warmth and sincerity of her greeting. "Who is Mr. DeWinter?"

"Never mind," I said.

"Good to be back," Carly said, ignoring the housekeeper's somber greeting.

"Might I help you with your baggage or I could collect Knapp to do so?"

"We've got it," I said.

"You could have let me know about your friend's arrival earlier, miss?"

I grinned at my housekeeper. "I wasn't sure myself."

Carly smiled at her. "Blame me. I'm as unpredictable as a tornado."

"Yes," Mrs. Dietrich said. "Let me know if I may be of any further assistance."

"Uh, yes, you can," Carly said. "Could you be a love and have some mimosas brought up to my room pronto? I'll start off with three. How about you, hun?"

"I'll just have the one," I said, feeling my face flush the color of the scarlet carpet.

"Mimosa?"

I smiled at Mrs. Dietrich. "It's one-part orange juice to one-part champagne."

"Make mine the one-part orange juice to *two*-parts champagne, darlin'," Carly said. "I've been a little under the weather. Doctor's orders."

"I will do the best I can," Mrs. Dietrich said. She whirled and vanished.

"You know," Carly said when she left. "As pissy as she is with her microaggression bullshit, it sure is nice to have someone wait on you hand and foot."

"Shut up," I said.

I helped Carly up to her room, lugging all of her suitcases up the stairs. I swear she'd packed some free weights in her bags. I should have had Knapp do this. But I wasn't used to telling people what to do. But damn, Carly, these bags. You could have used them for boat anchors.

"You got those bags there, Wonder Woman?"

"Yeah," I said, huffing under the strain. "Thanks."

"You know, I forgot to mention it," Carly said as we finally reached the landing and then headed to her room. "Your house looks breathtaking, hun."

"Oh, thank you."

"No, I mean Peggy's house back home. It's been landscaped and the lawn has been mown, leaves raked up. Did you hire someone?"

I was confused. "No."

"Oh," was all Carly said.

It had to be Roderick. But why would he go through the extra cost of doing something like that? He was only supposed to help me with the mortgage payment for a few months.

I would need to have a word with him about that.

3

After we settled Carly in her room and talked for a few minutes, there was a knock on the door. When I opened it, Mrs. Dietrich had four champagne flutes filled with what looked like orange juice.

"Your drinks."

She carried them on a silver serving tray, then set them down and started to walk out.

"Just a minute," Carly said, raising her hand.

The dour housekeeper stopped.

Carly picked up a champagne flute, sniffed its contents like it was a fine wine, and then sipped. She ended up chugging the entire thing, then burping.

"Excuse me. And I have to say, Mrs. Dietrich, for not knowing what a mimosa was ten minutes ago, you make a helluva great one." Carly grabbed another, then offered one to Mrs. Dietrich. "You should have one, hun."

"I never drink alcohol."

"Oh, you should. It makes life more tolerable, love. Trust me."

Mrs. Dietrich turned to me. "Will there be anything else, miss?"

"No, thank you."

She left without looking back, shutting the door smartly behind her.

"I don't think I've ever met someone who either needed to get laid or eat an edible so bad in her life."

"Shhh," I said, whispering. "She tends to linger. She'll hear you."

Carly polished off her second mimosa, and grabbed her third. She raised it in the air for a proposed toast. I grabbed my mimosa, raised it, and we clinked our glasses together.

"To a couple of good friends and two badass boss bitches."

"I'm no boss."

Carly gestured to the room. "Are you kidding? You own all of this. This is like, I don't know, some kind of aristocratic paradise and shit."

"Well, I *co*-own it. And it's not like I did anything for it. I just happen to be born with a certain last name."

"Yeah, I'm still having trouble calling you Madeline Usher. To me you're just plain ol' Mads. Mads Bland."

"I still am Mads. Nothing has changed."

"Didn't I tell you that you were destined for greater things? You should listen to your friend more often, love."

"Yeah, you were right, of course."

Carly grabbed a lock of my hair. "Speaking of which, when's the last time you had a total make-over? You need to seriously rock a new look for this shindig you're throwing."

"Liam and I have gone to the neighboring towns, but I haven't gone without him. Call me paranoid. People don't like Ushers and they somehow seem to know I am one. When I'm with a local boy, though, I don't get as much shit."

Carly polished off her last mimosa. "To hell with them. I'm available and I'm fixing up your ass, hun."

"But the party isn't until tomorrow night."

She winked. "No time like the present, darlin'."

4

"Still stinks like rotten egg farts."

I sat on the toilet as Carly washed my hair. She waved her hand in front of her nose. "Maybe a demon dropped a deuce in your water supply."

"It's sulphur," I said. "We're going to have a new well dug. Demon, why would you say demon?"

Carly shrugged. "Aren't demons and devils synonymous with sulphur?"

"How the hell would I know? We've already spent a fortune getting this place up to standards of this century."

"Sounds like a money pit," Carly said. "Like that old Tom Hanks movie."

"Well, it's not my money, because I don't have it. Roderick is dumping all of his savings into this house."

"That seems kind of risky."

"Well, if we can get investors to come to the party tonight who'll go for our pitch, then we'll have plenty of money—to restore the place and to live."

"What are you selling?"

"It's all software and web-based stuff," I said. "I won't bore you with the details. It's all Roddy's field, and I'm still learning it. He's piggybacking it off his company, Axis Security Systems. I feel like I've gone through an entire college course trying to bone up on the data."

"Well, it's gotta beat working in a grocery store."

"Yeah, they were kind of pissed when I called and told them I wouldn't be coming in anymore."

"I'm sure they'll get over it."

"Yeah."

"So, you're planning on staying here then? Not coming back to good ol' P.F.?"

"For the time being, I guess. There's not much back there for me. Maybe *you* should think about moving in here. We could hire you. Put you in charge of sales. I'm pretty sure you could sell ice cubes to penguins."

"Hmm, live in a once-lavish but crumbling mansion out in the middle of nowhere?"

"With your best friend. Don't forget that."

"God knows I'd love to get away from my mother. I was all set to move into your house. I mean, her and I would still be in the same town, but at least it's across town. She's becoming such a bitch lately. Always on my ass about this and that. Pretty sure she's just projecting all of her failings onto me in classic parent-offspring fashion."

"You two are so funny together."

"Yeah, I'm laughing my ass off. Hold still."

"Sorry."

Esmerelda poked her head into the bathroom. She looked like a walking ink spot with two green marbles for eyes.

"Well, there you are. Aren't you the perfect cat for Halloween?"

"I call her Esmerelda. Ezzy for short."

"Careful, she's seven years' bad luck."

"That's broken mirrors. Black cats aren't evil or bad luck. That's just some bullshit myths and wives' tales."

The black cat rubbed around my legs. I started to reach down to pet her, but I couldn't move with Carly having the hot iron in my hair.

"Sorry, girl, can't pet you."

The cat looked up at me, and then jumped up into my lap.

"That's one persistent pussy."

I laughed. "She likes attention. I pet her until my hand is raw, and she still can't seem to get enough."

Carly laughed. "I know the feeling."

Ezzy purred in my hands.

"By the way," Carly said. "Parker and Mary were in town and came into the store."

"You don't actually have to tell me."

"Well, I do, since he mentioned you. It's kind of the point of the story. Give me a chance."

"Sorry, go ahead."

"Anyway, he was looking bored as Mary was shopping around so he made small talk with me. You know, the usual plans and schemes about the future. What he's doing in college. What he's doing after college. And during it all, I got the feeling that he really wasn't happy. Not like he was when he was with you."

"Well, that's his problem. He had me and if he was happy with me, he shouldn't have let me go."

"Yeah. I told him all about what you were doing—the house, the inheritance, your handsome twin brother. He was really fascinated. And he said to tell you 'hi' the next time I spoke to you."

"Well," I said, annoyed. "That was nice of him."

"I bet he'd come crawling back to you if he saw what you're becoming—a business mogul who lives in her own goddamn country mansion."

"I don't want him anymore. Besides, I have Liam now."

"Yeah, you haven't told me the juicy details about your backwoods boy. When's he coming over?"

"Soon. He had a bunch of work to do first."

Ezzy jumped out of my lap and onto the sink's counter. Then she leapt up onto the shelf and started rubbing around.

"Your witch's cat is kind of distracting, Mads."

Ezzy knocked a candle and brass holder onto the floor. It made a metallic plunking sound on the honeycomb tile.

"Hold on," I said, rising. "Let me get her out of here. Then I'll shut the door."

I grabbed the sable feline and shooed her out. Then I picked up the brass holder and was about to replace the dusty candle back into it, but something was down inside the hole. A tiny black key.

"Can you hold on a moment, Car?"

"What?"

"I need a moment," I said, turning the candle holder upside down. The key dropped into my palm. Carly was distracted with her phone. "Wait here." I left the bathroom.

"Fine," she said, apparently texting somebody.

5

In my room, I opened up the bottom drawer of the vanity. Placing the third key in the lock, I opened it. Then, I grabbed the other two hidden keys, and I used them to open the other two locks.

Inside the metal box marked EVA USHER were two things: an amulet with a bird on it and a small book with a scarlet hardbound cover. The silver amulet resembled a raven with a tiny pentagram on his body. The eyes were inset with two purple amethyst stones. In the painted portrait, I realized that it was the same raven amulet with amethyst eyes that she was wearing. The book said A COMPENDIUM OF SPELLS, CHARMS, AND HEXES FROM THE SPIRIT REALM BY EVA USHER. Inside were pages and pages of handwritten notes and drawings in the most ornate, beautiful handwriting I'd ever seen. Spells for love. Hexes for cursing your enemies. One spell was to release your bonds, which apparently was if somebody tied you up or something. To do that, you were supposed to touch the silver amulet, clear your heart and mind of any negative or distracting energy, and repeat *vincula mea dimittere* in Latin three times.

"*Vincula mea dimittere*," I said in the mirror. My Latin didn't sound too good.

Wow, this amulet and compendium of spells book must've gotten her killed. She must've hidden these before she'd died. Maybe she'd hidden it to proclaim her innocence and deny her guilt? It seemed weird now that somebody could be killed for something like this, but one hundred years ago… people were different. The amulet would go perfect with my costume, so I unclasped the chain and put it on. As I did, I gazed at my reflection in the mirror. Eva's portrait stood in the background. With this amulet on, and with our similar dark hair and emerald eyes, we could have passed for sisters.

6

Returning to the bathroom, I showed Carly. I didn't tell her about the box or the spell book yet, or the keys. I asked her what she thought of the amulet. She thought it was creepy cool.

When I tried to take it off, to show it to her better, that was when I realized that I couldn't.

"What are you doing?"

"I can't get this thing off."

"What?"

"Help me."

Carly tried, but the amulet wouldn't move. It was like it had always been a part of me.

"How is this even possible?"

It's then that I told her everything I knew about Eva Usher—my dreams, what I'd found, and how she had been murdered.

"That's some kind of fucked-up witchcraft," Carly said later.

"You think it's witchcraft binding this thing to me?"

"Well, it's not Gorilla Glued on there, I can tell you that."

"What do I do?"

"We'll have to figure it out after the party."

What I didn't realize then was now I was more a part of Usher House than ever.

TWENTY-THREE

1

Carly and I carved the jack o' lanterns.

She and I had loved spending the time together. The pumpkins all came from Liam's farm.

We had two bulbous, orange sentries that stood guard at the gate's entrance. Several more were placed along the edges of the lane leading up to the house. Two more greeted guests at the front door. A total of thirteen jack o' lanterns in all—each featuring a horribly carved visage and a burning candle in them.

As one came in from off the main road and down the winding lane, they were each greeted with a burning, smiling face with a demonic countenance. Carly and I had tried to make some happy-looking jack o' lanterns as well, but they all had taken on a sinister look. When placed around the already-somber Usher House, which looked like it had come out of a horror movie anyway, the effect was all the more disturbing. Well, it was Halloween after all, so it was our time to be scary.

Roderick and I had professional party caterers come in. They set up all of the lights and decorations in the ballroom, which was where the crux of the Halloween Masque would be held. Guests were to arrive at 8pm. We had a full bar and all kinds of food. They were to mingle and dance until midnight. After that, we would have the unmasking.

Mr. Walsh would also make an appearance to celebrate and to help with any investor contracts and financial details since he was the Usher attorney. I had no idea what kind of costume that he would appear in, but I told him that no one would gain entrance without one. That was an absolute point. I didn't care if he was our attorney or not.

Rules were rules when it came to a Halloween Masque.

2

Mr. Walsh pulled up in his expensive car, arriving before the party guests. He greeted Mrs. Dietrich. I had noticed that our housekeeper took him into the parlor and I heard whispers. No doubt she was updating him on what had been going on. I decided to crash their private party, so I strolled in acting like I didn't know they were there.

Mrs. Dietrich saw the raven amulet and gave me a perplexed look. I was sure she had recognized it from Eva's painting. If I could have snapped a picture of Mrs. Dietrich's sour face right then, it would have been the expression to launch a thousand memes on social media. Classic. I feigned ignorance.

"Oh, hello," I said to Mr. Walsh. "How was your trip in?"

I wasn't one for small talk, but my interruption was like driving nails into Mrs. Dietrich. So I thought I would up the ante a little bit. "Could you get Mr. Walsh something to drink, Mrs. Dietrich? I'm sure he's thirsty."

She gave me a frozen-faced look, nodded, and walked off. I wanted to laugh.

"Enough with this 'Mr. Walsh' business," he said. "Ernest, please. We're practically family." He laughed. "The drive was uneventful. Until I came to the gates. All the decorations and lights, I love what you've done with the place. I haven't seen it look this festive since my youth. And I won't tell you how many years ago *that* was."

"We have a couple of investors arriving," I said. "Roderick and I wanted to impress them."

"Once an Usher, always an Usher," Walsh laughed. "Your predecessors were the same way—always putting on the Ritz. Well, I'm sure they'll be impressed. In my short time knowing Roderick, he's a shrewd businessman and very thorough. Despite his youth, he has an old soul about him. He reminds me so much of your father."

"You'll have to tell me more about my father. And by the way, I was wondering more about what's living up in the tower. I saw Mrs. Dietrich taking some food scraps up there."

"I was feeding the leftover supper scraps to the raccoons, naturally," Mrs. Dietrich said, re-entering the room as quietly as a spirit. "A family of them lives up there." She handed Mr. Walsh a glass of red wine.

"Well," I said. "That's kind and all, but I don't think we should encourage them. Don't you?"

Mr. Walsh regarded Mrs. Dietrich. She turned to me. "Yes, you're quite right. It's been such a habit that I'm afraid it's simply second nature. I'll quit feeding them and I'm sure they'll move on."

"I would very much like to see that room," I said. "Maybe if you gave me a key."

"Unfortunately," the housekeeper said, "I don't know where the key is."

"Oh," I said. "Then I guess we'll have to bring a locksmith in and have the lock replaced and a new one made." She was lying. I watched her face as I said that. Her expression, of course, didn't change. It rarely did. She'd be an expert poker player.

"That's a lovely amulet you're wearing," Walsh said, apparently changing the subject. "It looks familiar."

"Doesn't it?" I said. "I'm sure you've seen it before."

"I guess I may have," he said. "But I can't place it at the moment. Forgive me, it was a long drive."

"It belonged to Eva Usher."

With that I could feel Mrs. Dietrich's eyes on me. She seemed to watch my every move.

"I, uh, found it in my room."

"You should be careful wearing her things," Mrs. Dietrich said, her voice had a threatening air to it.

"Why?" I asked.

The doorbell rang.

Mrs. Dietrich practically ran to get away from me, which told me that she didn't want to talk about my great-great-great aunt apparently. A moment later, Mrs. Dietrich returned with someone in patched and ragged clothes and a burlap bag over his head. His head was stitched together in the most horrifying grimace. The scarecrow nodded to me.

Liam removed his burlap mask. "Whew, this thing is scratchy. I don't know how I'm going to wear it all night."

He said that he had found a costume and had laughed about it. I had no idea what to expect. Thankfully it wasn't something too ridiculous or embarrassing.

"Scarecrow," I said. "That's a brilliant costume, Country Mouse."

He shrugged. "Hey, I thought it was pretty damned clever, City Mouse. When I was a kid I saw *The Wizard of Oz* about thirty-seven times and the Scarecrow was always my favorite character."

"Because he didn't have a brain?"

"Because he was smarter than he was given credit for—and let's face it, he was Dorothy's favorite."

I gave him a kiss on the cheek. "I know how Dorothy feels."

"Well, we're definitely not in Kansas anymore, Toto," Mr. Walsh chuckled, attempting a joke.

"Uh, Liam, this is Mr. Walsh. He kind of runs things, legally speaking, here at Usher House."

"Liam Delaney." He outstretched his ragged arm and his gloved hand.

The name Delaney made Walsh wince. "Ernest Walsh. Call me Ernest."

"Pleasure to meet you, Ernest."

"So, you're from Delaney Farms down the road?"

"You know us?"

"Of course. I met your father, William, years ago. He's, uh, a very pragmatic man."

Liam laughed. "That's one way to describe Pops. Hardheaded might be another."

"Well," Mr. Walsh said. "I'm sure you two have much to catch up on. I'm going up to my room to rest before the gathering."

"You did bring a costume, didn't you?"

"Oh, yes. You won't even recognize me."

Liam looked around at the décor of the dining room. "Wow, I feel like I stepped into a time machine and slipped back about one hundred years. Where's your friend, Carly?"

"She's up in her room getting ready. Would you like a tour while we wait for her and for my brother to show up?

"Sure."

3

I showed Liam several of the cheerier rooms in the place like the library and ballroom, as I didn't want to scare him off. Then we absconded to my room.

"Wow," he said. "So old world. It feels like I stepped onto the set of *Downton Abbey*."

"It used to belong to my great-great-great aunt, Eva. That's her picture up there. I might have it taken down though, it kind of freaks me out."

"Yeah, it's weird how the eyes follow you no matter where you go."

I pointed to the silver raven amulet on my collarbone. "See, it's the same amulet in the picture." What I didn't tell him was that I couldn't remove it. In fact, it stayed in one place like it was attached to my skin. It didn't hurt, but I was aware of it every moment.

"Wow," Liam said. "It's kind of cool and, uh, kind of creepy."

"Yeah," I said. "And I think these purple stones are amethysts."

Liam leaned in closer. "Amethysts?" He reached for the amulet, then stopped like it might burn him.

"Yeah, amethysts are supposed to aid the mind to flow more freely between our realm and other realms. At least, according to Google."

Liam cocked an eyebrow. "Other *realms*? Well, they sure are beautiful stones. You should take it to a jeweler. If it's an antique, it could be worth a small fortune."

"Maybe I will someday."

I took Liam through the French doors and out onto the veranda. The evening was cool and blue. The jack o' lanterns along the drive looked like fiery orange flowers from up here as they trailed down the lane.

"Quite a view," he said. "I could get used to this."

I gazed at him—he was quite a view. I loved how he could be so classically handsome with his razor-sharp jawline, high cheekbones, and icy blue eyes, and at the same time, take on a boyish quality when he would lose himself marveling at something like the night. It was what made him so endearing.

"You're just a little too cute, scarecrow," I said.

He turned to me and smiled. I kissed him on the lips. A long and hard kiss. We were safe as nobody was outside. I didn't know why I felt like I needed to keep this a secret. Actually, scratch that, Roderick would hate seeing us like this. I didn't need his overprotection now. Luckily he was with his friends and most likely the investors. But my jealous brother would return at any time.

Something leapt at us. Liam jumped. "Holy shit."

The black cat peered up at *us*.

"This is Esmerelda. Ezzy for short." I picked her up. "Doesn't she have the most alluring green eyes?"

"Where did you get her from?"

"She showed up the day I got here. I guess she's a stray since nobody in the house claims her, but she sure seems to know her way around. She's been my good luck charm."

Liam stroked her sable fur. Ezzy purred. "Feels like pure velvet."

"I know. She's so soft, right?"

"Man, I'm so tired," he sighed. "I hope I can make it until midnight."

"You sound like an old man."

"After helping Herb and Pops all day in the shop with that damn combine, I feel like I'm eighty-four. They had me heave-hoing all of the heavy equipment."

I gripped his right upper arm with both hands. It was rock hard. "Who needs a gym when you have a machine shop?"

He laughed. "Yeah, right."

White-hot headlights knifed through the foliage of the trees. The Bentley crawled up the lane toward the house. Roderick was back— the prodigal son had returned. I grabbed Liam's arm and pulled him in. "Back inside, quick."

"Why?"

Once we were in my room, I shut the French doors and pulled the curtains. No peering eyes would be on us tonight. Ezzy weaved through Liam's legs.

"Why don't you climb out of your costume, scarecrow, and get more comfortable?"

"Uh, I don't have anything on *under* my costume. Wearing double layers was kind of warm."

"Oh," I said, smiling. "That's definitely a problem…for you. Let me go down and meet everyone. Then I'll be right back."

"Do you mind if I lie down on your bed?"

"Yeah, as long as you won't conk out on me. I want to do some dancing. Promise?"

He crossed his chest with a gloved finger. "Cross my straw heart."

As I started to head out the door, Carly stood in the doorway with her hand raised, apparently about to knock.

"I heard voices," Carly said.

"You should try therapy," I said.

"A *male* voice," Carly said, looking past me. She smiled at Liam sitting on the bed. "Hello again, hun."

"Oh, hey," he said, rising and extending his hand. "Nice to see you again. And, uh, under better circumstances."

"Why don't you two chat and I'll go down and talk to my brother," I said.

Carly smiled. "Fine by me, darlin'."

I turned to Liam. "Everything that comes out of this girl's mouth about me is probably a fabrication or an all-out lie. Be wary."

Liam nodded at me and blew a kiss.

4

Downstairs, I met our visitors. First, Darius Wolfe. He was a good-looking guy with long black hair and a three-day beard and piercing dark eyes from Miami. He was about fifteen years older than Roddy. Next, the investors were Michael Valdemar from Boston and Gordon Pym from Charlottesville. They were middle-aged men who seemed accustomed to the finer things due to their dress and manner.

Darius wore a gray sport jacket over a tight-black tee shirt. "A pleasure to meet you," he said, extending a strong, tanned hand. "Roddy has told me so much about you."

"How do you know my brother?"

"We both grew up in Boston. Mentored him in business and gave him a place to stay when he was at odds with his father."

"Adopted father," Roderick said. "And watch out for Darius, he's slick with the ladies."

"I'll try to remember that."

I said hello to the investors and we made small talk about the drive and the weather.

Finally, Roderick brought a DJ for the party. He was a good friend of Roderick's who had flown down from Boston the night before. He looked around twenty-five.

"The name's Ben," he said. "Ben Craven. DJ Raven on the stage."

"Ben Craven A.K.A. DJ Raven?" I said and laughed. "That's really interesting."

Ben was a charming and sweet-natured guy who wore a camel-haired overcoat, purple scarf, and a lime green tee shirt with Tiësto on it. I could see why my brother had liked him. His good nature seemed to bring out the best in Roderick, as I hadn't seen him smiling in days.

After I made nice with everyone, I went back upstairs to check on Liam. He was laying on my bed, sound asleep. Guess he'd had a long day on the farm? Ezzy laid on his chest. They looked so cute together that I didn't want to wake him.

I read Eva Usher's compendium of spells—she had love charms, hexes, and even one for necromancy. Apparently, she had been practicing witchcraft since she was around nine years old. She had compiled ten years of research and practice. I learned many things in this book that would save lives later.

TWENTY-FOUR

1

The Halloween Masque.

About one hundred people showed up, many of them were undoubtedly curious about the venue. This was the first time I knew of that Usher House was open to the general public. Yes, it was a reserved party, but it was well-attended. A few recognizable faces from Wilsonville and Folkston had arrived. Nobody from Barlow had showed up, which wasn't surprising as the locals seemed to hate the Ushers. Most of the costumes the guests wore had either been thrown together or quickly purchased from a department store like sexy nurse or sexy witch, but a few people had cosplay-level costumes. One woman was a comic book character I didn't know, but she had a purple costume with a mask and a crossbow; others were dressed like Spider-Man, Batman, or Captain America.

DJ Raven raged on the dais that we had constructed in the recently-renovated ballroom. He had a video projector and was showing scenes from old horror movies on the wall while he was spinning his infectious dance jams. I recognized Vincent Price, Bela

Lugosi, Boris Karloff, Vampira, and a few other cinematic ghouls in those flickering images.

The investors stood in the corner nursing their cocktails. They simply wore domino masks with their suits that Roderick had obviously provided. Mr. Walsh wore a ridiculous and obvious costume of a suit that had papers attached to it. It was his "law suit." He also wore a mask but it was pretty obvious who he was. He had told me earlier that nobody would recognize him in his costume, he was either joking or completely clueless.

Mrs. Dietrich and Knapp attended to the food bar, but they were dressed in their usual garb as Usher House employees. It was pretty impressive with a salmon and cheese bar, not to mention all kinds of finger foods like buffalo wings, ham and cheese sliders, steak kabobs, chicken wraps, Swedish meatballs, grilled veggie pizzas, and clusters of cookies, cakes, and pastries.

Most people were going to the open bar though. Darius Wolfe, wearing an orangutan costume, was pouring the beer and wine. He owned a bar in Miami and had jumped in to help when our bartender had canceled at the last second. He was grooving around to the music as he served the guests, looking like the happiest faux primate on the planet.

This old house had probably never had so much life in it before.

Carly had dressed in an old Bloody Mary outfit, which was based on Anne Boleyn's wardrobe. It had blood around the collar where she had been decapitated. She wore a domino mask that glittered. She was the perfect hybrid of the glamourous and the macabre. I wore a cute, nineteenth-century-like silver harlequin outfit, which was a silver and black jumpsuit with a full-sized mask with a leering face. Liam, of course was my scarecrow date. DJ Raven kept the place jumping. My handsome date didn't have his dance moves down, so I showed him a few things. Carly was having the time of her life, like she always does, dancing with Liam and me. We danced, drank wine, laughed, and danced some more.

Roderick's costume was astonishing. He had done something to make himself at least a foot taller and garbed in red with a skeleton mask. He called himself "The Red Death" and he wielded a shiny golden scepter. He glided around the room telling guests that he was giving them the "Red Death," and then would speak some indecipherable Latin phrases. He really got into his part—maybe a little too much so and it was scary. But I could tell he was enjoying himself. I don't think many people would have known who he was. Roddy has a distinct gait to his walk, so that gave it away for me.

2

When it was seconds to midnight, the time came to unmask. DJ Raven projected a clock on the wall and started the countdown music. Everyone counted down. When the bells chimed midnight, we all tore off our masks. And that was when the trouble started. I didn't know if Liam had too many drinks or what, but he grabbed me up and kissed me—hard. At first, I was taken a little aback by it, but then I sank into it, kissing him back. His warm tongue explored my mouth, and mine explored his.

"Do you mind?" Roderick said, a sour look on his face. "We don't really need the PDA, it's kind of embarrassing?"

"PDA?" Liam asked. "Public Display of Awesomeness?" He winked.

"Pretty sure that's not what Rod meant," I said and laughed.

"Sorry, Rod. When it comes to your sister, I guess I get a little carried away."

"Don't be sorry," I said, and this was liquid courage from the wine. "It's *my* house and I can *kiss* whomever the fuck I please, brother. Why don't you go find your *own* date?"

Roderick grew red-faced and looked like he was about to explode. But then he took a step back. "It's not just your house, *sister*. And I don't appreciate you speaking to me that way."

"Seriously, bro, chill the fuck out," I said, meeting him face to face. "I mean it."

Roderick gritted his teeth. "We're *not* done with this discussion."

Carly barged in, grabbing his hand. "Hey, Roddy, let me buy you a drink, darlin'. You look like you could use one, hun." She was obviously trying to diffuse the situation in her Carly way.

He snatched his hand away. "Get away from me." Then he stormed off into the crowd. Fortunately, the raging music covered our little family spat from our surrounding guests. In fact, we had to yell to be heard.

"Hey," Liam said. "I'm really sorry about that. I'm not usually that forward. I guess I just kind of got carried away in the moment. I've had one too many—you should probably cut me off."

"You don't have to apologize," I said, grabbing and kissing him again.

"I'll, uh, leave you two to it, loves," Carly said, shuffling off, heading toward the bar.

I don't know if it was the wine buzz or me being pissed about my brother, but I grabbed Liam's hand. "Let's go someplace a little less crowded. What do you say?"

He nodded and took my hand. As we strolled out of the ballroom, my ears rang from the loud music. Outside the double doors of the ballroom, we could finally talk again without shouting.

Liam pointed down the north hallway. "What's down there?"

"Oh, you don't want to go that way," I said. "It's the cellar door."

"What, like a wine cellar?"

"No, more like corpses," I said and shrugged. "It's a family crypt."

"Are you serious? There are *dead* people buried under this old house?"

"Well, it's not all that dramatic. They're sealed up in the walls of the mausoleum, you know, in caskets."

"Hmm, that's not helping."

"It's not as gruesome as it sounds. I've been down there."

"Well," he said, grabbing me. "I'm glad you're up here with me with the land of the living."

I guided him to the stairs.

"Where are we going?"

"Up. Do you have a problem with…up?"

"Uh, no," he said.

We climbed the stairs and were about to enter my room, when I heard a sound. Like a moaning.

"Do you hear that?"

"The music, yeah, how can you not?"

No, it was a moaning sound. It came again.

"That was not music," I said.

"Uh, yeah, kind of. Sounds like a dog."

I headed toward the sound. It was coming from behind the hidden door that led to the attic.

"It's behind there," I said.

"Let's check it out."

I shook my head. "The door's locked."

Liam felt the dark ebony wainscoting. "There's no knob."

"You have to push, and it clicks open."

Liam tried. The door didn't move.

Mrs. Dietrich had locked it again. The fact that she was so adamant about doing that made it all the more suspicious. "Good call."

The moaning sounded human. "Do raccoons make that kind of noise?"

"No," Liam said. "What gave you *that* idea?"

I kneeled down and peeked through the inconspicuous keyhole. All I could see was the flight of stairs led up to the heavy attic door.

"What's in there?" Liam said.

"Wait a minute," I said. Then I cupped my hands around the keyhole and yelled. "Hello?" My voice echoed up the hardwood steps.

The moaning sound stopped.

Liam gave me a puzzled look. So I shoved my ear against the door and listened. It was hard to hear anything since the music coming from downstairs was blasting so loud. The entire house seemed to have an electronic heartbeat from DJ Raven's blasting bass. But I listened through the stairway door the best I could. What I thought I heard was breathing, a steady in-and-out respiration. Like labored gasping from a person who had just done one million jumping jacks, not a bunch of raccoons.

"There's someone behind that upstairs door," I whispered to Liam, peeking again through the keyhole.

"Some*one?*"

WHAM. Something hit the secondary door. *WHAM. WHAM. WHAM.* The attic door rocked on its hinges. The reason for the steel bolts were now obvious. Whatever was on the other side was strong. Would that door even hold?

"Come on," I said. "I don't want to provoke it. Whoever or whatever it is."

When we'd come up earlier, I was feeling buzzed and wanting to have a long and scandalous make-out session with my date. Now I was awake, sober, and scared. I was also angry that I'd been lied to— Mrs. Dietrich *knew* who was behind that door. So did Mr. Walsh. I was certain.

"Where are we going?" Liam said.

"I want to find out what's going on. Right now." Grabbing his hand, I pulled him down the stairs.

"Ow," he said. "Your nails are digging into the back my hand."

3

Down at the gathering, only a few guests remained as most had left after the midnight unmasking. That was good, I had lost the mood to party. Mr. Walsh was chatting with Mrs. Dietrich. Perfect, I had them both right where I wanted them. As they saw me approach, they each looked a little pensive.

"Who's locked up in the attic?"

"I already told you," Mrs. Dietrich said, "it's a family of—"

"It's *not* raccoons," I interrupted. "They don't breathe heavily and pound on doors. Some*one* is locked up there. It's a human. And I want to know *who* it is and *why.*"

"You were up in the attic?" the housekeeper asked. The worry lines in her otherwise stony face were pronounced.

"No, but I don't need to be to know I'm being fed a bunch of bullshit."

Mr. Walsh raised his hands. "Please keep it down. The investors."

"I don't give a damn about them. If you're locking up someone against their will in this house, I'm calling the police. That's wrong on so many levels."

Mr. Walsh gestured to leave the ballroom. We left the din of hip-hop noise. He regarded Liam. "This is a family matter; I don't think it concerns…"

"It concerns him," I said.

Mrs. Dietrich shot me a stern look. "This is not the time or place, ma'am."

"I want the answer *here* and *now*."

"Hey," Roderick said. "What's all the shouting about out here? There's supposed to be a party going on." Carly was now with him. Guess she had worked her charms to calm him down from earlier.

"Mr. Walsh was about to tell me who's locked up in the attic."

"Someone's locked in the attic?" Carly asked.

"Yes," I said. "And someone's going to give me an answer right now."

"If I tell you," Mr. Walsh said, his eyes fixated on me. "Will you promise to keep this mute until the investors leave. If they find out, they'll walk—and all of this will be for nothing."

"*If* you tell me?" I said. "If you *don't* tell me they'll walk when fifty cops roll in here."

Mr. Walsh turned to Roderick. And then back at me. "It's necessary to keep the one upstairs contained."

"The one?"

"Throughout his life, he hasn't had any socialization. So he's more animal than human. He's dangerous, and can never be introduced into society. He would pose a serious threat."

"And who is this person?"

Mr. Walsh whispered: "Your brother."

TWENTY-FIVE

1

"What the actual fuck are you talking about, Mr. Walsh?" I said. "My brother is right here."

"We have another brother," Roderick said. "Apparently."

I didn't know what to say. What did you say to something like that? First, I'd learned that I was heir to a crumbling mansion and had a twin brother. Next, I learned I had another sibling, except this one was someone confined behind a locked attic door. Yeah, I had every right to be confused and pissed.

"You *knew* about this, Roderick? You knew about this and you didn't *tell* me? What the fuck is *wrong* with you?" I looked at Mr. Walsh and our housekeeper too. "What's wrong with *all* of you?"

"Calm down," Roderick said. "I only just learned about it. I didn't have a chance to tell you with all that's going on."

"Somebody'd better start talking," I said. "Or you can explain it to the Charlton County Sheriff."

"Your mother, Lenore Usher, gave birth to triplets, not twins. Two sons and a daughter. Roderick was born first, then you, and then Creighton. Unfortunately, his umbilical cord became wrapped around his neck. He nearly died. He was revived but, unfortunately, he had severe brain damage. It was one on the reasons that your mother had fled the house with both of you in tow when you were two years old. The strain of trying to raise the child was too much. He was violent, killing spiders and mice. He later killed the family cat. He grew more violent. And brutally strong. He had ponderous strength. It's as if his limited mental capabilities had somehow augmented him physically. He'd never be an heir to the Usher fortune, and he was an embarrassment to the family, so he was locked away in the attic. A scandalous secret, you might say. And he's been there, up in the attic, for sixteen years."

"But I saw someone, he looked human but not human, running around the grounds. He came after Carly and I."

"That's right," Carly said. "I saw him too."

"You saw him?" Walsh said.

"I saw some*thing*, hun. I couldn't tell if it was a human or an animal. It was big. And fast as a damned hurricane."

"Well, that's impossible," Mrs. Dietrich said. "Creighton has been locked away for sixteen years. I should know, I feed him every day."

"You're telling me he just lives up there? No human contact. Where does he go to the bathroom?"

"A toilet was put up there."

"So he's not fit to live with other humans but he's potty trained?"

"When he was around ten, he did get sick," Mr. Walsh said. "He was unresponsive. We had to bring in a doctor. The Usher's family doctor, who also oversaw the birth. We had to use a tranquilizer gun to bring him down, the kind you use on zoo animals. Apparently the dosage of the tranquilizer dart wasn't enough. He woke up as the doctor was examining him. He tore out one of his eyes, and then ate it. The doctor nearly died. He had signed a stiff confidentiality form earlier so he couldn't press charges. And that's when we were certain that Creighton could never have human contact."

"Out there in the darkness, someone is running around. Someone like him. How do you know he's always in there? Maybe he's found a way out?"

Mr. Walsh sighed. "I'll make a deal with you. Let's keep a lid on this tonight and the rest of tomorrow until after the investors leave. After that happens, we'll take the ol' tranq gun, go up there, and check it out."

"You still have the tranquilizer gun?"

"Yes," Walsh said. "A necessary precaution. And I warn you now, you won't like what you see. You can't treat him like a sibling. Creighton is an animal—a wild animal. And he must be dealt with as such or he can endanger everyone. And if he were to ever get out, who knows what kind of damage he could do."

"Is that why the gate is always locked?" I asked.

"The gate is definitely a precaution. To keep outsiders from the Ushers and to keep Ushers from outsiders." It was Mr. Walsh's attempt at lightening the situation with humor, but I wasn't amused. This wasn't a laughing matter, this was a person's life. My brother's life if they were being truthful. I wasn't sure what to believe. They'd been hiding the truth. I didn't know what was real or bullshit.

"I'm sorry," Roderick said. "I should have told you. I was worried how you would react."

"You have more to be sorry for than that. You've been acting weird ever since you've met Liam. Acting like a jealous boyfriend or something."

Mrs. Dietrich gasped.

"Uh, sis, can we have a more private conversation about our family affairs later?"

"Oh," I said. "We are. We're all going to sit down and have a long and meaningful conversation about everything as soon as those fucking investors jet."

"Those 'fucking investors' are going to save our family. And this house. You might cease being so disrespectful."

I gestured to our surroundings. "Is all of this worth saving?" I grabbed Liam and an open bottle of wine from the bar. "C'mon. Let's grab some air. It stinks in here."

I pulled Liam along. Carly came with me.

"What are you going to do, darlin'?" Carly asked.

"After being lied to about everything? I have half a notion to fly back to Pickman Flats with you."

"Is that a good idea?" Liam said. "Would you forfeit your inheritance?"

"Who cares. You should come along."

"Yeah, Pops wouldn't allow that to happen."

We walked upstairs to the second floor. I showed Carly to her room.

"Guess this is good night," Carly said. "For at least me, love. I have a quart of brandy and a few edibles that will finish off the party. There were some cute guys here, but, you know, hun, I don't fuck on the first date."

"Good night," I said. I gave her a kiss.

"Let's talk tomorrow, darlin'," Carly said.

"After this goddamn investor meeting there's going to be lots of talking. Good night."

I walked Liam into my room and closed the door behind me.

"I'm a little freaked out right now," he said.

"Yeah, me too. My nerves are shot. I came in here to fuck your brains out and now I feel like I'm going out of my mind."

"Fuck my brains out," Liam said. "Well, I appreciate that. It's been a long time since anyone has given me a carnal lobotomy."

"Spare me the details," I said, raising the bottle of wine to my lips. I took a long gulp, sucked in a breath, and then guzzled another gulp. Then I sat on the bed and felt the raven amulet at my neck. The amulet that belonged to my ancestor that wouldn't move. Impossible as that seemed. Some kind of fucking witchcraft. Just like this entire thing.

2

We ended up on the bed, our heads filled with wine. Mad, lustful, uncertain—I started to tear off Liam's shirt. The clutches of the alcohol made me want to escape with him. He kissed me on the head.

"No," he whispered. "I mean, I want to, I do, just not like this. Not the first time we're together. I want it to be special. You know what I mean?"

I was glad he slammed on the romantic brakes and brought me to my senses. I wanted the same thing, but part of me wanted to rebel against Roderick. With him trying to control me and lying, I wanted to exert any kind of control over him I could.

I grabbed Liam. "Hold me."

3

When I woke up at 5:08 in the morning, I was alone. What had happened to Liam? Then I saw a note on the vanity.

HAD A WONDERFUL TIME. WORK IN THE MORNING. HAD TO GO. LOVE, LIAM

My eyes focused on the penultimate word in the note, "love." He loved me? I was pretty sure I felt the same about him, but we hadn't discussed it. That word didn't pass our lips. No kind of statements or pronouncements of our fondness for one another. And now, here it was, out in the open. I was glad that he had "said" it first. That made it easier. When I had been dating Parker, the "I love you" had slipped from my lips so easy. It had hurt when he couldn't say it back for several weeks later. It was ironic that I was always protecting my heart, which was something I had to do bouncing from foster families, but dropping my guard at the first boy I felt something more than lust for. Someone with whom I might have a future. Even though Liam was the kind of guy you could have a future with, I still didn't want to make the same Parker mistake. And now, here in black and white, the word "love." Maybe it was easier for him to write than say it.

Ugh, shut up. You sound like a desperate wench. Get a grip. You're an adult. Take this all in stride.

I opened my door and went out into the hall. The house stood dark and silent. In these hours, the still house could be so overbearing. Often times I was afraid to stare down the darkness of the hallway. The last thing I wanted to see was the ghost of one of my relatives.

Not that I believed that could happen. But if it were, Usher House would have been the most appropriate place.

I went into the bathroom and relieved myself. Then, back out into the hall, I heard a low howling. I thought it might be coming from outside, but it was in the house. I walked down the hall and to the door of the attic. It was coming from up there. I turned the knob. Locked. No doubt Mrs. Dietrich had locked it. I thought about going to her chamber to get the key from her. Demand it. But if Creighton was dangerous, then it would be suicide to open the door to the attic alone. The howling was low and mournful. So full of sadness and self-pity. It broke my heart. This couldn't go on, not while I was in the house. Touching the silver raven amulet around my neck, I wondered what Eva Usher would have done.

Returning to my room, I felt wide awake now, so I grabbed her compendium of spells and hexes from under my mattress and opened it. She had written it in the most meticulous and delicate hand. It was dated 1918, two years before she'd died. This was something that she had put together at my age.

This is a compendium of spells, charms, and hexes that I have compiled over the years of my life. These will be kept under lock and key, as my family do not like me "consorting in the dark arts." They don't have any proof, but they suspect. I first learned of the dark arts from one called "The Swamp Witch," old woman Carlotta Wiggens. During one of my long, long walks far outside the property, I came upon her humble cabin. At first, I was frightened of her. But then I started to visit her almost daily. She became like a second mother to me. She showed me how to live off the land. What herbs could heal the sick and what were deadly poison. Carlotta had passed down wisdom of the ancients that was forbidden and lost in modern society. It's like ancient man had lost touch of who he was. A child of nature.

So, all of my thoughts and words lie in here. This is who I am and why I must hide this from the world.

It was a fascinating read. Mostly, though, I was trying to find out more about this amulet and its powers—and how to get it off.

This would take some time.

My eyes grew heavy and I fell asleep again.

TWENTY-SIX

1

In the morning, I wasn't expecting to see what I saw. Carly came out of Roderick's room wearing his robe, her red hair was tousled all over the place.

"Are you serious right now?" I said.

"Wait a minute."

Grabbing Carly's arm, I dragged her into my room, shutting the door. "What are you doing?"

"I was hoping to talk to you later about this, hun."

"Did you…sleep with my brother?"

Carly sighed. "I didn't intend to, love, honest."

"So you're saying by not saying it that you did."

"Last night, after you and Liam left me, he came to my door. We started talking. He wanted to show me his collection of guitars, so I went into his room. He started playing some chords. One thing led to another and, well, yeah.

"But I didn't go there with the intent of doing anything. I had zero interest in him. I wanted to hook up with his friend, DJ Raven, but some skank from town swooped him up first. I went to my room with zero intentions of being with your brother. He made all of the moves."

"Right," I said. "And you didn't stop him. He forced himself on you?"

"No," she said. "He didn't force himself. I was bored, lonely, and drunk. What did you want me to do, darlin'?"

"Uh, *not* sleep with my brother. Do you know how repulsive that is?"

"He's not that bad. After you get through his emo-ness, he's really a phenomenal lover. He was so in touch with me, hun, it was kind of refreshing from the usual close encounters of the strange and awkward kind."

"I don't want to be hearing this right now."

Carly put her hands on my shoulders. "Calm down, darlin'. It was a one-night thing. OK? It's not going to happen again. Let's pretend that it didn't happen."

"But I know it happened. How can I even look at him again knowing what you two did? How can I even look at you?"

"You're acting like some sanctimonious asshole, Mads. You practically throw it in my face that you have a rich and attractive boyfriend. What am I supposed to do when you're with lover boy?"

"Don't throw this back on me."

Carly nodded. "You know what…I think it's best if I just packed up my shit and went back a day early. Does that work for you, darlin'?"

"Do whatever."

"Fine." She opened the door to my room and stormed out.

Ezzy jumped off the bed and zig-zagged around my feet, staring up at me. "What are you looking at, little shit?"

As I got ready for the investor meeting, I was fuming and my hands were shaking. So much shit happened last night—finding this amulet, Roderick acting like an ass, finding out I had another brother, and then Carly and Rod. I couldn't handle it. It's like the world had gone insane on Halloween night. I knew the Usher family had a history of insanity, but was it the people or the place? This house seemed to make things happen. The air and energy here could make you crazy. What I decided *not* to do was yell at Roderick for seducing my best friend. Not now. It'd have to wait until after the meeting with the investors. After that, though, we were going to have words. All of them about his unacceptable behavior. If he was going to carry on like this, I didn't know if I could handle it.

2

I went down to the dining room. Steaming coffee and warm rolls waited. Mr. Walsh and Roderick met me a short time later, and then the two investors. Valdemar and Pym looked well rested. Apparently they'd hit their pillows early last night. Roderick appeared tired, his eyes baggy and a little bloodshot. I was a little grossed out knowing the reason why he didn't get sleep last night. He seemed hesitant to make eye contact with me. I don't know if Carly had told him that I knew or he had some kind of guilt. But, for now, I wouldn't let on that I knew.

"Sleep all right last night?" I asked him.

"When I *did* get to sleep," he said, sipping coffee. "Are you stoked for this meeting, sis?" Wow, he changed the subject quickly. He had no attachment to Carly. None. That pissed me off more. If he was going to have sex with my best friend, at least I would hope he'd feel something. If he used her only for a quick piece of ass, he and I would have problems. But now wasn't the time to bring it up. I had to clear it from my head the best I could.

"I have the presentation set up in the library," Roderick said. "Grab your coffee and your rolls, gentlemen, and then we can proceed."

3

Two hours later, the presentation with investors Valdemar and Pym was over. And then it was another two hours of them asking questions and talking. The meeting was brutal, only getting by with coffee and rolls and trying to stay interested and being "on" the entire time with a fake smile plastered on my face, but I got through it.

Finally, the investors rose from their chairs and mentioned that they'd had an early evening flight. We all shook hands and said our goodbyes.

We closed the deal.

It looked like we had two deep pockets that wanted what software tech Usher Enterprises had to offer. We'd get some research and development funds wired to us in a few days. We could use a little of that for personal expenses, Roderick said, and then pay it back with our profits. I wasn't sure that was entirely ethical, but maybe that was how business was done. Roderick certainly knew more about business than I did, so I assumed it was all right.

4

Now that I had some time to cool down from my earlier exchange with Carly, I went up to her room. I had hoped that she didn't leave. If she did, I was going to be sad. I didn't want us to end like this. Going into her room, it was empty. Her bags were packed.

"She departed about ten this morning," Mrs. Dietrich said, appearing behind me. "She told me to tell you thank you for all of the warmth and hospitality."

"Thank you," I said. I wanted to cry. This wasn't exactly how this morning was supposed to go. I texted Carly but I got no response. After waiting a long five minutes, I called her. It went directly to voicemail, which meant she had probably shut her phone off. Great. Now I felt like an asshole.

I approached Mr. Walsh and Roderick. "They're gone now," I said. "That business is done. Now we need to deal with the *other* family business."

"Sis," Roderick said. "Can't it wait?"

"No, it can't."

"He's been fine up there all of his life? Why change it? Why stir the pot? It's just going to get him excited."

"He's a human fucking being locked up in an attic. If you don't realize how sick and twisted that is, I don't know what to say."

"I'd strongly advise against it," Mr. Walsh said. "Your brother is right."

"I told you I'd go to the Charlton County Sherriff if you didn't let him out."

"He's like a wild animal, ma'am, that would be unwise," Mrs. Dietrich said.

"I want to see him," I said. "He's my brother. Our brother. Have some motherfucking compassion for Christ's sake."

"It's not necessary to take the Lord's name in vain, ma'am," Mrs. Dietrich said.

"Fine," Mr. Walsh said. "If it will assuage your curiosity." He turned to Mrs. Dietrich. "Bring me the gun."

5

Mr. Walsh held the tranquilizer rifle as he ascended the stairs. Roderick and I stayed behind him. Mrs. Dietrich had finally surrendered the keys to us. She didn't want any part of this.

"I must warn you now that this is an extremely terrible idea," Mr. Walsh said.

"Couldn't we have just put some tranquilizers in his food?"

"We've tried that before," Walsh said. "It worked the first couple of times, but then he caught on."

"How?"

"I don't know, perhaps his sense of smell or taste."

"Then those senses would be incredibly honed."

"As I said, he's more animal than human. All of his senses are heightened, despite his limited mental capacities."

We reached the landing at the top of the stairs. I pressed my ear to the door. "I can't hear anything… Maybe he's sleeping."

Walsh readied the rifle. He motioned Roderick to unlock the door. "Be ready to close it if I miss. I won't have another chance to load a dart before he'll charge."

"Will you miss?"

"Don't plan on it."

Roderick placed the tarnished gold skeleton key into the lock. He turned it. The door made an audible click. *Loud.* If Creighton Usher was sleeping, no doubt that that would have awakened him. My heart beat faster and I could barely breathe. Roderick turned the knob and opened the door.

The stench of rotten meat and feces was the first thing that hit me. Roderick pushed the door open more. I had to hold my hand over my nose and mouth to prevent myself from vomiting.

The room had an old fashioned wallpaper with sailboats and anchors on it. Something that would be in a young child's room. A bed sat in the corner. It was an old child's bed without a mattress. It had since been tossed onto the floor, and it lay empty with blobs of dark stains that resembled Rorschach test ink blots.

Roderick peeked behind the door in case the attic occupant was hiding. He wasn't there.

Dozens of plates with half eaten and discarded scraps sat near the door. Dried feces had been finger painted on the torn wallpaper. Flies buzzed everywhere. Maggots crawled in some of the spoiled meat.

"Where is he?" I spoke through my hand.

"This is not possible," Mr. Walsh said. "He's…gotten loose."

"I heard him last night."

"I have no doubt."

"Something has been stalking around outside at night," I said. "Do you think that's him?"

A half-eaten jackrabbit lay on the floor. It boiled with maggots. In fact, it was a gruesome menagerie of squirrels and birds and rabbits. There was even a deer's leg.

"That deer that had its throat torn out. I bet he did that."

"That was on the other side of the fence," Roderick said.

"I saw scratches near the main gate. He's getting in and out of the grounds."

Roderick rolled his eyes. "So you're saying that there's a monster roaming around the countryside?"

"How is he getting out?" I asked.

The room had a window with shatterproof glass. And it was also barred with some heavy steel bars. He hadn't gotten out that way.

"Look," I said. "The closet."

The closet door stood slightly ajar. Inside were more decaying animals, leaves, and wetness and mold. A ragged hole had been torn out of the ceiling.

"He burrowed through the boards and has been climbing out onto the roof," Walsh said.

"How's he getting up and down?" Roderick asked.

"That's easy," I said. "There's a tree next to the house. Esmerelda uses it all the time to get up and down."

"Who?" Mr. Walsh asked.

"My cat."

"Well," the lawyer said. "I guess that this little safari is cancelled considering that the animal has sprang the coop."

I shook my head. "This place is absolutely abysmal. He can't live in these conditions. It's unsanitary and it's cruel."

On the floor I found some faded picture books that were torn up. And some wooden blocks. Child's toys. Given to a child that hadn't been allowed to be one. Instead he had been locked up in here and forgotten.

"Mads is right," Roderick said. "This isn't the place for an Usher. This room needs to be cleaned up and fumigated. He needs to be moved to some facility that can take better care of him."

"It's a little late," Walsh said. "How are you going to explain this to the authorities? They'd lock us all up for negligence."

"Not all of us," I said. "Roddy and I just learned about it."

"Maybe you did and maybe you didn't."

I turned to Walsh. "What's that supposed to mean?"

Something landed in the closet with a *thunk*. The door creaked open. And two eyes from the darkness peered at us.

My other brother had returned.

He snarled and looked like he wanted to kill us.

TWENTY-SEVEN

1

"No sudden movements," Mr. Walsh whispered. "Don't even breathe."

Creighton stood about six feet tall. He had a thick black beard, long, matted hair covering his body, and wild, icy eyes. He only wore a torn pair of old black pants. Thick black hair coated the lean sinewy muscles of his torso. His fingernails were filthy and long. His feet were bare and filthy with long toenails. I hated to say it, but this was probably the closest thing to the Wolf Man that I'd ever seen outside of a horror movie. Once, I remembered reading about a condition called hypertrichosis, werewolf syndrome; I wondered if that was it. My body cramped. The sight of Creighton made my stomach ache and my bowels pang to be voided. The thing that was my brother made a low guttural growl.

Mr. Walsh raised the tranquilizer gun slowly. He spoke low and gently. "It's all right, Creighton. We're here to help you. Just take it easy, boy."

Fear had stiffened my muscles—I stood halfway between the man-beast and the door. If I tried to run with my concrete-heavy legs, he would no doubt spring at me. On all of us. Now I realized, too late, that coming up here had been a bad idea. I had only wanted to help, and I was now sure I was going to die.

Creighton stared at me, his cold blue eyes studying me. Then they scanned down to the silver raven amulet around my neck and hung there a moment. He then peeked back up at my frozen face. It seemed like the wheels of his mind were spinning, like he was trying to make a connection. A recognition perhaps, but how? Maybe he thought I was Eva Usher in the painting. We did look strikingly similar, especially wearing the silver raven amulet.

Whap! A tranquilizer dart struck him in the chest.

The man-beast screamed, one of the most blood-curdling shrieks I've ever heard. He leaped from his stationary position with his thickly muscled legs. He was upon Walsh in a split second, tearing at him, the muscles in his bare, hairy back knotting from the effort. Walsh held up the rifle to try and hold Creighton back. But Creighton was too strong, and with a swipe of a thick arm, tore it away.

"Get him off me!" Walsh screamed.

Creighton lashed at his face. Apparently the tranquilizer dart wasn't a strong enough dose or it hadn't entered his blood stream yet.

Roderick picked up the tranquilizer gun and reloaded it.

I ran up to Creighton to try to distract him from tearing Walsh to pieces with his talon-long fingernails. "Get off of him."

The hairy man backhanded me, hitting me on the side of the head. A burst of white light flashed before my eyes and my ears rang like a constant bell. I fell back into a rotting pile of animal bones.

Whap! Roderick hit Creighton with another dart in his neck. He immediately jumped off Walsh and went after Roderick. This time, though, Creighton's movements were sluggish, more sedate, the thick brawn of his hairy body working in slow motion. The second tranquilizer dart was definitely taking effect. Creighton then retreated to the closet. He stopped and uttered something that chilled me to the bone. One word, which I thought was incredible. That means he had the capacity for learning.

"Walsh," he said with a guttered tongue. And then he vanished into the closet, climbing up the wall and back outside.

I picked myself up off the floor. My face hurt where he had struck me and my ears rang from the blow. Creighton's strength was prodigious. If he'd struck me with his full force, I would have been hurt much worse. I rushed over to Walsh. Wide-eyed and panicked, his face was scratched up and his cornflower blue dress shirt was torn and blood spattered.

"He tried to kill me," Walsh said. "He wanted to kill me. I could see it in his evil eyes."

"Your name," Roderick said. "He said your name."

"How can he do that? He never learned to read and write."

"He must have heard it. Perhaps he has the ability to mimic sounds but not know their meaning."

"He seemed to use it in the right context," I said. "I think he's smarter than he's given credit for."

Roderick and I helped Mr. Walsh up. "He's a dangerous beast. And a menace. He's always been a menace. He should've died at birth."

"We've got to get out of here," I said. "He'll come back."

"Not with two darts in him," Roderick said. "Did you see how lethargic he got?"

"He'll go sleep it off somewhere," Walsh said. "And probably wake up with a massive headache on par with a morning hangover."

"Shouldn't we go try to find him while he's sleeping? Maybe we could relocate him somewhere better?"

"Where?" Mr. Walsh said. "Because if you have any suggestions without bringing the law down on all of us, I'm all ears."

I shrugged. "I don't know. Maybe we'll have to build him some kind of facility. On the grounds. Something that's cleaner. Maybe he can be taught to read and write. Maybe we can turn him more, you know, human."

"My, my, sis," Roderick said, "that's a lot of maybes."

"This is not the time," Walsh said. "I didn't want to do this to begin with. I did it to placate you. And it nearly got me killed."

We helped him out of the disheveled room. Roderick turned and locked the door.

"Have Mrs. Dietrich get me some antiseptic for these cuts. I don't need them getting infected."

"Maybe we should take you to the hospital."

"No hospital. This is family business. What happens in Usher House stays in Usher House. We keep it here."

We helped Mr. Walsh down the stairs. Apparently, Mrs. Dietrich heard us as she was waiting by the stairway door.

"Goodness," she said. "What happened?"

"Isn't it obvious?" Mr. Walsh hissed. "Now take care of me."

Mrs. Dietrich looked at Roderick and I, apparently taken aback at being publicly scolded by Walsh. "As you wish, sir."

2

"Where are you going?"

I'd grabbed the car keys to the Roadster and texted Liam that I was coming over. This was all too much. I marched to the front door.

Roderick stood in my way. "I asked you a question."

"I'm going over to Liam's."

"Now?"

"Yes, *now*. You have objections?"

"Walsh is hurt and he needs us. We need him."

"I think you can handle things here just fine. I mean, after all, you knew about Creighton before I did. Apparently I wasn't given the task of knowing some important information like that. So I guess that means I don't really matter. You handled the investors. So I might as well go off and have fun. It's certainly not that around here."

"We need you here. *I* need you here."

"I'll be back. It's not like I'm packing up my bags and leaving."

"Don't be gone long, then."

I wanted to tell him that I'm an adult and I could be gone as long as I damn well pleased. But I didn't. I needed to get away without any more incident.

Little did I know, the incidents were only beginning.

TWENTY-EIGHT

"Wasn't expecting to see you today." Liam was glad to see me. "At least, so early."

After I'd left Usher House, I had tried to call and text Carly. She wasn't responding. Either she was away from her phone, doubtful, or she had me blocked. More likely. So, naturally, driving away in the Roadster, with Usher House in my rearview mirror, I felt free again. Things had gotten so strange at the house. Now with Creighton, I was a triplet. I didn't know how to process it. I needed time to get away and think. To look at this objectively. To tell Liam. And this was something that a phone call or a text wouldn't cover, this had to be done face to face.

"Can I talk to you about something?"

He nodded. "Sure. I was just getting ready to go and pick up some combine parts in Folkston."

"Oh."

"What did you want to talk about?"

So I told him everything that had happened since he'd left the party in the early hours of the morning. Carly with Roderick. The investors. And then Creighton.

"The whole thing is so sick and twisted," Liam said.

"I don't even know how to feel about all of this. It's like, when I first got to this place, everything was weird and strange. Then I started to get settled in, thanks in part to you. I started feeling like I had the chance of a normal life, a better life. Something better than what was handed to me. And now, it's all falling apart. There are so many secrets and things that I don't understand. And now my best friend isn't responding to me. So now you're the only sensible, rational human being that I can talk to."

He held me. "Whoa, be careful there. You're getting yourself all worked up."

"Sorry." Hot tears streamed down my cheeks. My hands shook and I couldn't breathe. Everything seemed to be converging in upon me. The only thing that made sense right now was Liam's arms around me.

"I have an idea," he said.

"What?"

"Maybe you could stay here."

"I don't know about that."

"Yeah, it'd be great. We have this old mother-in-law apartment around the side of the house. My mom lived in it a while when she and Pops weren't speaking. Then we've mostly used it for relatives to stay there when they come down for Thanksgiving and Christmas. It's actually pretty nice. It's got its own kitchen and laundry room even."

"I'm afraid I don't have any money to pay rent."

"Rent? Are you crazy? You'd be staying here as a guest. You know, until you decide what you want to do. But you can stay as long as you like."

I liked this idea. It was certainly a viable one.

"Maybe a little while. I need time."

"No problem," he said. "Let me show you the place."

"I thought you had to get combine parts."

He laughed. "Another ten minutes isn't going to make a difference."

Liam walked over to a black and gold ATV with four big balloon tires. "Climb on."

I climbed on back. He jumped on, turned the engine over, and we headed toward the house. The day was clear and bright and the sun was warm. I liked being here, it was peaceful. I could clear my head. It was like this little island of normalcy. This last bastion of sanity. And right now, I needed to get away from the madness of the Ushers.

We headed around the sage-colored farmhouse with the wrap-around porch. On the far side of it was a cottage with a rocking chair on the porch. It was a cozy little place. Like a miniature version of the farmhouse. I could see myself living there. Waking up in the morning with the sun. Sipping coffee on the porch during the cool morning while the wind chimes that hung off the porch sang their metallic songs. Watching the tall stalks of corn sway in the gentle summer breeze. It was like I had this flash-forward of me doing that as an old woman, wearing a silk robe, my long gray hair in a ponytail, deep lines around my eyes. A look of peace on my face. I liked this vision. It seemed like the vision that I wanted to foster into reality. I wanted to be that person who I saw in my mind's eye. A person of peace and contentment. Could that be possible living in Usher House and being a part of a family who was each met with madness at an early age? Maybe it was time to get away. Maybe this was my mind telling me that I had made a mistake and this alternate life in my vision awaited me if I only escaped from my current domain.

Liam pulled up to the tiny house and cut the engine. We climbed off.

"Pretty nice, right, City Mouse?"

"Yeah," I said. "Why didn't you move in here?"

"I'd thought about it. But I'm pretty attached to my room. Also, it's hard for Pops to get around. I need to be close if he falls or anything. He's been doing that lately."

We climbed onto the porch. The cottage was painted sage and ochre like the farmhouse. I stood against the railing and looked out at the barren yellow fields and the thrush of green bushy trees beyond. Somewhere a pheasant crowed. The crisp autumn air smelled vaguely of cinnamon. I immediately felt at home in this place.

"I could stay here," I said. "I really could, Country Mouse."

"Great."

"For one night anyway."

"Stay as long as you like, Mads," he said. "I, for one, would love to have you."

Before I realized what I was doing, I leaned in and kissed him. Our warm lips locked and his salty flesh tasted good to me. I didn't want to stop—I wanted to keep kissing him.

"What's going on out here?"

Liam's father slowly came up on the porch, using his cane. The *shuffle-shuffle-thump* of his feet moving along the wooden floorboards and then the tip of the cane striking the surface made a kind of melancholy music. "Herb's been waiting on you, boy. Thought I told you to go into town for those engine parts."

"Yes, sir," Liam said. "But I wanted to show Mads this mother-in-law first."

"What business is it of hers?"

Whatever politeness Liam's father had shown me initially was now gone. He spoke like I wasn't even there.

"Well," Liam said, and I could tell that he was choosing his words carefully. "I was thinking she could stay here for a night or two."

"She has her own house to live in." His father spit a tobacco-laden gob off the porch. "That's where she belongs. Over there."

"It would just be temporary."

"Boy," his father said, leaning in close. His round face became the color of a boiled lobster. "Clean the wax outta your ears and listen. She's got no business here. I don't want her over here. And I don't want you seeing her. You've had your fun."

"But, Pops."

"The only place one of them Ushers belongs is in that asylum they call home." He turned to me for the first time. "Now pardon my rudeness and abruptness, miss, but you stay the hell away from my son and don't come back here. You're not welcome. I don't want any Ushers on Delaney soil. You got that?"

"What's the big deal?"

"Just do as I ask, boy. Don't need to say a reason."

Liam stomped his foot down. "I think you do…sir. This concerns my girlfriend. She might even become my wife."

Uh, what the actual fuck? Things were moving a little too quickly here. I wanted to butt in, but I didn't want to barge into this family squabble. It would be like trying to tear apart two fighting dogs—a bad idea as you'd be the one to get mangled in the end.

"Your *wife?*" His dad spit another brown gob again. "You don't have my blessing and that ain't happening. If you want to marry that girl, you'll do it far away from here. And you won't be coming back. I'll disown you as a son. Mark my words."

"I don't understand," Liam said. His face was flushed and his blue eyes were watery.

Red-faced, Delaney senior scowled at me. "Your mother. She…had an affair…with one of them. I can't even say its name."

"Vincent Usher?" I said. "My father?"

Mr. Delaney recoiled at the name as if I had tossed a cup of ice water into his face.

"Don't say that name. Not now, not ever."

"An affair? Pa, what are you talking about?"

"When your mom and I was having troubles, she used to go on long walks. Apparently she met up with this…individual…and the two started seeing one another. She moved out here so she could be with him. Some nights I'd go to bed and the two would be carrying on in here. I caught them one night. And I shot that son of a bitch."

"What?"

"Just some rock salt in the four-ten shotgun. But it was enough to hurt. What I'd do to any stray animal that would nose around my property where it didn't belong. He left and never came back. And that was the end of it. Your mother was happy again after that. Until the cancer took her away from us. And I'm convinced that that son of a bitch gave it to her. Nothing good ever comes from that family. Nothing at all."

Liam stood there looking at the floor, his face was now the color of sour milk. "Why…didn't…you…tell…me…?"

"Because that happened long ago, when you were a kid. It was no business of yours. Now that you dragged another one into our lives, it's time for me to end it. And if you insist, I'll go get my shotgun. I keep it loaded with rock salt just in case the coyotes come sniffing around. Or an Usher." His dad sighed. "And the bitch of it is…you look like your father. I see him in your face. Last time I saw you, I thought I was looking at him. And when Liam said who you were, well, it's like in one of those vampire movies. When they plunge the stake into the ticker of one of those miserable sons of bitches. It punctured me. Got me right through the damned heart."

Liam turned to me. He had tears in his eyes.

I went to him. "Liam."

He backed away. "I think. I think you should go."

"What?"

"I need to… This is too much… I need to think things through."

"If you would kindly jump into your fancy car and haul your tail out of here, missy, I won't have to get any more impolite and rambunctious than I already have. Now I know the past ain't your fault. Hell, I can tell that you didn't know anything about it. But now that you do, it's time for you to forget about my son. Forget about the Delaneys. Go home. And never come back." He spit again. "Ever."

My heart seized up in my chest. It felt like someone with a velvet glove was crushing it in their fist. I couldn't breathe. Tears started to burn my cheeks. I wanted to lash out and say something hurtful. To make them hurt as much as I felt hurt right now. But I didn't. The only dignity I could offer myself right now was to walk away. And so I did.

"Excuse me." Those were the last words I said to the Delaney men as I strolled past them, stomped off the porch, and then burst into a sprint across the lawn.

"Mads!"

My heart thumped so hard in my ears that I almost didn't hear Liam calling after me. But I didn't turn back. I wouldn't turn back. Not after this humiliation. This didn't even seem real. One minute we were kissing and the next, it was like life had come along and pulled the rug out under our feet as we were huddled together. It was like everything was keeping us apart. My brother. Liam's father. My family history. I had a home and I didn't want to go back to it.

I was done with everything.

TWENTY-NINE

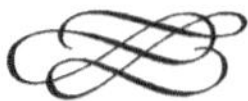

When I reached the Roadster, I was out of breath, sweating. I hadn't sprinted that hard since Mrs. Schneider made us run wind sprints for P.E. class last spring. My lungs ached. My heart hurt. My head swam with thoughts. The only thing I could do was drive away. Leave the Delaney farm in a puff of dust. And that's what I did. I turned the car around and roared down that dusty road at 60 miles an hour, leaving a trail of brown dust in my wake. Ashes to ashes, dust to dust. How could I ever face Liam again after knowing this? How could he ever face me?

When I hit the blacktop, I sped down the main road. I passed the gates of Usher House a few minutes later and kept driving. I didn't know where I wanted to go or what I wanted to do.

Ten minutes later, I hit the city limits of Barlow. Even though it was the middle of the day, the town looked like it was under quarantine. Not a soul around. I drove past Shirley's Diner. Empty. Somewhere inside was that waitress. That was the last person I wanted to see. Where would I go? I don't know. Maybe I would drive to Folkston, grab a chocolate milkshake, and think things over.

As I was heading out of town, which took an entire sixty seconds going from one end to the other, I saw the Airbnb that Carly and I had stayed at. And the rental car that Carly drove—the red Infiniti—was parked there. Grabbing my phone, I checked it—still no messages. I pulled off to the side of the road and hit Carly's number. It went straight to voicemail. She still had her phone off. Guess it was time to make a house call. Right now I needed a friend. And Carly was going to see hers whether she liked it or not.

I pulled up to the craftsman house. Fortunately, there was an entrance around back so I didn't have to talk to the owners, the sweet old lady, Mrs. Emerson. She would keep me there a half hour talking about the weather and the Bible. I strolled around to the back door. I was about to knock, but I didn't as Carly might not let me in. It's better to ask for forgiveness than permission, right? Whatever that means? Turning the knob, the door was unlocked luckily, and so I went inside.

The place was quiet and seemed empty.

In the bedroom, Carly lay sprawled across the bed in her underwear. She had a wet washcloth across her face. On the nightstand was an empty water glass, a bottle of Advil, and her phone.

She was lightly snoring. Then she let out a tiny sleep fart. It was the one thing I needed to set my mood from ragingly pissed and sad to on the verge of hysterics. I had to bite my tongue to stop from laughing.

I'm guessing that Carly sensed my presence in the room as she raised one corner of the washcloth.

"I feel like…hammered dogshit."

"You look like it."

"What do *you* want?"

"Good afternoon to you, too."

Carly raised up, sighed, and then laid back down. "I'm serious… my head feels like an overripe avocado that somebody curb stomped."

"Do you want some more water?"

"That'd be nice," she said. "Thanks, hun."

I went into the little bathroom off the bedroom and poured her a glass. Then I took it back to her. I sat on the edge of the bed. She took the glass and drank some.

"I thought your flight was tonight."

"It is," she said. "But I switched it to a red eye, and then called Mrs. Emerson and booked the house. Thought I'd get some sleep and get rid of this headache before I drove up to Atlanta."

We stared at each other a moment. And seeing my best friend's face, that's when I lost it. I completely started bawling.

"Hey," Carly said, hugging me. "I'm sorry, darlin'. I was being a completely insensitive, selfish asshole."

"Yes, you were," I said between sobs. "But it's not just that. So much more has happened."

"What?"

Then I told her about Creighton. About Mr. Delaney. And basically about the world I had adopted crashing in. It was like when I was younger, finding out that the foster family that I was with just wasn't the right fit. But this was different. I was an adult now. I couldn't just go out an adopt another family, hoping for the right fit. This was it. I was an Usher, but I didn't feel like one. I was Carly's bestie, but didn't feel like her friend. I was Liam's girlfriend, and now that was all lost. Everything was ruined. The only thing I had was Peggy Bland's house waiting for me. I could beg for that crappy job at Williamson's Market back again. But, right now, that kind of sounded good. Returning to the familiar felt like the ideal choice compared to all of this alien, whacked-out bullshit that I was dealing with. And all of this started with that letter in the mail. That invitation and plane ticket. How could a person's life change so quickly with so little?

"I think," I said, still choking out my words. "I need to go home for a little while."

"I can drive you back to the house if you want."

"No," I said. "Back to Washington State. Back home. With you."

"You're serious, hun?"

I nodded. "I think I am."

"But what about the house? Your brother? And your, uh, boyfriend?"

"I need time away from that. All of it. I just need time and space to think. This all happened so quickly. And I jumped in too fast. Now I need to step back. Step back and reevaluate everything."

"Are you sure, darlin'? This seems so, you know, sudden."

A text from Roderick buzzed my phone. I sighed. Checked it.

HEY, SORRY TO BOTHER YOU. I'VE BEEN TRYING TO REACH CARLY. TOTAL RADIO SILENCE. IS SHE WITH YOU? IF NOT, HAVE YOU HEARD FROM HER?

"Oh, Jesus," I said, setting my phone face down on the bed.

"What?"

"Can you check your phone?"

"Why?

"Just indulge me."

Carly groped over and swiped it off the nightstand. "I forgot that I had silenced it." She turned off Airplane Mode on the phone. Immediately, she was accosted by several dinging notifications. A stream of green text bubbles populating her home screen.

"What the actual fuck, stalker?"

"Sorry, I was upset. I was trying to get a hold of you."

"No, love, your weird-ass brother. He's acting like a complete stalker or something."

"What does it say?"

Carly shook her head as she summarized them. "Stuff about last night. How he has feelings for me. How he hopes that it won't drive a wedge between you and I. On and on about undying love. A couple of poetry quotes." Carly gazed at me. "That would be sweet and all if it wasn't so psycho that he just texted me like 23 times in the space of a couple of hours. All of this without me responding. Does he think this is charming or something?"

"He doesn't have a lot of social skills. As much as he thinks he's this entrepreneur of the future, he lacks the basic adeptness to act like a rational human being." I sighed. "This I am finding out more and more. It kind of scares me."

"No shit," Carly said. "This is one of those Swipe Left situations, hun."

"See what I'm dealing with? I need a break."

"But what about your things. Your cat?"

"I'm leaving with what I'm wearing. I'll call and tell Mrs. Dietrich to take care of Ezzy. She has to do what I say."

Carly gave me a hug. "I'm sorry how this morning went down, love. I feel like complete trash. On the outside…and in."

Giving her a big hug, I held her for a moment. I was mad that she had slept with my brother. But I had a feeling, based on the texts Carly received, that he had pushed the matter. Carly could get a little loose and careless when she's had too much to drink. It was not the first time she was regretful the next morning after an amorous encounter with a perfect stranger. The only exception being was this particular one was with my weird brother who was seemingly more unhinged by the minute. Insanity, it was said, ran in the Usher family like a raging river. That stream seemed to have formed within my brother. Would those waters roar through me as well; an unstoppable force that could not be dammed up? *Damn.*

"It's all right," I said. "We all make mistakes. I've made several of my own. There's something about Usher House that kind of gives you what you want, and then extracts a heavy toll for it."

"What do you mean?"

"I don't quite know. It's just how everything seems at the moment."

Carly climbed out of bed. "I need a hot shower and hotter coffee."

"I can drive if you're not up to it," I said.

"What are you going to do with your Roadster?"

"I'll have Knapp pick it up." Wow, it was kind of badass to have servants do what you want them to do. Feed your cat, pick up your car. But the weirdness factor rather offset these aristocratic perks. "Don't take too long," I added, suddenly feeling antsy. Feeling like Roderick might figure out where we were at and come for us. What if he had placed some kind of tracking device in my phone? What if he'd figured out what I was doing? *No, he's not that tuned into you.*

ARE YOU THERE? He texted back.

I couldn't answer. He'd try to call next. So I slipped my iPhone into Airplane Mode. It was the only peace of mind I could achieve as I was feeling anxious. I needed to leave Barlow. I needed to leave Usher House. *Now.*

The green highway sign revealed ATLANTA 120 miles.

Another two hours of driving. Carly shifted in the passenger seat. She had downed a venti triple-shot mocha that we'd gotten at the Folkston Starbucks as we'd left, and still conked out. I was already anxious and my stomach was bundled up in knots. I didn't need coffee or any kind of stimulants to keep me alert—I was on the precipice of an anxiety attack. Every mile I put between Usher House and myself, I seemed to be more anxious. My stomach churned and I burped up acid that burned my throat. I felt like I was going to vomit. I had to hold it together another two hours. Once we got to the Atlanta airport, turned in the car, and I charged an airline ticket to my credit card, I'd feel better. Thinking about doing that calmed me a little.

The song on the radio started to get to me. It was "Don't Fear the Reaper" by Blue Oyster Cult, according to the dash display. Lots of cowbell in that song. Not today. I switched it over to some light rock. I didn't need electric guitars ripping up my nerves. I still hadn't taken my phone off Airplane Mode. And I wished the curiosity hadn't gotten the better of me because that was exactly what I did. Like Carly, I had a dozen texts from Roderick and a few missed calls. Shit.

Before I could even scroll through them, my phone rang again in my hand, which caused me to jump. My anxiety stood on end seeing his name and picture pop up on my call screen. I could just ignore the call. But he'd call again. And my anxiety couldn't take it knowing that. So I slid the button over to answer.

"Hello."

The line was quiet for several seconds.

"Hello?"

"Glad to see you're answering your phone." I heard the wounded anger dripping from Roderick's tone. This was going to be an unpleasant call. Maybe I could be proactive. Possibly divert his energy a little bit.

"How is Mr. Walsh? Is he all right?"

"Yeah," Roderick said. "I took him to the doctor in Folkston and got him all stitched up. He had to get a tetanus shot and about ten stitches. We told the doctor it was a wild dog that attacked him. But we assured him that it wasn't rabid, or he would have had to get a shot in his abdomen with a hypodermic needle the size of a railroad spike."

"Where is he now?"

"He's here with me at the house. I'm glad you're so concerned about his health now. I could have used your help taking him to the hospital."

"What about Creighton? Where's he?"

"Who cares?"

"I care."

"He probably crawled off into the shrubs to sleep off his tranquilizers. I'm sure he'll return to his room. He seems to do that."

I was about to go into a long rant about our feral brother who was being locked in the attic of our weird gothic house in the middle of the country, but Roderick switched topics before I did. Apparently, he picked up on me trying to deflect his rage.

"I guess the question is: *where* are you and *who* are you with?"

"That's *two* questions, actually."

"Oh yes, you're such a stickler for detail," Roderick said with a sarcastic tone. "I forgot."

"Carly and I are hanging out before she leaves."

I couldn't let him know what we were actually doing. He'd come after me, I knew it. I'd call him again once I was back home.

"Oh, let me talk to her. She seems to have her phone turned off."

"She's sleeping right now," I said. "She had a long night."

"I'll say she did."

"Don't go there. It's bad enough."

"When are you coming home?"

Fuckity-fuck-fuck.

"Soon?"

Silence on the phone. Uncomfortable silence.

"You know, heading to Atlanta is not a very smart idea."

"How do you know?"

He didn't answer.

"*How?*"

He sighed. "There's a tracker in your phone."

"A what?"

"Oh my God, relax," he laughed. "It's only for your protection."

"I'm throwing this phone away and getting a new one then." Like I could afford that expense right now after I bought a plane ticket.

"There's no place for you to go," he said.

"What?"

"There's no home back home."

"What the hell is that supposed to mean?"

"The Bland house, I sold it. The funds are now in a trust. Can't say you got much for it—nearly two-hundred thousand. It needed lots of work. I hired some people to move out the furniture and place it in a local storage unit, and then fix it up. But it wasn't in great condition. I hired a professional stager to make it as presentable as she could."

"You can't do that."

"Ah, but I did do it…for you."

"But that would require me signing everything."

"Oh, Mr. Walsh helped me with all of the details. There were a few legal loopholes that we could slip through. And, well, I can write your signature as well as you. We *are* related, you know."

"But that's illegal. It's forgery. It's, like, fraud."

"It's done. The house is sold. In fact, the owners are moving in this weekend."

I couldn't say anything. I felt sick. Tired. Hopeless. The roadway ahead had once seemed like I was heading toward a future. Now it seemed like I was heading toward oblivion. I was heading nowhere as I had nowhere to go. Poor Peggy. Strangers were going to be living in her little house. Would they take care of her prized rhododendrons like she did, feeding and nurturing them with composted coffee grounds and eggshells? I doubted it. Peggy's only legacy to the world was a couple of flowered shrubbery in front of the quaint, yellow house. Poor, poor Peggy.

"Hello?" He said. "Did I lose you? Did you drive through a tunnel?"

"You fucker, Roderick. You fucking motherfucking fuck."

He laughed. "Wow, that's gratitude for you. I get you a spectacular country mansion, incredible car, sell off your superfluous assets so you have some cash, show you nothing but love and admiration, and this is how you treat me? By calling me crass, potty-mouth names? I know you weren't raised as well as I was in the manners department. But I'd like to think you were raised better than biting the hand that feeds you. Disrespect is so unbecoming, sis."

Sweat started to bead on my forehead. My eyes were bloodshot. I felt like I was going to vomit now. In a weird way, as I caught the reflection of myself in the mirror, looking tired and haggard, I flashed back to my brother, Creighton, in the attic. I looked just like him, a desperate, wild animal. And Roderick, he was the zookeeper. He fed me, petted me, and then locked the cage door. Except I hadn't known it. I'd suspected it, but I hadn't thought he'd stoop to this kind of devious, insidious behavior. But I hadn't known him. Until now. There was nothing he wouldn't do. He was ill. He had a mental sickness that trickled deep within his bones, infecting him to the core. Maybe I did too, but his madness eclipsed mine.

"So what I need you to do is turn that piss-ant rental car around, head back to Barlow, pick up the Roadster, and drive your ass home. Where you belong. Because that's the only home you have now.

There's nothing waiting for you in Pickman Flats. *Nothing*. Everything that matters to you is right here in the state of Georgia."

"There's something wrong with you, Roderick. You're not well."

"I feel as healthy as a one-hundred-dollar bill. Maybe even two hundred."

"You know what I mean. No normal person does this to someone that they care about."

"I've made you rich, and soon, respectable. We just closed a deal today with some top-level execs. They want to invest in us and are going to forward us a hefty advance. Do you know what an advance is? It's trust. It's monetary faith that they believe that what we have to offer them is worth something. How often has that happened in your life? And it's all because of me. I'm the one who is helping you realize your potential. To help you find who you truly are and where you belong."

"And where's that?"

"Here, with me, by my side."

The highway blurred in front of me. No, it wasn't the highway, it was my eyes. I dropped the phone and gripped the wheel with both hands. Carly woke up beside me.

"What's going on, hun?"

"I don't know," I said. "I can't see. I feel sick."

I pulled into the slow lane. A tomato red car coming up on my right side laid on the horn loud. I didn't see him. A young guy with long hair flipped me the bird. I pulled over, barely stopping the car before I crashed into the guardrail.

"Holy shit, love. You look bad," Carly said.

With just enough time to open the door, I leaned out and puked onto the roadway. My body shuddered and my heart felt like it was going to stop. I vomited again. Everything that I had in me, which wasn't much. It all came up with a bile yellow river on the cold asphalt. Large black ants already sniffed around the puddle I left on the road. And then I dry heaved.

"Oh my god, what's wrong with you?"

"I...don't...know..." The outside air felt like it was thirty-two degrees and I started to shiver. My teeth chattered.

"Are you sick?"

"Feels…that…way."

Carly climbed out of the passenger side. My phone rang again. It was Roderick. He must've disconnected and rang back.

"Don't…answer…it."

"No fucking problemo." Carly came around the car and helped me out. Everything hurt. All my muscles ached, feeling like sacks of broken glass had been sewn under my skin. I screamed in pain.

"Holy shit, hun, you're really bad off. We need to get you to a hospital."

I nodded, even though it hurt my neck muscles to do so. What had come over me? Was it some kind of stomach virus I had picked up? I'd never felt this sick in my life. I felt like only dying would make it better. Carly helped me around the car.

On the highway, cars zipped past, their headlights gleaming. The sound was almost unbearable and their stark white headlights were like shiny daggers that stabbed into my brain.

Carly helped me into the passenger seat. She grabbed her wool pea coat and laid it over me. I shivered under it. I'd never felt so cold in my entire life. The jacket wasn't enough. I needed more warmth that this. But this was all I had.

Carly climbed into the car and grabbed her phone. She Googled the nearest hospital. "There's one in Clydesburg," she said. Then she set the coordinates in her map app. "It's about 15 minutes away. Hang in there, hun."

She checked for traffic, then pulled the Infiniti out onto the highway. My phone rang again under my feet on the floorboard. The sound felt like somebody had shoved a large metal pot over my head and banged it with a ball-peen hammer. "Make it stop."

Carly leaned over and groped for it, still driving with one hand. She picked it up, then silenced it. "What's that cocksucker's problem?"

I couldn't say anything. It hurt to talk. And I was pretty sure whatever I had to say didn't matter because I was going to be dead soon anyway.

THIRTY-ONE

1

When I woke up, I found myself in my bed in Usher House. How did I get here? Had I passed out? Whatever had happened, I felt better. In fact, I felt terrific, like I had gotten about 12 hours of sleep. The sun had just gone down, the rosy fingers of dusk still stretched across the sky, its last grasp before the night consumed all.

I felt at my neckline. Yes, the raven amulet was still there and in place. It hadn't moved. I was fully clothed in a long, old-fashioned dress that I'd never seen before, and yet looked familiar. It was the old kind with the bustier and girdle at the waist. A silken dress over one hundred years out of date and violet in color. I rose. My room looked the same. Maybe a little newer. The wallpaper and furniture weren't as sun-faded.

Walking over to my vanity, I gazed into the mirror. It wasn't my face; it was Eva's face. The face in the oval portrait above the fireplace. How was this possible? Wait a minute. This was a dream. Like the ones I'd been having before. And knowing it was a dream, I needed to wake myself up.

"Wake up," I told myself in the mirror. "Wake up, Madeline." But nothing came out. It was only the silent words that I mouthed.

A knock at my door stirred me from my thoughts. I crossed the bedroom to answer it. Corbin Usher waited for me on the other side of the door. He was pale and handsome with stringy hair the color of soot. He was bundled up in a long, dark overcoat.

"It's time, little sister," he said.

"I know," I said. But I didn't say it. The person who I was occupying, Eva, was saying it. I was a sleeping observer inside this wakeful person. Merely a camera capturing this footage, nothing more. Only a receiver and not a transmitter.

Corbin grabbed my hand. "Come," he said. "We're going to be late."

I pulled my hand aside. "Father will see."

"I don't give a damn about father anymore," Corbin said. "I love you." He touched my belly. That's when I realized that there was a bump there. "Our son will live."

"How do you know it's a boy?"

Corbin smiled. "I don't—but that is my hope. He'll grow into a strong-willed man."

"Father won't accept this. After the baby is born, we cannot hide our love from him anymore. And what of your wife, Annabel?"

"It won't matter. If father doesn't accept us, we'll move from here and be free of him. Free of Usher House. Free to live the life we want to live out from under his iron fist. And you bewitched me, not Annabel—I have no love for her. I only married her because father demanded it. He's an oppressive, insensitive autocrat."

"You're so dramatic, Corby. Our father isn't that bad."

"That's because he likes you best. Now stop dawdling. We're supposed to meet the physician at midnight. He won't wait."

"Let me grab my cloak."

"We'll take the secret way out."

2

A brief ride later in Corbin's black Ford Model T, and we stopped at a little cabin at the end of some dark woods. It was a quaint log cabin with warm, amber light seeping from its windows. When my brother Corbin helped me down the carriage steps, he walked me to the cabin. I wore a black, hooded cloak that covered my hair and face.

"Now don't be afraid."

"I'm not afraid, dear brother. You should be the one who is afraid."

"Oh, why?"

"Because father likes me best. And your wife will not accept this."

Corbin laughed. "They matter as much as the wind." He rapped on the door.

A bald man with a large head answered. I recognized him. Yes, he was the man I had seen in the previous dream. He looked nice and gentle here, serene even, but when I saw him before, he was shouting.

"Here she is," Corbin said.

A moment later and all went black.

THIRTY-TWO

1

"We're here, darlin'."

Carly pulled up to the hospital in Clydesburg, to the Emergency Entrance. The lights under the car port stabbed into my eyes like white-hot needles.

"I was having some fever dreams."

"I know," Carly said. "You were saying all kinds of things in your delirium like 'the baby' and 'Corbin.' It was kind of freaking me out, hun."

She climbed out of the car and walked around to the passenger side. She opened my door. "Let's get you inside so they can see what's wrong with you."

An attendant, a good-looking black man of about thirty, came outside. His nametag said Maurice. "Can I help you ladies?"

"Uh, yeah, Maurice," Carly said. "We were driving to Atlanta and my friend got really sick. Think she has a fever."

"Oh," Maurice said. "If she's contagious, let me go get my mask and some gloves, and then we can take her around and get her checked in. I'll get a mask for you too, miss."

"It's not an infection," I said.

"What?"

"It's not a sickness. It's the house."

"Excuse me?" Carly said.

"What is she talking about? A house?" Maurice said.

"The house. It has something to do with me being away from it," I said, trying to be as loud and clear as I could, but my voice was cracking. "I saw it in my dream."

"Saw it in a dream," Carly said, staring at me like I was crazy.

"Yeah, except it wasn't a dream. It was a vision. It was like I was being shown something. Like an old movie clip. A memory, I guess."

Maurice looked at us like we were a couple of whacked-out white girls. Guess I was—I am an Usher after all. Happy to see I was carrying the family line of insanity. Flying that freak flag proudly with a capital U on the field, fluttering in the breeze.

"It looks like y'all need to work something out," Maurice said. "If you need me, I'll be inside."

"Don't go, darlin'," Carly said, waving at the retreating caregiver.

"Get me back to the house," I said to Carly, grabbing her wrist.

"What? Why?"

"Get me home."

"But you're sick, hun, and we're at the hospital."

"Get me home or I'll die," I gasped. "I can't explain."

"If you fuckin' die on me Mads, I'll kill you."

"If you don't get me home soon, you won't have to worry about doing it."

"OK, love, you're freaking me the fuck out."

"Try being me."

Carly slammed the door and ran around the rental car, then climbed in. She started the car, put it into drive, and roared off into the night.

2

I could tell we were getting closer to Usher House without even knowing where we were going. That velvet glove that felt like it was crushing my heart and lungs had started to release its grip ever so slowly. I could breathe. My mind wasn't racing. The cold sweats and shivering that had clenched me had lifted like dark clouds after a spring storm.

Carly looked over at me. "Holy shit, hun. Your color. It's returned to your face. You were as pale as a fish's belly."

"I feel better." I pointed to the silver raven amulet. "It's this. Whatever this is, it's bewitched or something. It's why I can't take it off. And it's why I can't leave. As long as it's on me, it will keep me prisoner in Usher House."

"You feel sick every time you leave?"

"No," I said. "But the further away I get, something happens. Even at Liam's, I felt a little twinge. It's like I didn't belong there. As much as I tried to believe I did. Then after his dad told me about my family. Well, I guess I don't have a home anymore. Not even in Pickman Flats."

"Are you serious, love? We'll get a place together just like we planned."

I shook my head. "It's too late for that now. This amulet—it *wanted* me to find it. Ezzy helped. I feel this was all planned. Like it was some big cabal."

"You sound like those crazy conspiracy theorists on YouTube, hun. Are you saying this was all a conspiracy against you?"

I nodded. "Yeah, I think it was. I really think that it was." I stared out into the darkness. "It's like this big chess game and I was one of the pieces on the board, only I didn't even know I was a part of the game. Thought I was queen, but I guess I'm a pawn."

Carly stared into the darkness. "All of this shit is crazy, Mads. I love you. And I know that you're not crazy. It's that place that's making you that way. And now you're wanting me to take you back. I don't want anything to happen to you, darlin'. It'd kill me."

I placed a hand on her arm. "I'm going to figure this out for both of us. Maybe you can help me find some answers. Keep close to me. Roderick is on his best behavior when he and I are not alone."

"OK. Harrington's is expecting me back. But I'll tell them I need a few more days. They'll have to run the store without me."

"Thank you, Carly. I love you, too."

3

When we arrived at the Usher House gates, they were swinging open, as if we were being expected. In fact, I knew that we were expected. Roderick knew where I was now that he was tracking me through my phone. Did he know about this raven amulet? Was he the one behind all of this? Was he capable of something like this?

Carly rolled down the dark lane of Usher House. After all that had happened in such a short amount of time, I remembered the first time it had been us together going down this dark and winding lane to the mysterious house at the end of it. That same kind of fear and anxious anticipation struck me again. I thought about calling the Charlton County Sheriff and having him come out here. But what would I say, exactly? What could I tell him? About Creighton? Sure. About my brother being mean to me? Well, it wasn't like he'd hit me. I didn't think there was much the law can do about mental cruelty. About gaslighting. About weirdness. No, I needed to see what Roderick wanted. But this I could tell you. Everything ended tonight. It was getting resolved. I couldn't go on like this. If I was truly trapped at this house thanks to this amulet from my great-great-great aunt who had been killed for allegedly being a witch (let's face it, she was), then things must run at this house my way. I'd use all my powers to keep Roderick in check. I'd find a way to get the upper hand. But how?

I had some ideas.

If I played the weak one, made him think that he'd beaten me, that I'd play the game, then I might trick him when he's defenseless. Lure him into a trap. What trap? I didn't know. Tie him up to a chair and waterboard him? Play the same kind of mental tricks that he'd played on me? No, that wasn't my thing. There was always love. Killing him with kindness. Would *that* work?

Carly pulled up to the front of the house. All of the lights were on.

I had to say, for initially being a creepy house, it still appeared festive and welcoming from the Halloween party the night before. All the jack o' lanterns were lit—a welcome home to a Halloween nightmare world. But a world they welcomed you with open arms and hidden agendas.

"How do you feel, hun?"

"Like my old self—desperate and deranged."

"How are we going to handle your creepy brother?"

I sat for a moment. "We're going to be nice."

"Seriously?"

"Yep. Let him think he's won. Also like it's no big deal. He'll let his defenses down."

Carly shook her head. "I know he's your brother and you know him better than I do, but he's too smart for that. He'll know what you're doing. He's like one of those Bobby Fischer chess grandmasters who's always two moves ahead of everyone else."

I shrugged. "It's all I've got."

"You can always call the cops."

"Don't you think I want to? There's nothing I can really tell them. This has to stop here. With me. With us."

"Guess this is what you call a dilemma," Carly said, nodding. "Either option kinda sucks, hun."

"Yeah, it's a dilemma. But no matter what happens, it's getting resolved tonight. I'm sick of manipulative men. Parker, Roderick, and Liam. Well, he's not manipulative, just spineless. I can't even count on him. He ran away from me at the first sign of trouble."

"Yeah, your track record for men has been total shit." Carly laughed. "Join the club. Maybe all men are shit."

"No, I don't believe that. We've only chosen a few bad eggs from the dozen is all. But one thing I've learned—you really have to count on yourself. No Prince Charming will save you. Sleeping Beauty has to wake up and kick ass alone."

Carly nodded. "Fuck yeah, sister."

We climbed out of the rental car. As I walked to the house, I felt like I had eyes on me. Here outside with me, and from inside. Now I knew how a bug felt under a microscope.

"We should probably hurry inside," I said. "I think Creighton is out here. He's stalking us."

"So you have a bloodthirsty brother outside and one on the inside? Lucky girl."

"Shut up."

The stone gargoyle babbled sulfurous water from its yawing mouth into the putrid fountain. With its horns jutting upward into the night, it seemed to warn Carly and me in its monolithic, fiendish way that we were in imminent danger.

"That thing seriously creeps me out," Carly said. "That's a serious feng shui faux pas, just sayin'."

I went to grab the door handle but the door opened on its own. Mrs. Dietrich stood there.

"Welcome back, miss. And your friend. We've been expecting you."

"No doubt," I said.

Mrs. Dietrich didn't say anything. We stalked in. The electric lights were dimmed, and all the candles in their sconces and on tables were lit. They cast the room in an amber glow and it almost looked like we were stepping into an ancient cathedral. I couldn't help but to remember the first time I'd stepped into the family crypt with all of the wall torches lit. Venturing through the door and across the threshold into Usher House again, I had never felt stronger. But at the same time, I felt like I was walking into my own wake.

"You'll find Master Roderick in the billiards room," the house-keeper said.

Ah, yes, the games room. Where the gamemaster waited for me to make my play.

THIRTY-THREE

1

The tell-tale crack of ivory pool balls.

Six teal frilly lamps hung over the fern-colored cloth table. Portraits of Ushers watched the game from the floral hunter green-wallpapered walls. An orange fire hissed in the hearth.

Roderick wasn't alone in the billiards room. Mr. Walsh was there. So was Darius Wolfe. They were shooting pool. A pitcher of beer on the nearby table and three mugs. It was like they were a few dudes at a pub playing a friendly game. But that wasn't the case. The real game was between me and Roderick.

"Sis," he said, all smiles and bright eyes. "So glad you're home. We were all worried sick about you. Hey, Carly. Want a beer? Mrs. Diet rich can fetch us a couple more frosty mugs. Beer tastes best in a frosty mug, right?"

Be nice. Be nice. Be nice.

"Let's cut the shit, Roderick," I said. "You know why I'm back here. And it wasn't by choice."

"Ms. Usher, please let me explain," Mr. Walsh said.

"No thank you. I'd rather hear it from my dear brother. Alone." I turned to Carly and whispered. "Can you handle these guys for ten minutes?"

She rolled her eyes, walked over, and grabbed a pool stick. "I'll mop the floor with their carcasses." She turned to Darius. "What kind of wager do you want to make, handsome?"

"Wager?" he asked.

"Yeah. I win and you guys come clean with what your real plan is."

Darius smiled. "And if you lose?"

"I don't lose to losers," Carly said with a wink.

"C'mon, Rod," I said. "Let's go to the library. I don't need an audience."

"I'm in the middle of a game with my friends."

"Oh, yes, you're in the middle of a game all right." I snatched the pool stick out of his hands and passed it to Mr. Walsh. "He's going to forfeit the game. Carly will play in his place."

"You're a beautiful beast," Darius said, smiling at her with his perfect teeth. "Get ready to be tamed."

Carly smiled at him. "Wager your bet, darlin'."

2

"What the hell do you think you're doing?"

That was what Roderick asked when I slammed him up against a wall of Proust books in the library. Normally I didn't get violent, but today wasn't normal. Far from it. He pushed me away from him. I fell back a few centimeters, but my fists were clenched. I wanted blood.

"You bastard," I said. "Why are you trying to ruin my life? What did I ever do to you besides having the misfortune of being related?

Like I knew he would, Roderick when from aggressor to victim role. This was typical narcissist, gaslighting behavior. And the more I'd thought about it, the more I realized that's who I was dealing with —a full-blown brother with narcissist personality disorder. The superficial charms, the gifts, the promises, all to get me on his side. It was all gold plating on the bird cage.

"You're so mean to me," he said. "I've done everything for you and you treat me like complete shit." Oh, he was throwing in a martyr complex, too, great. Should I offer him some long nails and a dogwood tree so he can crucify himself properly?

"You did this. All of this." I pointed to the amulet. "Not only have you been interfering with my life—tracking me, selling my house, being jealous around Liam, but you somehow arranged it so I would find all the keys that opened the box that had this amulet in it. This amulet that now prevents me from getting too far away from the house."

He gave me a look of utter surprise. And I knew it was real. Roderick was a good actor, but not that good. He'd never go on stage and thank the Academy for his Oscar-winning performance. But I had to say, his astonished look was the most authentic emotion I've ever seen from him.

"Based on your stupid expression, you have no idea what I'm talking about, right?"

He took a step closer to me to look at the amulet. I kept my guard up, expecting anything from him at this point. "You're saying that that piece of jewelry won't let you leave the house?"

"Oh, I can leave. Only not too far. It's like this weird tether. And I think that if I do get away, I will die. I almost did tonight. I'm bound here in some way I don't completely understand."

"So why don't you take it off?"

"Do you think I'm that stupid, Roderick? Of course I'd take it off. Then I'd bury it out in the swamp. But I can't get it off. It's like it's affixed to me."

He reached out. "Let me try."

I backed away. "Don't touch me. In fact, don't come anywhere near me again. You've acted inappropriately and I'm shutting that shit down now. If we're to have any future, you're going to start acting more like a brother and less like a spurned lover."

Ugh, just saying that made my guts curdle like sour milk.

"So you're stuck here at Usher House," he said, to no one in particular. Mulling it over, I guessed. "But what is it? And why?"

"It belonged to our great-great-great aunt, Eva. She hid it or someone hid it after she died." No, thinking back to my vision, she had it on when she was hanged. That means that somebody had taken it off her corpse, placed it in the three-lock box, and then hid it in the hearth of her fireplace. But who? Corbin? Why would he do that? Nothing made sense. "I don't know how or why it works. I've been having…visions…I guess you could call them. I thought they were only dreams. But they're visions. And they're telling me something. But I only get bits and pieces, so I kind of have to put them all together like a jigsaw puzzle."

"And what have these, uh, 'visions' told you?"

"That Eva and Corbin had had some kind of romantic affair."

Roderick looked aghast. I guessed that was good.

"I don't know if it was mutual or if Corbin had forced himself on Eva. Maybe she had created the amulet and hexed it to protect herself from her brother."

"Maybe. But magic isn't real."

"In the visions," I said, ignoring his comment, "he betrayed her. Made her think she was going to have their baby and they were going to run away. But, instead, a lynch mob, led by Corbin, hanged her. She was wearing the amulet at the time. I found it hidden. I don't know what it all means. Nothing makes sense anymore." I walked toward the window and looked outside at the rising moon ascending over the dark blur of trees. "Nothing has made sense since I first set foot in this house."

"So you're a prisoner here," Roderick said. The way he said it creeped me out. It's like he was weighing the possibilities in his mind and then a little elated that this was my current situation.

"Not necessarily," I countered. "I will figure out a way to undo this spell. It seems to be some kind of black magic. I have means."

"What means?"

Oh, I spoke too quickly. He didn't need to know about Eva's compendium of spells. Somehow he might take it away from me or use it against me. Either way, I had to treat Roderick like an antagonist, an enemy. The only ally I had right now was Carly. And what I needed was to go up into my room with her, lock the door, and figure this thing out. Talking to Roderick was getting nowhere. I had to devise a better plan. Maybe somewhere in Eva's book she'd created a dark spell against Corbin but never was able to conjure it? I wouldn't know until I looked. Now, I was feeling anxious to flee the library, grab Carly from the billiard room, and escape upstairs.

"Where are you going?" Roderick said.

I was heading away from the window and marching toward the door.

"Girl talk time," I said.

Roderick put his hand on the bust of Pallas on the table. It was about the size of a loaf of bread. He picked it up, hefting it.

"'And the Raven never flitting, still is sitting, still is sitting on the bust of Pallas just above my chamber door.'"

"What's quoting Poe supposed to mean?"

Roderick smiled. "It means the Raven is rapping at your chamber door, sis."

"What are you talking about?"

It happened in slow motion and yet I couldn't do anything about it. He raised the bust of Pallas in a threatening manner. Although I raised my hands to defend myself, he struck me in the head with it.

A moment later, everything went raven black.

THIRTY-FOUR

When I woke up, I thought I'd gone blind. My eyes opened up into complete darkness. My head throbbed and when I reached up to touch it, I could feel a stickiness that felt like warm syrup. But I knew it wasn't syrup. My hand grazed the top of something. Then I quickly reached out to the sides. I was in a box. I kicked with my legs. No, not a box, a coffin. And that probably means that I was down in the crypt, in the cherrywood coffin.

Here's where I basically freak the fuck out. I screamed as loud as I could, hoping someone outside of the coffin could hear me. I mean, Roderick didn't put me in here and leave me, did he? He was outside, right? This was some more of his gaslighting bullshit. He was probably outside the casket, wanting to hear me freak out, and then he'd open up the lid and say that he was joking, and why couldn't I take a joke?

It wasn't a joke. No one came to my aide. I screamed myself hoarse.

Then something clicked next to my head.

And a voice. Roderick's voice came over some electronic device.

"Hello, Madeline Usher, are you awake? This is your wake-up call."

I fumbled for where the voice was coming from. It was a two-way radio. The red light was the only glow within this dark tomb. Somehow reassuring. I pressed the talk switch.

"You locked me in a coffin? Get me out of here. Get me out of here now!"

Roderick laughed over the radio. "You should save your breath. I figure you probably have about thirty minutes of air in there. The more you scream and cry, the more you're going to use up. And you don't want to do that, do you? After all, I'm the only one who knows where you're at. If you make me mad, I might just, you know, forget where you are. Think of all the money we'd save on a funeral and burial."

"You're fucking insane, Roderick. Do you hear me? Let me out of here right now. This isn't fucking funny! I will kill you. Do you understand? I. Will. Kill. You."

"Like I said, you should save your breath. And idle threats are a waste of it. What we should really be discussing—in your very limited time—is the future. *Our* future."

"We don't *have* a future."

"Well, now, that's up to you. I can do this alone, but, believe it or not, I like you, even love you. I feel like you're a part of me. We're twins after all. Well, triplets if truth be told, but you know, that member of the family is a write-off. Locked away in his own prison. Don't make me do the same with you."

"You're going to kill me? Bury me alive?"

"No, not necessarily. As I said, the choice is yours. Promise that you'll play nice and I'll let you out of the penalty box. Keep being the bitch and you can remain there for the rest of your short life. If you keep that ego in check, you might just live."

He was insane. He was beyond a narcissist. He was a narcissistic sociopath. What kind of normal person could lock somebody in a coffin—alive? Their own flesh and blood? I had underestimated Roderick. And that may have been a fatal move.

"OK," I said. "You win. I'll do whatever you want. Just let me out."

Roderick laughed over the radio. I was beginning to really hate that laugh. "Yeah, you see, I knew you'd say that. Any rational person will say whatever to avoid death. They'll say that they'll 'do anything' to end the torture. But what then? Broken promises afterward? No, that won't do. I need some kind of guarantee that if I let you out of your early grave that you'll concede. You'll end this idea of running away or being anything but Madeline Usher, my sister."

"What do you want, a signed declaration?"

"You know, that's not a bad idea."

"Fine, bring it down and I'll sign whatever. Just get me out of here."

"So, if I brought down paperwork that would impart all your shares to me, and that you are indebted to me—your love and any future wages—will all be mine. That if you ever leave, you will forfeit everything? You will sign that?"

What do I do? Die in less than thirty minutes suffocating to death in my own coffin or sign my life away to my mentally ill brother? Decisions, decisions. Talk about dilemma. This was about the shittiest dilemma that I've ever had to choose between. Absolute shit.

"Before you answer," Roderick said, "you'd better think long and hard. But don't take too long—or you'll run out of oxygen." He laughed. He was mad, truly mad.

I brought my knees up as far as I could toward my chest. Maybe I could push the lid open. Shove with my hands and push with my knees. Maybe I could free myself. I pushed with everything I had. It was useless. First, I didn't have the momentum to move the lid, secondly, it was probably locked from the outside. I was going to die in here unless I played his game.

"Fine," I said. "I'll just die in here." Yeah, I was bluffing, but I wanted to see if I could freak him out a little bit. Get him to change his tune.

"That's what you want? That's your big decision? Cash in your chips, metaphorically speaking, and push yourself away from the poker table of life."

"Yeah."

"Alright," he said. "I thought you were smarter, but I guess I overestimated you. That's on me. Have a nice, long sleep." He clicked off.

What did I do, did I just seal my fate?

The radio clicked. "In case you change your mind, I'll check back in in five minutes. We'll see how cast iron your will is then. Until then, enjoy your respite."

The radio clicked again.

I closed my eyes. Tried to think, which was hard with my heart racing. I needed to calm down. But I couldn't breathe. Did Roderick know I was phobic of tight places too? Breathe. Calm. Deep breaths.

Tears streamed from my eyes. This was it. I couldn't let him win. But he would no matter what decision I chose. If I played along and gave up, he would ensure that he would dominate me. He was calculating. The chess grandmaster had figured out all of the moves ahead of time.

I wiped my eyes.

Meow.

What was that? A faint sound near my head.

Meow.

It was Esmerelda.

Had he put her down here in the crypt? No, I doubted it. He would have probably put her in the coffin with me. She must've followed Roderick down here.

"Hey, girl can you get me out of here?"

Silence.

You have led yourself into this box willingly and now you must lead your way out?

I wasn't sure if the voice had come from outside the coffin or inside my own head. It seemed to be everywhere, and yet, nowhere, if that made any sense.

"Where are you?"

You already know the answer to that.

The voice from my dreams. It's the same voice.

"Eva?"

You will die soon if you do not remove yourself from this casket.

I pounded on the heavy lid. "I can't get out."

If you did get out, what would you do? How would you stop your brother?

"I don't know. He's so powerful and was playing me this entire time."

Why did you willingly step into his trap?

"I don't know. I guess I needed to belong to something. Maybe that's been my problem my entire life. Growing up an orphan and needing to belong. Needing a family. And never finding one. And then, when I do, it again turns out to be shit."

I am your family—the only one that you ever need.

"But you're dead."

Could the dead interact with you? Could the dead have led you to find the keys? The box? The amulet? The spell book?

"You did all that?"

I never died, I simply changed forms. A form I have lived in for a century. And I have waited a long time for your arrival.

I felt around inside the coffin for some way to get out. The air had grown stuffier, harder to breathe. My heart beat faster. My breathing more rapid. Panic was setting in.

You have the means of escape.

"But how?"

The solution I cannot give. The answer must come from within you. If you do not discover the solution, you will die, and I will have underestimated you.

I breathed slower. Controlled my breathing. Counted the breaths one-two-three-four-five exhale. Yes. *Calm.* Growing up, when I was stressed out, this old hippie lady in the park one day had taught me how to meditate. I'd asked what she was doing sitting alone with her eyes closed and her legs crossed under her skirt. She'd taught me about counting breaths. Since then, I'd used it to calm myself down when I got stressed out. A few times in the store after dealing with nasty and rude customers, I'd had to take a break and retreat into the bathroom, doing deep, slow breaths, to calm myself.

One-two-three-four-five-one-two-three-four-five-one-two-three-four-five.

Feeling calmer, I attempted to collect my thoughts. Answer. What answer? What solution? Damn it. Then, I recalled something

I'd read in Eva's compendium book of spells. That first day that I found it. It was strange, but that was the first page that I had turned to. It was a spell for releasing your bonds. Could it work here? Oh, if I could only remember it. I concentrated. Concentrated hard. I tried to recall the words on the page. I had had an advanced English class in high school where we studied Latin to learn all of the root words. I tried to recall what "release my bonds" might be. The tightness of the coffin made me lose my concentration. Then, yes, as plain as day, I had a total recall of the words, as if looking at them on the page.

I spoke them aloud: *"Vincula mea dimittere."*

Nothing. I tried again.

Nothing. OK, third time's a charm?

I concentrated and said each word with conviction: *"Vincula mea dimittere."*

A clack sounded somewhere inside the box. Holy shit. With my feet and hands, I pushed the heavy lid open. The stagnant air of the crypt smelled so sweet to me in that moment. Fresh air. Or fresher air than being stuffed in a corpse box.

Lit torches in their metal sconces lined the dark brick walls. They crackled. The shadows of the crypt seemed to swallow all of their light, making what would normally be cheerful firelight seem lifeless and anemic. The bronze placards of the Usher names all glimmered in the firelight.

Meow.

Esmerelda waited for me. Then she jumped up into my arms and purred.

"That wasn't you talking to me, was it?"

The cat only peered at me with her perfect emerald eyes.

"No, I guess not. That would be crazy." Did I imagine that interaction?

I stroked her fur, particularly on her breastbone with the creamy white patch in the shape of a crescent moon. Then I noticed something. The patch of fur was the same shape as the raven amulet. It had been there the entire time and I hadn't noticed.

"Are you really Eva? Are you, what they call an animal familiar? Did you really change forms after you were murdered?"

The cat gazed into my green eyes with her own.

The radio crackled. "Mads, you there?" It was Roderick. If I don't answer it, he'd either think I was dead or I somehow escaped or I was ignoring him. It might bring him down here. But if I did answer him, I'd have to deal with him. But maybe it would buy me some time. Damn.

Esmeralda jumped from my arms. I picked up the radio and pretended like I was out of breath.

"I'm...here..."

"Are we still feeling strong or has some of the wind gone out of your sails?"

"You might kill me...Roderick...but you'll never possess me... And if I have to die in this box...I'd rather do that than have to live with you..."

"You goddamn bitch—I'll fucking kill you!"

"You already have."

I sat the radio back down in the open coffin.

"Mads? Madeleine? *Answer* me?"

Then I shut the lid to suffocate his voice.

Shit, I was hoping that would buy me some time. But I may have just pissed him off. I needed to get out of here. The only problem was that the only way out of the crypt was through the iron gate and up the stairs. Undoubtedly, the iron gate and the cellar door beyond were locked. Maybe the Ushers had hid a key? I headed toward the gate. Maybe by some miracle of miracles there was a key? But even if I escape the crypt, I may be spotted on the main floor and end up right back down here. Shit, I'm trapped.

Esmerelda meowed.

"Not now, girl, we're having a serious situation."

What was I going to do? I was still trapped down here. Guess I would have to fight. But with what? He'd no doubt have his cronies with him. Out of the coffin and into the fire. *Fire!* Maybe I could grab one of the torches and use it as a weapon. Try to burn them?

I was about to tell that to Ezzy when I noticed that she'd vanished.

"Ezzy?"

A faint meow from somewhere but it was not inside the room.

"Ezzy, where are you?"

She meowed again. I followed where I thought the sound came from. A brick wall. How did she pass through it? Then, down by my feet, I noticed a wide crack between the bricks. It was narrow but she must've squeezed in there.

"Ezzy, you get back here."

She went quiet.

I grabbed the torch to get a look down there and see if I could find her. As I pulled it out of the metal sconce on the wall, the bricks shook. At first it was like an earthquake, and then the wall opened into blackness like a gaping wide mouth. The smell was musty and damp. The air made the torch flame flutter. That meant air was coming from inside. It didn't smell like fresh air. More like stagnant air. I searched the murky darkness for the black cat.

"Ezzy?"

Her emerald eyes appeared in the firelight. She meowed and then vanished into the darkness. It was like she wanted me to follow her. I guess she hadn't steered me wrong so far. There was a sound behind me. Footsteps on the stairs. It must be Roderick and his friends. Time to go. I'd rather take my chances in this spider-infested hole than deal with my blood-sucking brother.

I pushed the brick door closed so they wouldn't follow me.

And then I wandered into the darkness.

THIRTY-FIVE

*I*t was a tight squeeze in this dark passageway. I didn't know if Roderick or Mr. Walsh knew about this secret passage (pretty sure the latter would), but I was not waiting around to find out. I wondered if this was the secret passage that Eva and Corbin Usher had used one hundred years ago? Where did it lead? Were there connecting passages?

Spider webs clasped at my hair. I used the torch to burn them out of my path the best I could. The flames licked the dirty, silky strands and scrambled up the sides of the walls, then burned themselves out. Creepy crawlies scurried away from the light.

I couldn't even think about it or I'd scream. I focused ahead only.

I couldn't see anything beyond the light of the torch.

Ezzy's occasional meows guided me. Just my luck there was a secret passage in Usher House. Of course there was. If you lived in a crumbling haunted mansion, it had better have at least one secret passage or it would get its B-movie horror license revoked. But why have one in the crypt of all places? Who would want to secretly visit a crypt? It was made by Ushers, though. Who was I to question their reasons and sanity, or lack thereof? I was pretty sure I'd had a conversation from inside a casket with a cat.

As I wandered through this passage, I couldn't help but remember that invitation and airline ticket I received in the mail. It seemed like it was years ago. And now, here I was, somewhere down in the bowels of Usher House, running away from my vicious twin brother. *Have a good time in Georgia at Usher House. We'll have some laughs.* Yeah, right.

I wondered where this passage lead. If it went up into the house, then there should be some stairs somewhere, right? Or maybe a ladder? Then I had a chilling thought. What if a secret passage was started but never completed? What if it didn't go anywhere? What if I was trapped within the walls of the house and died? I shivered. A draft was coming from somewhere.

Stop freaking yourself out and making a bad situation even worse.

A moment later, I nearly collided with a rusty iron gate. It was completely enveloped in ivy. I set the torch against the wall. The flames licked the bricks in an attempt to find fuel, starving. There didn't seem to be a lock, just a bolt. It took all of my effort to slide it open. Then I pushed on the bars. They wouldn't move. Dammit. I'd come all of this way and I was still trapped. I pushed and pulled on the bars. I even lay down on my back and attempted to push the gate open with my feet. It didn't work.

"Ezzy, where are you at?"

She was silent.

No doubt she'd climbed through the bars and the thick veil of green ivy leaves.

"Ezzy?"

Two hands burst through the ivy and seemed to grab at me. I screamed.

No, they didn't grab for me, they grabbed the bars and pulled. Dirty, strong hands.

The iron creaked and then the papery rustle of ivy as the gate was torn loose.

I stood there, now looking at the exit. Who did that?

The hand appeared back through the ivy. It wanted me to take it.

Great, no choice—there's no place to run.

So I took that hand and I was pulled through the ivy. The leaves clung to my head and shoulders. I felt like I was being borne out of Usher House and back into the world once again. The cold and dark night November world.

My savior smiled at me. The first time he's ever smiled at me. He displayed his yellow, crooked teeth. Smoker's teeth. It was Knapp.

Then he placed his thick, dirty finger to his lips. I found that odd and funny considering he cannot speak. Of course, he was telling *me* not to speak. Ezzy wrapped herself around my ankles. I scooped her up. Then I trailed Knapp who was heading off into the moonlight.

Where was he taking me? I should be wary. He worked for my brother and Mr. Walsh. If he wanted to harm me, though, he could have. So I continued to follow him.

He led me to what appeared to be a wall of ivy. He fished out a large skeleton key from his soiled tan dungarees and jammed it into the metal lock of an ancient-looking wooden gate. He opened the gate and like a gentleman, stood aside and allowed me to enter first. I couldn't see much in the darkness. The silvery moonlight revealed these grotesque, phantomic shapes within. Fear gripped me.

"It's safe," Knapp said, his voice raspy like an old, untuned piano.

"Wait, you can *speak*?"

He gestured inside the gated area. "Inside. Quickly, please."

Sucking in a breath, I took a step inside. As I did, the song of trickling water danced in my ears.

Knapp closed and locked the gate behind me with a resounding metal *thunk*.

"How can you talk? What's going on? And who puts a secret passage in a crypt?"

Knapp smiled. "One question at a time, please, ma'am."

"I'm all ears."

"I can speak, miss, when there's something that must be said."

"That's good."

"From my understanding, the original Mr. Usher had the passage built so he could abscond off for evening strolls." He lowered his eyes. "I know your father, Vincent Usher, used it in his lifetime."

Of course he did. To sneak out at night and go see Liam's mom no doubt.

"What *is* this place?"

The garden was protected by a seven-foot high wall covered in ivy surrounding it. As my eyes better adjusted to the darkness, the phantomic forms took on more benevolent of structures. Ghostly shapes under the pale moonlight. Marble statues of chubby cherubs and beautiful goddesses. The trickling water originated from a fountain which was round in shape and teaming with lily pads. A pale stone sculpture of two children, a boy and a girl playing, was near the rising water. Even in the darkness, I couldn't help but think that those two children resembled Roderick and I, perhaps in an alternate universe when we might have grown up together here at Usher House.

"This is my sanctuary," Knapp said. "My own private place. It was built by Edgar Usher for his wife, but she didn't prefer it. The children are supposed to represent Corbin and Eva. Allegedly they met here in secret after nightfall. After her death and Corbin's suicide, Edgar ordered the garden sealed off. It became a secret garden, I guess. When I came here fifty years ago, it was nothing but ragweed and ruins. But over the years, I restored it in private. None of the Ushers either noticed or cared that it's here. So it has become mine. But, of course, it's yours, ma'am, it rightly belongs to you."

"Uh, no, I'm good. Really. You put in the hard work. I wish I could see it. I'm sure it's beautiful in the daylight."

"They won't find us here, but there's no time. You're in danger, ma'am. You have been ever since you've arrived."

"And you're just telling me this *now*, Mr. Knapp?"

"Josef, please, ma'am. Call me Josef. If you wish."

"OK, Josef. I know that I'm in danger. My brother basically has destroyed my life and locked me in a fucking coffin. It's pretty obvious he's not throwing me a goddamn surprise party."

"Mr. Walsh had plans. I've heard them. To get you and Roderick together. Then you were to die and Roderick would own everything. And, I believe Mr. Walsh wants you both dead so he can benefit. At least that's what I've heard. I'm a good listener."

"But that doesn't make any sense. Why wouldn't he just take it all when he had the chance and we didn't know who we were?"

"As long as your deaths weren't verified, he couldn't legally do anything. And then when your brother met you, things changed. He has an…unwholesome…attraction to you."

I cringed. "Yes, I've noticed. Thanks for reminding me, Josef."

"Roderick wants you alive. But he will kill you if you don't do what he wants."

"He, uh, made that perfectly clear when he locked me in the family crypt."

"You need to get far away from here, ma'am, and never come back. Protect your life."

I pointed to the amulet around my neck. "There's a problem. I can't leave. I nearly died when I tried to. It seems that I'm stuck here. Some family curse or witchcraft or some shit. Basically, I'm as fucked as a fox in a fur farm."

Knapp peered at the amulet that glinted in the moonlight. He gasped. "That belonged to Lady Eva Usher."

"Yeah, I'm aware."

"There are stories that she was a powerful witch and that she had sold her soul to the devil. That she made some kind of pact with him."

I nodded.

"What keeps you here… What's in that piece of jewelry is the devil's power. It's evil."

Do I really want to tell him that I basically used "Satan's power" to free myself from a casket? Naw.

"Thanks. I'd love to take it off, but I can't."

Knapp retreated a step back from me as if I were going to hurt him. "You have her power. Eva's power. The devil's power."

"Well, I don't feel too powerful. In fact, I feel like a goddamned failure."

"I can help you no further."

"But my friend is in there. I've got to get her out."

Knapp shook his head. "I am sorry, miss. I wish I could. But as long as you walk with that amulet on you, you walk alone. I cannot consort with its evil."

"So what the hell am I supposed to do now, handyman?"

Knapp gave me a vacant look.

"Fine, you know what, it's fine." I nodded to the gate. "Can you let me out?"

"Of course."

He rummaged the skeleton key back out of his pocket and unlocked the secret garden gate. I made a mental note that if I survived the night, I must come back and look at it in the daylight. I was sure it's absolutely gorgeous.

"Oh, uh, Josef, one more thing."

"Yes, ma'am."

I handed him my cat. "Take care of her for me, she's special."

He looked at the cat, holding it as if I had handed him a sopping wet rag drenched in sewer water. He set her down. "She is not a cat. I have seen this beast during my decades of working here, never aging a day. It is the devil's power that makes it so, too."

"Fine," I said. "Can you make sure the devil spawn doesn't follow me?"

The moon had vanished behind some clouds. It grew darker.

I started to head off, then stopped. "Uh, Josef? Do you have some kind of flashlight?"

Josef produced a silver pen from his tattered tweed jacket. Then he depressed the button. It was a penlight. Not too bright but it would have to do. "Thanks."

Rain began to pelt down. Large drops the size of dimes. At first they came slowly, but within a couple of minutes, a cloudburst opened up. The cold November rain soaked me to the bone. I would have to be wet and cold; I had no other choice.

I headed for the fence line. It'd be ideal and shorter to go around to the front of the house and go out that way. But there was a good chance I could be spotted by Roderick or Mr. Walsh. Or Creighton. In all of this excitement, I had forgotten about him...

A chill ran through me.

What if he was out hunting tonight? All I had to defend myself was a measly penlight. I wondered how Mr. Knapp fared with Creighton. He'd likely would have had his run-ins with him over the years. Maybe Knapp hid after dark? Maybe Creighton didn't stalk him or find him a threat? Who knew?

I tried to climb the fence in a place, but as I reached the top, I slipped on the wet metal and the razor-sharp spike slashed my index finger. Hot blood jetted from my finger and streamed inside the palm of my hand. Time to find that hole in the fence. Hopefully Creighton, if he was out, was in the swamp. And that he couldn't smell fresh blood from a few hundred yards. That would be bad. Perhaps I'd be safe in the rain.

Lightning flashed. In front of my eyes, my surroundings, for a moment, looked like a camera negative. Thunder rumbled a few seconds later. The storm was closing in.

I dashed along the fence line, sloshing my feet in the wet leaves. My only hope was to climb through the hole and head to Liam's house. We left on bad terms, but I needed his help. The penlight barely lit my way as I scrambled over the uneven ground.

Brambles lashed at my hands and face.

Thorny branches whipped at my eyes and slapped my cheeks. Kudzu vines grabbed at my arms and clutched my legs like floral octopus tendrils.

My heart pounded in my ears.

The rain stung my eyes.

Lungs gasped for air.

I stopped to catch it. I wished I had my phone right now. It'd be so easy to just call him. To call anyone, really. But would he answer? Would he even be happy to see me if I go to his door? Guess I would have to find out. As I got ready to run again, the crack of a branch somewhere in the darkness grabbed my immediate attention. That was just a deer or a rabbit, right?

I shined the penlight in the direction of the sound.

Lightning flashed and in that millisecond, a face was illuminated from the darkness.

Peering through the brush was the face of Creighton. He had found me. He snarled his sharp teeth at the light, strands of saliva dripping from his mouth. The rain had matted his hair.

And then he charged me.

THIRTY-SIX

1

I ran.

When a feral person who has had his meals shoved under a door and no socialization whatsoever surges toward you—you stand in place and die—or run. He caught up to me quickly. I ran behind an old hickory tree, trying to keep it between us; he would charge one direction, I would run in the opposite. I tried to figure out what to do. He would rip me to pieces like he did that deer. He had nearly killed Mr. Walsh—and he would have if it wasn't for the tranquilizer gun. I wished I had that gun now.

"Creighton! It's me, your sister." Yeah, I knew, he didn't understand language. But I had to try. "Please, I want to help you." I did my best to not make direct eye contact with him or act scared. I was once at the zoo in Portland and certain signs of aggression, like direct eyesight, could provoke them. Some people too. And if a wild animal sensed your fright, you were also in trouble. Except I was terrified and I'd never been that good of an actor.

Lightning flashed again and the image of his contorted face burned into my brain. I'd seen that look before—the same look before attacking Mr. Walsh. Creighton was out on the hunt. He wanted blood. And apparently my blood would do.

I couldn't keep this game up though; I was getting tired. Soon enough he'd overtake me and I'd be done for. I didn't even want to imagine being torn apart by his overgrown nails or jagged-looking teeth.

Lightning flashed again. This time my silver raven amulet caught the light. It flashed. Creighton seemed interested in it. He stopped, staring at it. He even turned his head trying to understand it, the way a dog would when they heard a sound they didn't quite recognize. I wished I could remove it and give it to him. Maybe the amulet had some kind of fascination to him. Maybe not. Could he sense the supernatural properties of it? There was no chance I could make it to the hole in the fence. It was too far away—and I couldn't hold him off. This would all end in a matter of seconds. Would it be with me dead? How ironic would that be? Escaping one brother trying to murder me by imprisoning me only to be killed by my other brother who's imprisoned.

Whatever mystical sway the amulet might have held over Creighton had ended. He jumped one direction, and then doubled back. Clever boy.

He grabbed me by the arm. He jerked it so hard I was worried he would pull it from my shoulder socket. I screamed in pain. My scream would be the death of me—I knew it. But he jumped back. Maybe my loud voice hurt his ears? Could his hearing be more developed? His strength and sense of smell seemed to be, why not? I slowly walked backwards. Maybe he'd let me get away. He just stood there, watching me.

But I tripped over a tree root and fell on my back.

He was upon me in a second.

His hot breath in my face stank like rotten meat. I knew it was the end.

Lightning flashed again.

Then, for some reason, a word popped into my brain. Ignite. No, not ignite. *Ignis*. The Latin word for fire. Why did that happen? The lightning? Something told me to say it aloud. So I did—as loud as I could. I figured it was the last word I would ever say.

"Ignis!"

Creighton stopped what he was doing and looked at me. Drool fell from his mouth and onto my cheek. I was too terrified to be disgusted. The word seemed to stop him.

I repeated the word. This time throwing everything I could in it.

A light exploded all around me. At first, I thought the lightning had struck close. But no, it came from the amulet. A flash of blinding light that lit up the woods as far as the eye could see.

Creighton immediately covered his face with a hairy arm and jumped back. He screamed. He came at me again. Only this time, he stumbled. The light apparently had blinded him.

"IGNIS!"

Light blasted from the amulet again. Creighton screamed. And this time, he turned and ran. The blinding light seemed too much for him. Curious as the light didn't harm me. Only like another flash of lightning. This must be one of the defenses of the amulet? If I survived tonight, I must study the compendium of spells. Pretty sure I'd find it in there. Cold from the rain, I aimed the penlight and headed for the hole in the fence. A few minutes later, I had found it and slipped through the iron bars.

2

Leaving the fence, I ran across the muddy fields of Delaney farms. Out in the open, the penlight and the occasional flashes of lightning provided enough light for me to see without tripping myself. It was hard to believe that a fortnight ago, Liam and I had been riding horses across here in the noonday sun without a care in the world. And now, here I was, literally running for my life in a world of rainwater and mud and thunderous rumbles.

My stomach started to knot up a little. I knew that it wasn't from me running. It was the amulet. I had that queasy feeling again. *Strange.* Carly and I were miles away before when I started getting sick. Now, I was maybe a mile from Usher House and I could feel it coming on. Why was that? Could it be that I had used its abilities? Did that have something to do with it? Did that make it stronger? Guess it was a good trade off. I had to save my life twice using whatever witchcraft was in this thing. Was it the power of Satan? I didn't believe in Satan. Not that I was a total atheist; I'd always been more of an agnostic. But what I'd experienced with this amulet I would say that there's a supernatural realm. This wasn't any ordinary power that I'd ever seen.

A brilliant flash and an elm tree exploded beside me, struck by lightning. The stench of ozone made the moist air burn. The broken tree, burning, extinguished quickly in the drowning rainfall. That was close. It felt as though that that bolt had been meant for me. Had it?

The Delaney farm looked so welcoming with its warm glow of lights from the house. What a truly welcoming sight. I hoped that Snooker the Border Collie was inside or my arrival would be announced. The house looked so warm and cozy. My teeth chattered in the cold rain. I kept moving to try and keep warm. As I climbed on the porch, something black and fast jumped in front of me. At first I thought it was a giant rat.

Meow.

"Ezzy, what are you doing here? You escaped from Mr. Knapp and followed me, didn't you?"

Meow.

Guess that meant yes. Esmerelda was soaking wet and looked like a drowned rat.

I peeked in the windows at the blue flickering light in the living room. Mr. Delaney sat in a rust-colored Barcalounger chair with his stocking feet propped up eating what looked like an entire Dutch apple pie out of the pan and watching Sean Hannity on Fox News. Snooker laid passed out in his bed at his master's feet.

Could I sneak in through the front door and up the stairs without him hearing me? Guess I'd have to.

I wiped my feet on the welcome mat the best I could. The last thing I needed to do was trail in a bunch of wet and muddy footprints.

Then I tried the front door, it was locked. Damn. I could try the back door, but there wasn't time. Then I had an idea. It worked once.

I touched the locked door, and then concentrated and said each word I with quiet conviction: *"Vincula mea dimittere."*

The door unlocked. It worked—first try!

Opening it, I stepped inside hoping that the old oak door didn't creak. It gave a little squeak but the commentator's blaring voice on the TV must have covered the sound as Mr. Delaney didn't turn his head. He kept his fork moving from pie tin to pie hole in a fairly rhythmic motion. Was Mr. Delaney self-medicating with food from today's events or did he always eat like this?

The narrow staircase lay right in front of me.

Fortunately, it was an enclosed staircase so that Mr. Delaney wouldn't see me going up. I only hoped that the worn wooden stairs wouldn't squeak as I climbed them. The warmth from the house warmed my chattering bones a little.

As if showing me how easy it was, Ezzy skipped past my feet and scrambled up the stairs as silent as a shadow. She waited for me up on the landing.

I sucked in a frigid breath and crept upon the first stair, trying to stay on the sides of the stairs so my weight wouldn't make them creak and groan as much as I knew they would in this old farmhouse. It felt like it took ten years to slink up the stairs, and I panicked that Mr. Delaney would stop his pie-and-TV fest and walk right past as I was doing my best ninja impression.

"You stay the hell away from my son and don't come back here." I remembered of the last things he said to me. *"You're not welcome. I don't want any Ushers on Delaney soil."*

3

I reached the second-floor landing without discovery. The hallway was dark, but a light on under a door and the faint sound of Sam Smith crooning "To Die For" clued me into Liam's room. I tip-toed to the door, turned the brass knob, and cracked it open. Ezzy scooted in past my feet and squeezed through the opening.

Liam, sitting cross-legged on the hardwood floor, had a sketchpad on his lap and drew a portrait. I didn't recognize the woman, but I guessed it to be his mother. He was drawing it from an old photograph paper clipped to the page. The charcoal drawing looked photorealistic. He was good, really good.

His room was neat and orderly, everything in its place. Not a room you'd expect a teenage boy to have. He didn't have any sports posters or bikini-clad girls on his walls. Instead, he had framed prints of famous art—I recognized Edward Hopper and Van Gogh among them. Even his bed was made. Points for classiness, Liam.

Ezzy leapt into his lap.

Liam jumped. "Hey, where did *you* come from?" He stroked her wet fur.

"You *might* want to set her down," I said, tip-toeing into his room. "I'm not one hundred percent sure she's a cat. She may be an animal familiar sent from hell who was once my great-great-great-aunt hanged for witchcraft."

Liam dropped the cat on the floor and wiped his hands. He gazed up, and then he knitted his eyebrows together. "What are you doing here?"

"The door was unlocked."

"Pops let you *in?*"

"Uh, no, he was kind of occupied, so I didn't really want to bother him."

"You shouldn't be here."

I wanted to cry, but I held back my emotions. "I didn't have any place to go."

"Wait, were you serious about the cat?"

"Yeah," I said. "Things have gotten a bit weird. I'll explain later."

Liam shook his head "You're soaking wet." He dropped his sketchpad, face down, I noticed, so I wouldn't see his drawing. He grabbed a fleece blanket with a Bengal tiger on it off his bed and wrapped me up in it. The cocoon of warmth made me relax a little.

Liam peered again at my disheveled appearance. "What happened to you?"

"I, uh, got into a fight with some brambleberries. I lost. And then it rained."

"You're all dirty. You look like you crawled out of a grave or something."

"Yeah, I kinda did."

"What the hell are you talking about?

"I need your help."

Sam Smith sang about wanting somebody to die for. Apropos, Sam, apro-fucking-pro.

"Excuse me?"

I explained everything that happened since I left his house. Everything. And when I was done, I wasn't sure if Liam was going to hug me or hate me. Fortunately, he did the former. Thank goodness as I'd had it with loved ones trying to murder me.

"Will you help me?"

He looked at me. His eyes misted. Then he hugged me again. "I was so miserable without you. Nothing seemed right. I was beside myself."

"I was only away from you like twelve hours."

"It was too long."

He kissed me, long and hard. It warmed my shivering body. He broke free. I caught my breath. "Let me, uh, get you some dry clothes at least."

"You don't have anything that would fit me."

He held up a finger. "Wait here."

He vanished for a moment. Ezzy pawed a pencil on the hardwood floor. Then Liam returned. In one hand, he had a bath towel; in the other, some folded clothes. A white blouse, a gray cable knit sweater, and some jeans. "They were my mom's. I think you two are about the same size." He handed me the towel and the clothes. "I'll, uh, just turn my head."

He did. I dropped the blanket, and then danced out of my dishrag-wet clothes down to my bra and underwear. I wished I could change them too into some dry ones but I wasn't about to wear Liam's mother's underthings. It was already weird enough to be putting on her clothes, a dead woman's clothes. I toweled off my hair and body. After that, I climbed into the jeans. They were warm, comfortable, and even a bit stylish, not your typical "mom jeans" at all. So was the blouse. The knit sweater was snug and warm against my cool skin. He was right, the clothes fit me as if they were my own. His mother was a small woman. Thank god for small favors, literally. "OK," I said. "I'm decent."

He turned around. "Wow, you look…better."

I pushed the dark, damp tendrils of hair out of my face. "Do you have a rubber band or something?"

He handed me one from his desk. I tied my wet strands into a ponytail. "We don't have much time. Carly needs my help."

Liam picked up his phone. "Then I'm calling the police. Your brother's behavior is criminal. He has to be reported."

"If you call the cops, your dad will know I'm here. What will he say?"

"You're right. Nothing good."

The *thump-thump-thump* of footsteps came from down the hall.

"It's Pops," Liam whispered. "Hide."

A moment later, the man of the house threw open the door.

And he seemed upset.

THIRTY-SEVEN

1

My heart racing, I squatted behind Liam's bed, clutching the black cat from hell.

"Were you outside?" his father asked.

Then I noticed my discarded wet clothes and towel in the middle of the floor. I held Ezzy close to me, my hand over her mouth so she wouldn't make a peep.

"Why?"

"There's water droplets all over the stairs and floor. And mud in places."

"Yeah, I had to grab something out of my truck. Sorry, I'll clean it up."

"I didn't hear you come and go."

"Uh, you were pretty engaged in Hannity. And I didn't want to bother you." Liam noticed my clothes in the middle of the floor. With a surreptitious nudged of his stocking foot, he scooted them under the bed.

"Your hair's not even wet."

Liam pointed to the towel on the floor. "Dried off."

His father sighed. "Well, I'm going to bed. You should too. We have a long day tomorrow. But take that towel and clean up that mess first."

"Yeah, I will, Pops. Good night."

"G'night."

His father lumbered out of the doorway and Liam shut his door. He waited a moment, listening, and then gave the all-clear sign with a wave of his hand.

"We've got to get you out of here," he said.

"Yeah. Can I make it out without being seen?"

"If we go now. He'll be in his bathroom. He'll be in there a few minutes. Now, excuse me. You can avert your eyes."

Liam slipped off his heather gray Charlton County High School t-shirt. I turned my head, but I kind of cheated and looked at his reflection in the window. He had lean arms knotted with muscle from working long hours in the fields. His torso was also slender with well-defined abdominal muscles. I bit my tongue. He slipped off his plaid pajama bottoms down to his black boxer briefs. He looked like an Olympic swimmer or a fitness model. But this wasn't a body built by vain hours in a gym, this was hard-earned farm muscle. Liam slipped into some faded jeans and a black Henley shirt. He stuffed his feet into some weather-beaten work boots.

"You can turn around now," he said. "I'm decent."

I turned and smiled. *Yes, you are decent, my handsome friend.*

He then reached under his bed, fishing around. He pulled out a nickel-plated automatic pistol with a mother of pearl handle. And then he stuffed it in the waistline of his jeans.

"Do you really need a gun?"

"Can't hurt," he said with a shrug. "Why?"

"I'm not used to them. They've, uh, always made me nervous."

"It's just a precaution," he said grabbing his Carhartt jacket. "Let's go."

I turned over his face-down drawing on the bed. "By the way, you draw really well."

"Oh, uh, thanks. I was, you know, doodling."

"By drawing a picture of your mother while listening to Sam Smith?"

Liam shrugged. "I miss her sometimes. She was about the only person in my family to really understand me. Ready?"

I nodded and scooped up the cat. Liam opened the door, waited, and then motioned for me to go. I slipped past him. Liam shut off his bedroom light and closed the door. He crept down the stairs behind me.

On the porch, Liam silently closed the front door behind him. "Time to make a run for my truck." He grabbed my free hand; my other one clutching Ezzy. "You ready?"

"As ready as I'll ever be."

We darted off the wooden porch together, hand in hand, and made a run for it to his Tundra parked at the edge of the yard. He let go of my hand. I ran around to the passenger side and climbed in. He jumped in the driver's side. We shut our doors quietly.

Liam turned the ignition key, then put his truck in neutral. There was a slight incline and we rolled silently down the muddy driveway. The house became smaller out of the back window. When we were far enough from the house, Liam turned the key and his truck started. Putting it into drive, he drove slowly down the dirt road. Further away from the house, he snapped on the headlights.

"You, uh, seem like you've done this a few times."

Liam shrugged and smiled. "Only a few times. When I can't sleep. Which is a lot."

"What do you do?"

"Mostly drive around. Listen to satellite radio. Think."

"Sounds lonely."

He reached over and rubbed my neck. "I'm not lonely now."

Then he pulled out his phone. Except he didn't dial 911.

"Who are you calling?"

"Chief of police. He's a family friend. His name's Del. I have his home number."

"Del?"

Liam asked the chief to meet him on Highway 13. It was important, he couldn't explain it over the phone, and to please hurry.

2

Ten minutes later, a police car rolled up to Liam's truck in the rain. Inside the brown and gold cruiser was a chunky man with waxy pink skin and eyes that looked at little too close together. He had a toothpick between his teeth. This was Police Chief Del Westworth, according to his gold badge.

"What can I do you for on such a filthy night, Liam?" He spit out the toothpick, which was all chewed up, and then slipped in a fresh one into his mouth from his khaki shirt pocket. "You'll have to excuse me. I quit smoking three weeks ago and it's been tough. Toothpicks help a little bit. The cinnamon-flavored kind. They taste a little like that kind of Fireball Whiskey, and I can't exactly drink that on the job…most of the time."

"Del, I've got a serious problem."

"Yeah, I'd say you do. By not introducing me to your lady friend."

"Oh, this is Madeleine."

I gestured to him. "Hello."

"Howdy back," he said with a smile, showing his crooked yellow teeth. Then he looked at Liam. "So what are you doing dragging me away from Candy Crush?"

"It's at the house."

"Your daddy all right?"

"It's not at Pop's house. It's at the *other* house. The Usher House."

Del's friendly demeanor dropped away. It reminded me of that time when what's-her-name waitress back in Barlow found out Carly and I were going to Usher House. The exact same look.

"You don't got any business there, son. You just stay away."

Someday I needed to find out why the town of Barlow hated the Ushers so much. Eva died a century ago. Why all of the hate today?

"It's serious, Del. Mads' brother, Roderick, he's holding a girl in there against her will."

Del spit his fresh toothpick out the window. "I don't give a damn if he's holding the First Lady. That place is like a damned plague that has to be quarantined—you let it loose and who knows who it'll infect. I had some bad business with that family about twenty years ago. They can all rot. It's none of my care or my concern. And yours neither, Liam."

"But Del—"

"And as far as your girlfriend, well, you might just drop her off at the side of the road and get the hell back home. An Usher is going to do nothing but get you killed." He slipped in another toothpick. "They'll kill you faster than smoking."

"But I thought you could help. You're the law. You're supposed to do the right thing."

"Tell you what I'm gonna do, son. I'm gonna go back home and 'do the right thing' by forgetting this whole conversation. And then, I'm going to finish my Candy Crush game."

"Del, I—"

The deputy nodded his over-sized pink head. "Go home, Liam. Y'all have a nice evening. G'night." He sped off into the rainy darkness. The red taillights of his car winked out like the eyes of a dying animal.

"Well, *that* was a waste of time."

Liam shrugged. "Hey, I tried."

"Now we're going to have to do it *my* way."

"Fine, I'll drive to the front gate."

"No, take us around the side."

"You really think that's a good idea?"

I glared at him.

3

Five minutes later, Liam pulled up next to a portion of the fence close to the house.

"Tell me you have some tools in this truck."

He smiled. "Who do you think you're talking to?"

Liam had a hammer, chisel, and a jack. He stuck the chisel at the base of one of the iron spokes of the fence, then he pounded the chisel with a hammer. The spoke broke loose. With the jack, he stuck it between the spokes, inserted the jack level, then pumped it. The jack bent the iron bars back enough for us to slide in. "They're probably not going to be too happy about the fence."

"They can deduct it from my salary. Let's go."

Handing Ezzy to Liam, I climbed through the fence hole first. He handed me the cat and then he climbed through. The lights of Usher House were dark. Hopefully, everyone was asleep. Oh, who was I kidding? Of course they weren't. It felt like we were a small special forces unit about to break into my own house.

The rain had let up some but the wind picked up. The pine trees around the house swayed and creaked like ship's masts. It was a lonely, unsettling sound. We ran across the wet pine needles scattered in the barren yard and hid along the south edge of the house. I held Ezzy close to my chest. She purred, obviously not affected by the wind and rain or all of the excitement.

"I don't know if Creighton is still out," I said, scanning the area for possible danger. "I got lucky last time with the raven amulet. But I don't know if I could do it again."

Liam pulled out his nickel-plated .45 from his jacket. "Relax, I've got it covered."

Our faces reflected dully along the pistol's shiny barrel.

"Are you good with that thing?"

He smirked. "I can shear off a gnat's pecker at fifty paces."

"Uh, I don't think gnats actually have 'peckers.'"

"Have you checked?"

"Would you please stop."

"So, what's the mission now, GI Jane?"

"This way."

We hunched down to avoid being seen in any of the first-floor windows and ran along the rear of the house. I found the ivy that grew up along the wall. I knew the iron gate was somewhere inside. "In here. There's a secret passage."

"It's the Munster's house. Of course there is."

"Shut up. You said the Addams Family before. Not the Munsters."

He shrugged. "Whatever."

I found the gate. It was still open enough for him and me to squeeze through.

The grim darkness and mustiness of the passage was a relief from the wind and the rain. I snapped on the penlight that Mr. Knapp had given me.

"Smells like a grave in here," Liam said.

"Well, it kind of is."

"Seriously?"

"This leads to the family crypt. From there, we'll have to go up the stairs and break in quietly."

"That sounds…promising."

"Hey, if your law-enforcement friend could have helped, maybe we wouldn't be here right now."

"Del isn't a bad guy, he's just not a very good cop."

"No shit."

The inky shadows surrounded us as the penlight fought to illuminate the almost impenetrable darkness. Ezzy, who sauntered ahead of us, stopped in the middle of the passage and stared at the wall.

"Uh, what's the deal with your cat? Is what you said true?"

I gave a nervous laugh. "Best that I can tell."

"What is an 'animal familiar' anyway?"

"They're supernatural entities that help witches. Usually demons. In this case though, I think this is a relative."

"Uh, that's creepy. And weird."

"Have you met me?"

Ezzy started to paw at the bricks.

"There's nothing there, girl," I said, and scooped her up. Liam backed away from the cat.

"Wait a minute," Liam said. "Hand me your light."

He took the light and studied the wall. "The grout in the bricks doesn't match up. There may be something here." He felt around the wall. "There's a hole between the bricks."

There was a hole all right, covered with dusty cobwebs. And who knew how many spiders that lived inside. Liam peeked in the hole with the light. "I see something."

"What?"

He shook his head. "It looks like a lever." Liam reached inside the hole. I was about to protest, but then looked away. I couldn't imagine how many black widow bites he was going to get. Liam grunted and shifted. Then the wall rumbled and opened. He stood back and wiped the cobwebs off his hand.

"Open sesame, right? Guess your Satanic cat knows what she's doing."

A dark staircase stood in front of us.

"Well," I said, "she's not Satanic per se… Where do you think these stairs lead?"

Liam started to head up the dusty stone steps. "Only one way to find out." He held the light with one hand and his pistol with the other the way cops do.

"You look like you know what you're doing."

"You do a lot of shooting on a farm. Day and night. A sure killer for boredom."

I followed him up the spiral staircase that wound around. Metal sconces on the walls held unlit torches. A secret staircase. Of course, why wouldn't Usher House have one? If Ezzy was Eva, or maybe Eva's animal familiar, then it made sense she would have known about this. Maybe this was the staircase that Corbin and Eva escaped the house that fateful night?

We came to a wooden door at the top of the stairs. Liam turned to me.

"Any idea where in the house that this might open up to?"

"I don't. I'm completely turned around right now."

He sighed. "Let's hope that this doesn't open into a room some-one's in." He handed me back the penlight, keeping his pistol at the ready. "You do the honors."

I turned the tarnished brass lever on the door and it slid slowly open.

Volumes of books lined the walls. We found ourselves in the

library. It was dark, save for a single lamp at the reading desk. The secret passage loomed behind the shelf of books in the corner of the library. The one by the window. Where I found the key for Eva's three-lock box. Another secret that was right beside me and I didn't even know. I could imagine Edgar or Vincent Usher "retiring" to the library for the evening and then going for some covert midnight stroll on the grounds; and Corbin and Eva, too. The rain pattered on the window glass and the wind shook the frame.

"We're in," Liam whispered, peering around in the dimness. "And it doesn't look like anyone's home."

I set Ezzy down. She padded around in the shadows, blending in with her inky color. "Oh, they're home."

"So what's the plan?"

"Simple. We find Carly. And we make them release her at gunpoint and then leave."

Liam nodded. "And after that?"

I shrugged. "Haven't thought ahead that far."

"Fair enough," he said. "Where do you think that they're keeping her?"

"Well, the last place I saw her was the billiards room. Guess we try there first."

"Do you know if any one of your guests is packing heat?"

"I don't think so. I didn't see them carry any guns."

"Good. I like those odds much better."

We crept to the library door. Since I came in here often, the door had a slight creak, so I cracked it open slowly…

Creeeeeeeak.

So much for subtlety.

Liam grimaced at me. "You *have* heard of WD-40, right?"

"If we survive the night, I'll take it up with Mrs. Dietrich first thing."

I left Ezzy in the library and shut the door. I didn't want her hurt. We entered the dark hallway. Like in the library, most of the lights in the house were out. Only a few wall sconces were on, and low. "It looks like everyone got bored and went to bed," Liam whispered.

I nodded. It seemed that way. Was Carly still in the billiards room or had they locked her in one of the rooms upstairs? I guess it made sense that they would do that. But I might as well be thorough. I motioned to the billiards room. Liam followed me. Opening the door, it was dark. Nobody there. I closed my eyes, listening for them. Except for the wind and rain pounding outside and the occasional creak and groan of the old dark house settling in the night, it was silent.

"I don't think anyone's down here," I whispered to Liam. "It's a good chance they're upstairs."

"Where upstairs?"

"Guess we'll have to check all of the bedrooms. Starting with my brother's." I shuddered at the thought. I didn't think I can handle seeing his smug, self-satisfied face right now. I might just have to put a fist into it. And I was by nature not a violent person.

All of the candles that were lit before were extinguished. The entire house was dark except for some muted moonbeams from the skylight. We headed up the stairs.

"Are you sure this is safe?" Liam whispered.

"No, I'm not."

And when we reached the landing, all of the electric lights popped on at once.

Mr. Walsh and Mrs. Dietrich appeared from the hallway shadows. Mr. Walsh held a large pistol that looked like it was made of gold. Then Roderick and Darius showed up a moment later, exiting one of the upstairs bedrooms. Roderick was smiling, holding a crystal glass full of dark wine.

"Welcome to the party," he said, raising his glass. "We've been expecting you. What kept you so long?"

THIRTY-EIGHT

"Wʜat are you talking about, Roderick? You locked me in a coffin, how could you be expecting me? And where's Carly?"

Roderick smiled. "First, have your drippy little friend here lower his Super Soaker. Mr. Walsh has a nervous trigger finger. Trust me, I've been to the range with him."

Liam looked at me as if asking permission. "You'd better do it," I said.

He sighed and set the pistol down on the carpet.

"Kick it over here, Mr. Delaney," Mr. Walsh said, aiming the 24-carat pistol at Liam's heart. "Gently."

Liam did as he was told. The nickel-plated pistol with mother of pearl handle slid across the burgundy carpet. A strange déjà vu moment. The image of that silver pistol on the wine-colored carpet. It was like this moment had happened before. Strange.

Darius Wolfe picked up Liam's pistol. He turned it over in his hands, admiring it. Then he nodded to Liam.

"Quite a collector's item, kid, thanks."

"Pops gave me that forty-five for my sixteenth birthday," Liam said. "I'll be needing it back."

Roderick shook his head. "Shut the fuck up. The adults are trying to have a conversation." He turned to me. "Your friend Carly is fine— she's sleeping with Captain Ambien tonight." Then he pulled out Eva's three-lock box and the scarlet-covered compendium of spells book. "And when were you going to tell me about this, sis?"

"It's none of your business."

"Actually, it is. It's my business, your business, family business. And we're in the business of being a goddamn family. Why did you keep this from me?"

"I wasn't. I just found it."

Roderick looked to Mrs. Dietrich. "This is the genuine article."

"It is, Master Roderick," the stone-faced lady said.

"Well," Roderick said. "You passed the test, sis. I'm proud of you."

"What are you talking about?"

"Well," Mr. Walsh said. "It seems that before Corbin Usher hanged himself, he wrote a letter of confession stating everything he'd done, including hiding the keys, the amulet, and the book. The letter was never revealed, instead hidden in some family documents that were lost."

"Mrs. Dietrich and Mr. Walsh only found those documents a few months ago," Roderick said. "The location of the keys and box weren't revealed, only that they were hidden in the house. Due to your uncanny appearance to our late-great relative, our benefactors here, who believe in Eva Usher's curse, thought that you might be of some help."

"And when you were seen wearing that long-lost amulet on Halloween," Mr. Walsh said. "Well, let's say things got all the more interesting."

"Did they?" I said.

"You used the powers of your great-great-great aunt's amulet to set yourself free," Roderick said. "I wasn't sure you could do it." He gestured to Mr. Walsh and Darius. "We all had our bets placed. I'll pay up my debts later with you, gentlemen."

"You locked me in a coffin to see if I could get out?" I said "You could have killed me."

Roderick took a long slug of his wine and then waved his hand. "Don't be so dramatic. You had enough air for a couple more minutes. Do you think I was actually going to *kill* you? I'd set a timer. When the alarm went off, I went downstairs. And lo and behold, you weren't there. Naturally, I was expecting you to be there in the flesh. I didn't know about the secret passage until Mrs. Dietrich told me about it after the fact. Nice work."

"What are you even getting at?"

Roderick pointed to the raven amulet. "The sins of the father weighed upon the children. Or, rather, the sins of our great-great-great aunt weighed upon dear Madeleine."

"How did you know?"

Roderick opened Eva's spell book. "I can read. It's easy, you know, right to left, top to bottom. Words form sentences. Sentences form paragraphs. Paragraphs form ideas. Ideas transform into actions. Actions affect change." He smiled. "Your actions have affected change, haven't they?"

"Whatever this power is," I said, "I don't want it. I renounce it."

"But why?" Roderick said. "It's the power of the dark lord. Do you know what kind of magic that is? Do you know how formidable the Usher legacy could become?"

"This is power that has a price, Roderick. A heavy price."

"Don't you get it? Corbin and Eva. They had something together. They could have made Usher House into anything. The name Usher could've been synonymous with Vanderbilt, Rockefeller, Hearst, shit —Kennedy, Bush, Clinton, Walton, hell, Trump!"

"That's ancient history," I said.

Mrs. Dietrich crossed herself. "Our Lord in heaven, hallowed by thy name."

"Did I say something upsetting, Mrs. Dietrich?" Roderick asked.

"Sir, I agreed to help you influence Ms. Madeleine, not to consort with Satan."

I stared daggers at Mrs. Dietrich. "So, *you* were behind all of this?"

"The amulet and spell book were never meant to be found," the housekeeper said. "I was against it but Mr. Walsh forced my hand. This should have never happened."

"I've got news for you," I said. "I've been dreaming this before I even came here. I guess it was meant to be."

"I want no part of this, miss and sir," the sober housekeeper said. "I wish to retire to my quarters now."

"Get out of my face," Roderick said.

"Good night," she said. "And I am sorry, Lady Usher."

Mrs. Dietrich left. Good riddance.

I was about to say something when a scratching sound stopped me. It came from up above. The skylight. I first thought it was the wind or the rain pattering down. But no, it was scratching. Not the branch of a tree. But animal scratching. Had Ezzy gotten out?

No. It wasn't Ezzy.

Two fierce eyes looked down upon us through the glass.

It was the form of Creighton.

And then he smashed the glass.

THIRTY-NINE

1

The skylight above exploded, raining down shards of colorful broken glass onto us.

Creighton plunged through the glass, seized the chandelier, and like a ramshackle trapeze artist, swung from that, released himself, leapt onto the bannister, sprang over, and landed on the carpet. Slashed from the glass, his hairy skin was torn and bleeding in places, but that didn't seem to make a difference. He growled.

"Shoot that son of a bitch," Roderick said to Darius.

"With pleasure."

BLAM! Darius leveled Liam's pistol and shot Creighton. The bullet ripped through the beast man's muscled shoulder and he howled in pain.

Before the assailant could shoot again, Creighton had sprang upon him. He slashed the pistol from Darius' grip with his long fingernails—and bit into his throat. Darius groaned as a ragged strip of flesh was ripped by Creighton's jagged teeth, revealing the glistening meat of muscle and stringy sinews beneath. A scarlet waterfall of hot blood surged from the vicious gash.

Darius screamed and placed his hand over the fresh wound in his neck to stem the flow of life that pulsated from him with every rapid heartbeat. Blood gushed through his frantic fingers as he fell to the floor. His face was now the shade of raw bone....he died.

Liam used the distraction to go for Mr. Walsh's gun.

"Liam, no!" I screamed.

Mr. Walsh shot Liam in the stomach. He groaned and fell backwards, clutching the wounded area.

"No!" I tried to help Liam.

Creighton hunched over his kill, fresh blood flowing from his shoulder wound. He growled at his brother.

Roderick stood there, looking stupefied. "Do something, Walsh."

Mr. Walsh leveled his pistol at Creighton and fired. The bullet tore into Creighton's chest He staggered away from Darius' corpse, took a couple of lunging steps toward Walsh and Roderick, and then slumped face-first onto the floor. I didn't know if my other brother was dead, but I couldn't worry about that right now.

"Give me Eva's spell book, Roderick!" I said.

"Why?"

"Because Liam is dying!"

"What's a spell book going to do?"

"Give me the goddamn book!"

Roderick surrendered the spell book.

Mr. Walsh, apparently perceiving me and Liam as no longer a threat, lowered his pistol. He walked over to Darius, kicking him. Darius didn't move, his eyes wide open in horror, his mouth agape, and his throat completely torn open as if savaged by a wild animal. Mr. Walsh then walked over to Creighton, his pistol trained on my feral brother's body, and kicked him.

The beast man didn't move. More blood spilled within the halls of Usher.

I thumbed through the spells looking for something, anything. I seemed to remember one on necromancy when I read the book earlier. Not that Liam was dead yet, but maybe there was some way I could heal him. The powers from this amulet of evil had worked to save me, maybe they could do the same for my love.

Liam grabbed my hand. "It's OK," he said. "You don't have to do anything. Let me go."

"Shut up," I said. "I'm saving your life."

Mr. Walsh savagely kicked Creighton again. My feral brother sprang up. Mr. Walsh shot him again. This time in the stomach. Creighton slashed the pistol from Mr. Walsh's hand, and stumbled back. Walsh screamed in pain and then retreated up the attic stairs, desperate for any escape. Creighton, wounded and bleeding, limped after Mr. Walsh. Walsh tried the door, but it was locked. Catching up to his antagonist, Creighton sprang, missing Walsh. Instead, he ripped the door loose. The attic door fell open. Walsh, having no other place to retreat, sprinted up the stairs. Creighton pursued.

"There has to be one," I said as I thumbed through the spells in the book. "There has to."

"Let him go," Roderick said. "It's too late."

"Shut up. If he dies you're directly fucking responsible. *You're* the reason all this is happening."

"I only wanted us to be together as a family."

"You're not only a liar, Rod, you're pathetic."

Liam's eyes began to roll back into his head. His breathing shallowed. He was dying. A moment later, I found a spell in Eva's book. "Hold the book open and don't say another goddamn word, do you understand me?"

Roderick nodded.

It was a necromancy spell. In the notes, Eva had mentioned that she had brought a dead crow that she had found in the garden back to life. I didn't know if this would work on a human, but I didn't care. I had to do *something* to save Liam. Touching the silver raven amulet at my neck, I read the Latin aloud. Many of the words were tricky, but I pronounced them as well as I could.

Nothing happened.

Liam lay on the floor.

"It's a waste of time," Roderick said.

"If it's a waste of time then why did you lock me in a coffin? It works. I've seen it work."

I tried again.

"Surge qui dormis, surge. Sicut aer iterum respirare non animantibus. Beat cor tuum quasi iterum facit animam viventem. Aperi oculos tuos creatura iterum habet in animam viventem. Surge qui dormis, surge."

As I did, the room seemed to go dark and I was alone with Liam's body. Then, I realized that I wasn't alone. The brutish men from Barlow stood around me. All of the them from my dream, from the vision that I had where Eva was hanged. Their dark expressions focused on the oak tree. Eva's body swung back and forth from the branch of the oak tree like a pendulum's blade, the noose tight around her neck, which was twisted at a severe, gruesome angle. Her hands were bound behind her with a leather strap.

Corbin Usher watched his sister's corpse sway. "Take her down."

"She needs to hang to let all see what happens to devil worshippers in this county."

"She's dead. I need to take her home."

"Let her down."

One of the men untied the end of the rope from around the trunk of the tree and unceremoniously let Eva's corpse drop to the ground. Corbin leaned over his sister's body, loosening the noose from around her neck and pulling it off. He then untied her bound hands.

Corbin whispered in her ear. "Please forgive me, sweet Eva." He rose. "I will get my car and take her home." As he did, the men moved back from the corpse, which was almost shrouded by the mist.

Eva's eyes sprang open. Then she rose, her neck broken and twisted. She reached up, straightening her head, snapping her neck bones back into place with a sound like the snap of dry kindling. She rose, and with her mouth still gagged, she walked over to me, the low fog swirling around the tails of her black cloak. This seemed less like the power of active imagination and more like it was happening in the flesh, as if I had entered the past so completely I had brought Eva bodily into the present. It was overwhelming.

"If you're going to do this, I need to do it," Eva said, having pulled the gag from her mouth and capturing me with the intense expression of her green eyes. I felt her intention join my desperate need.

Eva started to speak again, but only a cat's grotesque meow came from her lips. And then, a moment later, she shrank, growing smaller. The black cloak she was wearing seemed to envelop her, and then she became a black cat—with green piercing eyes and a white spot on her breast where her silver amulet once was.

"You are the cat," I said. "You *are* the familiar."

Before I could react to that realization, the cat sprang onto my face. I tried to pull her off me, but I couldn't. I fell back onto the ground, fighting with the animal, screaming. The black cat forced her head into my mouth. I choked, gasping, trying to breathe, pulling out a handful of black fur. The demon feline scrambled the rest of the way into my mouth—her head, shoulders, and body, becoming smaller. I felt the impossibly large lump writhe down my throat. I coughed and gasped, pulling ragged breaths into my lungs again. My body didn't feel like mine anymore. It's as if I had strings tied to my joints, and I was being moved like a marionette. Eva from down inside me was pulling the strings.

I will help you if you help me, Eva's voice within said.

"What is it that you want?"

Kill Roderick. All the men Ushers must die for what they did to me.

"My brother's done wrong, but he doesn't deserve to die."

And neither does your lover.

"Well, he's not my lover. He's more like a boyfriend."

Do you want him to live or not, cow?

"More than anything."

Then we have a deal, the voice said.

"No, I—"

Silence!

I watched as my hands turned the pages of the spell book to a part I hadn't seen before. Then I was speaking words that had never passed my lips before. Rhythmic, musical words in a determined cadence. It was a spell of some kind, a conjuring spell.

Eva guided my hands and placed them on Liam. She then spoke

the words through me. The men from the village surrounding us watched. They either seemed curious or too afraid to move.

I felt weaker. As if I had gotten over a bad virus, drained and depleted. I nearly crumpled to the floor. When I touched Liam's stomach wound, the blood was still there, but the angry bullet hole under it had vanished. He opened his eyes, staring up.

"Where am I?"

"You're safe," I said.

And then Eva's voice within me said. *And now you got what you wanted—it's my turn to get what I want, what is due me.*

A moment later, I was diving over Liam's prone body and grabbing Roderick, choking him. My hands crackled with blue bolts of electricity, filled with new strength.

Die! Eva's voice inside me said. *Die!*

"No. He doesn't deserve to die. Release him."

You promised, girl. You made a deal.

"There's already too much death in this family, and I'm not going to let you take everything away from me the way they took everything from you." I fought her presence inside me for control of my limbs.

Then I remembered a spell from Eva's book. It was a binding spell, which could be used to stop others from harming you. It was fairly simple.

"I bind you, Eva," I cried out. I pulled the clot of black cat hair from my fingers with one hand, and then reached up and pulled the hair tie free. My dark locks fell down around my shoulders. Quickly, I twisted the hair tie around the cat hairs while chanting, *"I bind you, Eva, from harming me and all I love and care about. I bind you, Eva, from harming me and all I love and care about. I bind you, Eva, from harming me and all I love and care about."*

NO!

I continued the binding chant, despite her pleas from within me.

The men surrounding me grabbed me and picked me up off of Roderick. They dragged me over to the noose.

"The witch is not dead yet!" one man said. "She speaks the devil's words."

I fought, kicking at them while still holding onto the bound cat hair and chanting.

"She's got the devil in her," another of the men said, getting too close.

I scratched the man's face with my nails. He stepped back.

Then I felt nauseous and was going to vomit. Clutching the bound cat hair in my grip, I rolled over onto my hands and knees. At first, it was only gasps of air squeaking out of me—and then black fur. The cat slithered out of my mouth in a wet, embryonic ball. It lay on the ground kicking its hind feet, yowling as if in pain. Then, it grew bigger, the fur fading, until it became Eva once again.

The men ignored me. They grabbed Eva.

"Leave me alone," she screamed. "I curse you—I curse you all!"

Corbin returned. "Eva?"

"Help me, brother!"

The men pushed Corbin aside.

"You betrayed me, Madeline!" the witch said, fixing me with anguished hate-filled eyes.

"I didn't," I said. *"But I bind you, Eva, from harming me and all I love and care about. I bind you, Eva, from harming me and all I love and care about."*

"I curse you! And your brother too! And all of Usher House! It will be brought down stone by stone on top of you! You will rue your deceit, cow!"

One of the men gagged Eva so she couldn't utter another curse. Another threw the noose around her neck. I felt sick seeing the past repeated, knowing I had somehow brought Eva fresh suffering. I never meant to do that.

"This time," the bald man said. "She hangs until she rots."

I kept repeating the chant.

2

A moment later, I was fully aware of being at Usher House, the terrible mists of the past-made-present having parted. The walls of the manor and the stairs were visible and solid again. Roderick sat against the wall rubbing his throat. He had purple marks around his neck. I had really grabbed him, moving into present reality while surrounded by the powerful vision of the past. I knew what had happened was real, though. Not visible to those around me, perhaps, but real.

I stopped chanting. In my hand, I had the cat hair bound with the rubber band. It had happened. This was the proof.

Liam sat up slowly. "I feel like I was hit by a truck."

I kissed him. "Welcome back to the world."

"I missed you," he said. He saw the cat hair in my grip. "What's that?"

"Uh, just some witch shit. I'll explain later."

He chuckled. "I can't wait."

A commotion on the roof ripped our attention away from one another. Through the broken glass of the skylight were shouts and screams.

"It's Walsh," Roderick said.

"What's happening?"

I picked up Liam, helping him up. Roderick rose too, keeping his distance from me. We rushed down the stairs from the second floor and outside into the wind, rain, and darkness.

On the roof, Creighton and Walsh circled one another like prize fighters. They must have climbed through the hole in the attic. Walsh had broken off one of the lightning rods and was using it as a spear, a metal scarab beetle on its head. Creighton, moving slower due to his wounds, screamed and circled Walsh, looking for an opening. Walsh happened to see us on the ground.

"Get a gun!" he screamed. "Shoot him! Shoot him now!"

Apparently agitated by Walsh's voice, Creighton rushed Walsh. Walsh plunged the tip of the lightning rod through his abdomen. My beastly brother fell back, trying to pull the tip of the makeshift spear out of him. Walsh pushed the rod, trying to back Creighton off the roof. The wind-swirled rain tousled around them. In horror, I realized the tip of the lightning rod had pierced through Creighton's back.

And in all of my years, I will never forget what happened next.

Creighton grabbed the shaft of the lightning rod and pulled himself closer to his assailant. Apparently too weak and stunned, Walsh held on to the rod for a moment too long. The rod protruded from Creighton's back, stained with glistening fresh blood and fragments of tattered flesh. Then Creighton, the rod still buried half in and half out of him, picked up Walsh over his head. Walsh flailed and screamed. The beast-man threw him off the roof.

Walsh crashed onto the gargoyle fountain—his body impaled by the two horns on the stone demon's head. The rush of water that foamed endlessly from the gargoyle's gaping mouth turned bright crimson as it mingled with the attorney's blood. Walsh, impaled through his back, stared at us, his face upside down, with a horrified grimace.

Creighton let out a final victory scream and then tumbled backward against the roof. He didn't move after that.

I turned to Liam. "Think we call the state troopers this time?"

Liam nodded. "You Ushers sure know how to throw a crazy house party, City Mouse."

I shrugged. "It's in our blood, Country Mouse."

And then he kissed me.

3

Liam and I went back inside. He dialed the state police.

I dashed upstairs to the room that Roderick and Darius came from. I had to step over Darius' corpse, which lay sprawled on the second-floor hallway.

In the room, Carly's body was slumped in a chair. She looked pale. Dead.

I shook her. She still felt warm. This was a good sign. I cracked open one of her eyes. It was dilated. She may have been drugged. Then she writhed and woke up.

"Holy fuck," she said. "Why do I keep drinking so much?"

"I don't think you did. Pretty sure my brother or his idiot friend drugged you."

"Last thing I remember was playing pool and drinking beer. Then everything went fuzzy." She then noticed me covered in blood, dirt, and soaking wet. "What the hell happened to you, darlin'? Did I miss a party?"

"Yeah," I said. "Something like that. A hell of a party. We're lucky to be alive"

She hugged me. I hugged my best friend back.

FORTY

1

Springtime arrived in the South.

The thick, warm air smelled sweet with honeysuckle. The secret garden that Josef revealed to me during that fateful night last November had grown into a regular spot of meditation and reflection for me. Often, I strolled through the library and ventured along the secret passage down to it. In addition, I'd had the secret stairs under the house opened back up and fumigated of spiders and creepy crawlies, as well as some electric lights installed. It's much more pleasant now. Most mornings I visited the garden for an hour or so of reflection before I began my day. I loved the trickling water of the fountain—so peaceful and meditative. Often I do meditate, usually twenty minutes at a time, but I had also done so for up to two hours a session. I'd discovered it a gentle and yet spirited way to strengthen my mental resolve.

Mrs. Dietrich brought me my morning cup of tea daily. Over these past months, she grew much kinder toward me. The events of last autumn seemed to scare her into submission. I practiced being kinder toward her, too. We seemed to have a mutual understanding.

Esmerelda studied the colorful koi swimming around in the babbling fountain with an intense fascination. Ezzy kept my spirits bright. After binding Eva, I also bound Ezzy by casting a spell and fitting her with a silver collar I fashioned especially for her. It required me to melt down some of the Usher silverware, which was pure silver by the way, and to fashion the trinkets onto a leather collar. However, I'd gotten quite good with such arts and crafts as jewelry making. Now the black cat stayed out of mischief for the most part. I'd read where binding a witch with silver could limit her powers. I also entwined Eva's portraits with black ribbon, binding her image, as an extra precaution. Call me paranoid, but I could not let her destroy Liam, Roderick, Usher House, or myself. As long as Eva was bound, I believed we could remain safe against her curse to destroy us.

2

The state troopers that Liam had called were all shocked by the bloodshed. It certainly didn't help Usher House's already troubled reputation. Later, I spoke to the press to place it on record that the Ushers were a normal family now, nothing like our past, eccentric relatives. However, interviewers who wanted more lurid details still hounded me occasionally. They went ignored. The passing of Mr. Walsh and Darius were reported as defensive deaths, so no criminal charges were filed, thankfully. With the loss of Mr. Walsh, I accepted the role as lead administrator of Usher House—quite a task since I had no formal training, but I have studied online courses of family law. We could hire another "Mr. Walsh," perhaps, but outsiders made us wary. Roderick now handled the business affairs, but nothing was done without my permission. After the incident, Roderick stepped back from his inappropriate obsession and control over me. I believe that I scared him. For someone who had doubted witchcraft and the supernatural, he seemed now to be a true believer after a little practical magic was applied.

3

Liam and I have grown fond of one another. We spent time together, mostly on weekends and a few weeknight dates for dinner. He visited here, as I am still not welcome on Delaney soil. Liam's father needed his son too much to disown him. William senior, however, had no idea about his son's fatal shot, dying, and being resurrected. He would never allow Liam over if he knew that. Liam had the faintest of scars where the bullet entered, but it looked like a birthmark more than a bullet wound. I would love nothing more to run off to a tropical beach vacation with my lovely and handsome beau, but I have still not figured out a way to remove this unearthly curse of the amulet. Yes, Eva Usher was bound, but it seemed, so was I. This amulet cannot be removed—though I have attempted many unbinding spells. So, I remained here at Usher House, its master and its prisoner.

4

Carly returned to Pickman Flats. She has expressed interest in staying at Usher House again, but the events of her last visit made her uneasy. On numerous occasions, I'd told her that she could move in here, or even to nearby Folkston, which was nice, but I cannot seem to convince her. Yet.

5

Creighton miraculously survived. After multiple blood transfusions and months in the hospital, he returned home. Roderick, Liam, and I testified that Creighton was acting only in self-defense against Darius and Mr. Walsh when they had drawn their weapons upon us, and so no murder charges were filed. My feral brother no longer resides in the attic. Contractors were hired to repair the roof, and it was thoroughly cleaned. The repaired skylight was more beautiful now than ever.

My other brother lived in his own room on the second floor with us. A few hours of my day I read to him, mostly from children's books like *Pat the Bunny*, *Goodnight Moon*, or *The Big Red Barn*, and I have taught him the alphabet and spelling. He's become a personal project of mine. In addition to a love of listening to music, classical, oldies, and even some modern stuff, finger painting became his new form of artistic expression. For now, daily sedatives were administered. Occasionally, he had violent outbursts when he grew frustrated or couldn't understand something. He once broke a chair when fingerpainting class wasn't going well. Though I avoid using the amulet's power, I did administer its power once when he became unmanageable. I am one of the few he trusts and obeys. He seemed to enjoy the company of Mr. Knapp, the groundskeeper as well, and my brother often spends afternoons outside with him. Through love and trust, I have tried to foster Creighton's obedience, but that hasn't always worked. Dominant behavior had to be displayed too. However, I retained hope for Creighton, he was my brother.

6

Thanks to our initial investors, Michael Valdemar and Gordon Pym, the stocks for Usher Enterprises rose. Roderick and I have sought to expand the software security business, as well as some real estate holdings. Roderick, of course, has done all the traveling meetings since I am unable. I believe that Roderick looked forward to these trips and spent many weeks away. The events of last November shook him to his pitiless soul.

7

As far as my great-great-great aunt's curse on the house and of us, I hoped and prayed that the bindings held. As I mentioned, I toiled to undo the curse she had cast upon us within that netherworld, but I fear it was done in vain—the silver amulet was absolute power from the prince of darkness himself.

A curse loomed over Usher House still.

But all I could do now was make this house into a place that I could finally call home.

<u>Coming soon</u>: ***Usher House: Reckoning*** (Book II)

ACKNOWLEDGMENTS

When I was around seven years old, I once told my sister I wished we lived in *The Munsters* mansion instead of the one-story rambler that occupied South Elizabeth Street in Milton-Freewater, Oregon. "But nobody would visit us," she said. "They'd be too afraid." I shrugged. As an introvert often distracted by daydreams, I didn't find that a problem.

My first book in the *Usher House* series is a life-long obsession with wanting to live as a Munster or an Addams. Growing up, my babysitters were Vincent Price, Christopher Lee, Bela Lugosi, Peter Cushing, Boris Karloff, Barbara Steele, Ingrid Pitt, and Lon Chaney, Jr. as I watched monster movies on Saturdays at 3:00 PM on *Creature Feature* from Spokane's KHQ-TV Channel 6. On my dusty bookshelves stalked the Aurora models of Dracula, Frankenstein's Monster, and The Wolf Man (all of which I still have). Feeling like a weirdo in elementary school class for reading *Creepy*, *Eerie*, and *Famous Monsters of Filmland* magazines, moving into Usher House, literarily speaking, seemed like a natural progression decades later.

Originally, *Usher House* started as an ambitious but unfinished screenplay I wrote back in May 2005. However, the story never left my mind. Fifteen years later, I'd decided it was time to pack up, move back into Edgar Allan Poe's crumbling manor of dark insanity, and try to tell Madeline and Roderick Usher's tale again. (Sorry, Mr. Poe.)

I want to thank my family—for a story like this wouldn't be possible, and my weirdo friends, many of whom were monster kids, who've been with me on this long day's journey into eternal night,

ALSO BY DON ROFF

Clare At Seventeen (2022)

Clare At Sixteen (2021)

Snowblind (2016)

Ghost Detective (2016)

Terrifying Tales Vol. 1 (2012) Vol. 2 (2014)

Heebie-Jeebies: Volume One (2012)

Ghost Hauntings: America's Most Haunted Places (2011)

Haunted Tales (2011)

Zombie Tales (2010)

Real-Life Hauntings (2010)

Werewolf Tales (2010)

Zombies: A Record of the Year of Infection (2009)

Ghost Quest (2009)

Vampire Tales (2009)

Creepy Stories (2008)

True Scary Stories (2007)

Dragon Adventures (2007)

Tales of Terror (2007)

Scary Stories (2006)